THE DREADFUL HOLLOW

Also available in Perennial Mystery Library
by Nicholas Blake:

END OF CHAPTER
THE SMILER WITH THE KNIFE
THE WHISPER IN THE GLOOM

THE DREADFUL HOLLOW

Nicholas Blake

PERENNIAL LIBRARY
HARPER & ROW, PUBLISHERS
Cambridge, Philadelphia, San Francisco
London, Mexico City, São Paulo, Singapore, Sydney

A hardcover edition of this book was originally published in the United States in 1953 by Harper & Brothers.

 For information address Harper & Row, Publishers, Inc., 10 East 53rd Street, New York, N.Y. 10022. Published simultaneously in Canada by Fitzhenry & Whiteside Limited, Toronto.

First PERENNIAL LIBRARY edition published 1979. Reissued in 1988.

LIBRARY OF CONGRESS CARD CATALOG NUMBER: 87-46118
ISBN: 0-06-080493-9 (pbk.)
88 89 90 91 92 OPM 10 9 8 7 6 5 4 3 2 1

Contents

PART ONE

1. The Financier's Interests

The lift, moving like greased lightning, whisked Nigel Strangeways up to Sir Archibald Blick's private apartments at the top of the immense postwar building. "*Facilis ascensus Averno,*" Nigel found himself muttering to the lift boy. A strangely prophetic misquotation, it was to turn out, though at the time it seemed sufficiently irrelevant to an appointment with a famous financier: the lift boy, who believed he had been given a red-hot tip from the stables, was quite visibly racking his brain to remember what race this outlandishly-named horse had been entered for.

Nigel was shown into a room so anonymous, so impersonal that he felt himself changing on the spot into a cipher. It was the kind of room for which the word "functional" might have been invented, except that one could not imagine what function it possibly served; unless it was just this—to reduce the visitor to a mere statistical unit. A desk, with a clutch of telephones and a positive control board of colored buttons to push. Walls paneled with some shiny, ox-blood, Australian wood. A long board table, of the same wood, in the center; neat, new, businesslike chairs set around it. In spite of the panoramic view southward over the Thames which the windows offered, the room afflicted one with claustrophobia. It was like the inside of some monstrous lift, or a cabin on a luxury line. He had only to push a handful of those colored buttons, thought Nigel, and beds would emerge soundlessly from the walls, a cocktail cabinet from the floor; a radio would start playing; valets, manicurists, waiters, secretaries would stream through the door. At present, no indication of the private life was to be seen—not a book, not a picture, not an ornament, not even a copy of the *Financial Times* on the desk.

Wait a moment, though. As Nigel prowled round to the other side of the desk, he saw that what he had taken for the back of a large calendar was really the back of a photograph: a studio photograph, expensively framed, of a beautiful young lady. She sat upright, one leg crossed over the other, gazing at Nigel with all the unenthusiasm of Knightsbridge. She was evidently made for pearls and a twin set; but unaccountably she had omitted to put on the uniform of her tribe. The young lady was, in fact, stark naked. So powerful, however, was the room's impersonality that the fair sitter set up no vibrations at all; she neither allured nor shocked; her total nakedness might have been an advertisement for a skin tonic or some course of mental hygiene. To Sir Archibald Blick, she seemed to be saying, figures are facts—no more, no less.

Nigel was still studying this anomalous creature when, a minute later, Sir Archibald entered the room. Thin, small, dapperly dressed, wearing an old Etonian tie and a thick black ribbon attached to his pince-nez, his face a map of wrinkles, he looked at first sight like a dandified, haggard baby or a certain type of art connoisseur. He walked stiffly up to Nigel, with what in a less distinguished man would have been called a strut, touched his hand, gave him a keen, assessing glance, and motioned him to a seat at the board table.

"Glad you could come along. I've a proposition to lay before you." Sir Archibald meticulously straightened out a writing pad on the table in front of him. "What do you know about anonymous letters?"

"Have you been getting some?" asked Nigel, making an effort to prevent his eyes wandering toward the Knightsbridge nude. Sir Archibald ignored the question.

"You've had experience in dealing with them?"

"A certain amount. But the police are much more—"

The eminent financier brushed this aside too. "What is your theory about them? How would you set about tracing the writer of anonymous letters in—let us say—a country village?"

Nigel Strangeways was too old to get onto a high horse at this kind of *viva*. If Sir Archibald proposed to interview him like a candidate for some junior post, he was quite prepared to accept the role; much of his success as a private investigator had been due to a deceptive air of docility, and to the passionate interest in human nature which precluded any taking offense at its more offensive manifestations. Besides, as an old Oxford man of a vintage 1920 generation, Nigel could never be averse to a bit of theorizing.

"Anonymous letter writing is generally taken to be a symptom of mental disease. You look for someone with sexual repressions—it depends, of course, upon the tone of the letters. Sexually unsatisfied women, particularly at the change of life, are often the culprits; there have even been cases of such women writing obscene letters to themselves. It is sometimes linked up with a certain type of so-called 'religious mania.' These are the stock explanations." Nigel's pale-blue eyes gazed abstractedly upon Sir Archibald's wrinkled, pink, baby face, with its petulant mouth and frosty expression. "I myself prefer to state it in rather different terms. Sexual inhibition is at once too narrow and too loose a way of defining such aberrations. For example, it does not cover satisfactorily the cases where parents, whose child has met with a fatal accident through no fault of their own, receive malicious letters accusing them of neglect or murder. I believe there is such a thing as pure, irresponsible malice in human nature. But generally I'd look for the source in some failure of personal relations: the writer wants to take it out on someone else for something in which he himself has failed or feels guilty." Nigel held up his hand, like a lecturer anticipating an objection. "All this boils down to the question of power. Nearly all of us, from the village busybody to the great financier, need the feeling of power over other people's lives. If we cannot satisfy this need through our work or our human relationships, we may be driven to some substitute activity: we may keep lap dogs or write anonymous letters. I would always look for someone who has been denied power, or lost it—someone in whom the springs of love have found no outlet and turned brackish."

"So you equate love and power?"

"Not by any means. It's a matter of—"

Sir Archibald pursued his own line of thought. "So women, being more possessive than men in personal relations, are more profoundly affected by a failure of love or power, and will be more likely to take up lap dogs or anonymous-letter writing."

He nodded to himself briskly, as if some view of his own had been confirmed, took a small silver matchbox from his waistcoat pocket, and began fiddling with it.

"At any rate," he went on, with a sharp glance at Nigel, "you'd say there is always an element of—er—mental abnormality at work? The anonymous-letter writer is never quite sane?"

"Which of us is?"

"Nonsense, my boy. That's modernistic cant. For all practical purposes, most people are sane. Stupid, if you like, but—"

"Leaving that aside," Nigel broke in, "poison-pen letters could well be written for quite different, objective reasons—to damage a man's business, for instance, or to break up his home—as a move in some criminal conspiracy. That would be sane enough, according to some definitions of sanity."

Sir Archibald perceptibly froze at this ironic comment on his own words. He was unused to such treatment. Removing his pince-nez on their broad black ribbon, he directed at Nigel the glare which had petrified high officials of the Treasury. Nigel gazed back at him mildly, innocently. The great man tried another method of putting him in his place. Walking over to the desk, he pressed a button and spoke into the house telephone.

"Jameson, bring up the Prior's Umborne file."

He sat down again, at the far end of the board table from Nigel now—the employer-applicant relationship was to be underlined—and waited in silence for his secretary to appear. A smooth, horn-rimmed, higher-executive type slid into the room, as if on skates, laid a file before Sir Archibald, and stood back a pace.

"You have obtained Mr. Strangeways' ticket and reservation for tomorrow?"

"They are in the file, sir. A taxi will be awaiting him at Moreford. Mr. Raynham will expect him for lunch."

Sir Archibald lifted a little finger, and the secretary skated out. Nigel smiled faintly at the act which had been put on to impress him; the vanity of the great could be so naïve as to be almost pathetic.

"I make it my business to employ the best men. I've had good reports about you. I want you to go down to Prior's Umborne, in Dorset, and sort out some trouble there. They've had an outbreak of anonymous letters recently, and it's got to be stopped. You'll find full details in this file, together with three of the letters which Raynham—he's the vicar—has passed on to me."

Sir Archibald stood up, to terminate the interview. Nigel did not.

"There are a few things—" he began.

"What? Isn't the fee I have offered big enough? Didn't you say, in reply to my first letter, that you were free to take the job any moment?"

"Oh, yes. That's all quite satisfactory, thank you. But I like to know what I'm letting myself in for."

"I didn't realize that people in your profession could be fastidious," snapped the financier.

"We don't mind rolling in other people's mud. We just like to be told the reasons why. For example"—Nigel had been flicking over the papers in the file—"does this tell me why Sir Archibald Blick should concern himself with unpleasantness in a remote Dorset village?"

The small black eyes stared unwaveringly at Nigel.

"I have interests there."

"Financial interests?"

"Financial, and personal. My elder son lives in the Hall there—our family home. I have installed my younger son as manager of a new machine-tool factory in

Moreford. I'm behind the firm which started this factory. One of the foremen committed suicide last week, after receiving an anonymous letter—quite a number of the factory employees come from Prior's Umborne, I should tell you, and efficiency is suffering."

"I see. Curious place to start a machine-tool factory—an old market town like Moreford. Policy of dispersal in case of war, I suppose. You certainly wouldn't want the work held up just now."

Sir Archibald glanced at Nigel with something like respect. "You're right. But don't go chasing red herrings. Too many people in this country nowadays jumping at their own shadows. I don't believe these anonymous letters are part of the Russians' policy to impede our rearmament program."

"Well, then, on the personal side—whom do you recommend I should get in touch with? Apart from the vicar? Who would know most about the place? You say your elder son lives there?"

"You won't get much out of Stanford. He's a recluse. Bit of a genius in his way, but a born dabbler, I'm afraid—never settled down to anything except his damn-fool hobbies. There's Charles, of course; but he's got his hands full with the factory."

Sir Archibald Blick was a transparent man in some ways, thought Nigel. The shadow of impatience that passed over his face when he mentioned the industrious Charles, the indulgent twitch at one corner of the mouth when he spoke about the unsatisfactory Stanford—these told their tale. A buzzer sounded on the desk. Sir Archibald pressed a switch, and a dim voice crackled.

"Mr. Danvers to see you, sir."

"Tell him to wait."

The voice crackled an obsequious protest. Mr. Danvers was evidently an important man, in a hurry.

"If he can't wait a quarter of an hour, he must make another appointment. Give him a drink. And bring some up here." Sir Archibald turned to Nigel. "These Ministry officials—the plague of my life. Well, now, the best person for you to concentrate on is Miss Chantmerle—Celandine Chantmerle. A very gifted woman. Lived at Prior's Umborne all her life. Her father was an old friend of mine. She doesn't like me much, but that's by the way. She's idolized in the village, and what she doesn't know about it isn't worth knowing. Yes, a remarkable woman. Anyone else would have gone sour after being a cripple all these years. Then there's her sister, Rosebay: much younger, a difficult girl; you won't get much out of her, unless"—Sir Archibald's voice suddenly took on a note of shocking brutality—"unless she makes you fall in love with her. . . . Here are the drinks. What'll you have?"

Over a gin and tonic Nigel gave Sir Archibald a noncommittal look. There were wheels within wheels here, but the mechanism seemed to have come to a stop. Nigel gave it a nudge.

"Unusual name, Rosebay."

"The father was a botanist. Distinguished fellow, but a bit unbalanced, you know. Killed himself, actually. Thirty years ago. The elder daughter inherited his brains: the younger, I'm afraid—"

"She's mad, you mean?"

Sir Archibald frowned, pursing up his small, petulant mouth. "Rosebay is very highly strung."

There was a marked pause. Sir Archibald played with his matchbox again.

"And the vicar?" asked Nigel.

"Mark Raynham? A disappointment. I put him there. I have the gift of the living. He got knocked about in the war. Not altogether reliable—politically, I mean. Rather a firebrand. He's quite popular, I believe, with some sections of the village; but there's a strong Plymouth Brethren element there too, and when zealot meets zealot—"

"I presume the police have been called in."

"The village constable is an individual named Clotworthy. A perfect illustration of the results of inbreeding in these remote country districts. Well, our works at Moreford will remedy that, as time goes on."

A glint came into Sir Archibald's cold eyes. One of his "interests," Nigel remembered, was the Society for Practical Eugenics. Scratch anyone in the right place and you find the fanatic: it was charming to view the machine-tool factory at Moreford as an instrument for improving the Prior's Umborne stock. Nigel's eye turned involuntarily for a moment to the photograph on the desk.

Sir Archibald could be disconcerting in his shrewdness. "I noticed you looking at that when I came in. Put me down as a dirty old man, I dare say." He gave a little, rusty laugh, disagreeable in its false gaiety. Rising from his chair, a slim, brittle figure which showed his age in its stiff movements, he took up the photograph. "I'm interested in eugenics, as you have gathered. This is the winner of our Potential Motherhood Award for 1950. We go by more than a photograph, of course: medical history of family is investigated, and so on. We're a practical society. The winner gets a monetary award, which we increase by weekly payments if she marries one of several mates selected by ourselves. A good type, this, physically and mentally."

Sir Archibald seemed about to enlarge on her points, like the judge at a cattle show, when the buzzer sounded again.

"All right, all right, send him up. . . . I've got to see this Danvers fellow now. Good-by, Strangeways. Keep in touch. I'll expect a report from you in a week."

Back in his club, Nigel ruminated on this astonishing interview. What chiefly emerged from it was the financier's evident wish to keep Nigel's mind fixed, by means more or less subtle, upon the general proposition that poison-pen writers are (a) mentally unbalanced and (b) women. Had Sir Archibald some candidate already in view? Rosebay Chantmerle, for instance, who was so "highly strung"?

Nigel opened the file. Clipped to the inside cover were a first-class return ticket, a seat reservation, a slip of paper with the registration number of the taxi which would meet him, and a check for his first week's salary and expenses. Sir Archibald's staff work was good; no doubt it had better be. The file itself consisted of a large-scale map of the Prior's Umborne area, a list of its leading residents, with addresses and telephone numbers, a few typewritten sheets, signed by the vicar, which gave a summary of the poison-pen campaign to date, and a sealed envelope containing, no doubt, the anonymous letters themselves.

Running rapidly through the vicar's statement, Nigel gleaned the following main facts: the poison-pen campaign had started—or, at any rate, the first letter to be publicly acknowledged by its recipient had been posted—ten days before, on April 6; the recipient was the vicar himself. The next day, one Daniel Durdle received a letter; he took it round to the vicar the same evening—a circumstance which evidently tickled the latter, since Daniel Durdle was a leading light of the Plymouth Brethren. The vicar was convinced that some of his parishioners had had anonymous letters too; he felt "an atmosphere of tension and suspicion" in the village; but, in spite of his appeal from the pulpit that Sunday, no one came forward. Late on the Monday evening Greta Smart, returning from a visit to her married sister in the next village, had found her brother John lying in their cottage with his throat cut and a razor beside him. This John Smart was a foreman in the Moreford machine-tool works. Under the body, Police Constable Clotworthy had discovered an anonymous letter. All three letters had been posted in the village. The police had impounded the originals and envelopes for John Smart's inquest; but the vicar enclosed typewritten copies of them, with the information that the letters and the addresses on the envelopes—a cheap brand of stationery—were written in capitals, in ink. He added that, owing to the low standard of education among his adult parishioners, a good many of them wrote in capitals anyway.

The vicar's report, apart from its occasional flicker of amusement, was written in the driest, most banal communiqué style. It conveyed nothing of the man, except, perhaps, Nigel fancied, a sub-ironic comment upon the employer-employee relationship between Sir Archibald and himself, as the former envisaged it. Nigel thought he was going to like the vicar. He opened the envelope which contained copies of the anonymous letters. Over the first the vicar had scrawled "My own billet-doux." It was short but not sweet:

Get up in that pulpit, holy Joe, and tell them your wife was a whore.

The letter which had been addressed to Daniel Durdle was equally outspoken:

You hypocrite, I know about the strong liquors you swill privily.

More cryptic, and still more economical, was the letter which had caused John Smart to kill himself:

I'll tell Blick about 1940.

Thoughtfully, Nigel put the letters away. To the outsider, he reflected, there was always something comic, even unreal about such missives. It took a strong effort of imagination to feel them as the recipients would, to understand the real consternation and despair which these thrusts from the dark could cause. It was not the way they might reopen old wounds; a man who had lived for years with some guilty or tragic secret must have grown a pretty hard skin over it. No, the poison of the poison pen lay in its anonymity—in the victim's sudden awareness of bitter hostility playing upon him from an unknown quarter, the sense of being pursued by a thing without a face.

The letters ran true to type. They were directed against three men who held prominent positions in the life of the village, and they aimed to take these men down a peg. Envy, malice and uncharitableness were at work. If the letters contained any truth, they argued a surprising range of knowledge—surprising because of the widely different backgrounds of their recipients. They also suggested a certain artistic flair in the writer. The Plymouth Brother's letter was couched in Chapel jargon; the vicar's had a note of irrepressible sardonic humor. And poor John Smart? Whatever had happened in 1940, it must have been something which would lose him his job if it were revealed. Why else "tell Blick," his employer? Something so grave that it made Smart reach for his razor. There was a line there, and no doubt the police would be following it up.

To speculate further was futile. Nigel walked round, at a venture, to the London Library and looked up the name Chantmerle. He was rewarded by three volumes, with which he settled down in the reading room. Putting aside, after a glance, an austere monograph by Edric Chantmerle, F.R.S., *On Some Variations in Sub-Arctic Flora*, he dipped into the author's two earlier, less exacting works, *Sunny Woodlands* and *Come Out to Ramble*. These turned out to be far more distinguished than their titles. Written in the Edwardian period—the golden evening of belles lettres, as of so much else—they were leisurely essays about the flowers, trees, landscapes, topography, etc., of Dorset, at once charming and scholarly. The style was sensitive, humorous, supple, a delicate phthisic flush substituting for the purple patches normally found in such works. What chiefly emerged for Nigel, though it was never underlined, was the author's passionate attachment to his county. How deep the roots went could be seen in the essay "On Prior's Umborne," from which Nigel learned that the Chantmerle family had lived there since the Conquest. In James the Second's reign they had built the Hall; but toward the end of the nineteenth century, their fortunes presumably having dwindled, they had moved in to the Little Manor, once the Dower House, and the Hall was let. Some of Edric Chantmerle's most lyrical writing was evoked by this Little Manor, the house in which he had been born, and the countryside around it.

Steeped in the vicarious nostalgia which Edric Chantmerle's essays had induced, Nigel returned to his club. Their idyllic tone clashed horribly with the idea of poison-pen letters. No doubt the place had changed a lot in the last thirty years. No doubt, for the matter of that, a great deal had gone on at Prior's Umborne, beneath Edric Chantmerle's fastidious nose, of which he had been unaware. No, he's too good to be true, thought Nigel impatiently.

Yet he could not shake off this phantom from the past, irrelevant though it must be to the case upon which he was embarked. One of the amenities of Nigel's club was that it offered a human reference library, including in its membership experts upon almost every branch of knowledge under the sun, most of them all too willing to hold forth upon their subjects. This evening, before dinner, he tracked down to his lair beside the bar an ancient and tortoiselike gentleman.

"Hallo, Flumps, how are you? What'll you drink?"

"Very ill. A double whisky," replied Sir Henry Flumpington, whose book on plants in English folklore is unlikely to be superseded.

"Did you ever come across a chap called Chantmerle? Edric Chantmerle?"

"Young Chantmerle? Yes, we corresponded. Never met him actually. I put him right on a Clare reference. What was the damned thing now?" Sir Henry waved his flippers feebly, like an overturned turtle. "Anyway, there's a flower mentioned in one of Clare's poems. Chantmerle said it couldn't ever have been found up there. Actually, there's one place in the country where it still grows; you can read about it in Druce's *Flora of Northants*. Bit of a dilettante, but not bad. Has he murdered someone?"

"He died. A long time ago."

"I know Clare died a long time ago," replied the octogenarian with some heat. "I'm talking about this Chantmerle of yours."

"So am I. He died about 1930. Killed himself, I understand."

"So he did. So he did. You're perfectly right. Yes. Lost his money in the slump, they said. Don't you believe it."

"I've heard he was a bit unbalanced mentally. You think it was just that?"

Sir Henry's beady eyes kindled. "All experts are unbalanced. Look at me. Monomaniac. Mad as a hatter. No, what I'm telling you is that he couldn't have lost his money."

"Why not? Lots of people did."

"Lots of people didn't have first-rate financial advice. Now I happen to remember Snippy telling me—and Snippy knows about these things—that your Chantmerle's affairs were handled by that awful fella what's his name." The flippers waved convulsively. "You know. A stinker if ever there was one. But he's got the Midas touch. Couldn't lose money if he tried. Just a minute now. Don't fuss me. Ah, I've got it!" Sir Henry clawed the name triumphantly out of thin air. "Black."

"Blick, d'you mean? Archibald Blick?"

"Yes, yes, yes. Blick. That's what I said. Blick."

2. The Vicar's Troubles

"You're quite sure you'd rather stay at the pub?" asked the vicar.

"Yes. Thanks very much. It's better that I shouldn't become identified with either of the warring factions in your village."

"I understand. Though staying at a pub won't commend you to the Plyms."

"They do their drinking at home, do they?" asked Nigel, remembering the letter which Daniel Durdle had received.

"Only cider. Though why they make an exception of that, I've never fathomed. The local rough cider is diabolically strong stuff." Mark Raynham paused, and an impish gleam showed in his fine, wild eyes. "Also, I dare say you don't want to be taking my bread and salt when it might be me who's writing these letters?"

"It might be you," Nigel echoed, looking straight at the vicar's face—a craggy, tortured face, older than his years, with a strong nose and deep furrows running from it to the sides of his mouth.

Mark Raynham's laugh rang out over the hillside they

were climbing. It was a strenuous laugh, nervous yet uninhibited, matching the spring growth and sunshine all about them along the old trackway. At lunch he had postponed discussion of the anonymous letters, telling Nigel that he always preferred to take his problems out of doors. Now the cue had come; but Raynham seemed unwilling at first to take it. The track was steep and rough, and the vicar prodded himself up it with a stick, limping quite heavily. Presently, before they reached the summit, he turned off into a field on their left, led the way to the brow of the hill, and sat down.

"There you are," he said, waving his stick at the view before them.

Prior's Umborne lay below, a cruciform village straggling along the main road southward to Moreford, and a secondary road which crossed it at right angles. Near the crossroads were grouped the post office and the inn where Nigel was to stay—The Sweet Drop. A hundred yards to the west of the crossroads stood the church and vicarage; and beyond them again a drive led from the secondary road to the Hall, which was sheltered from the north by a plantation of beeches. Immediately below the hill brow where they sat was a group of stone buildings, the largest farm in Prior's Umborne, and a small road wandered westward past this farm up toward the Little Manor, concealed from them at present by a fold of ground. Where this road joined the main road at the northern end of the village stood a smaller pub, the New Inn. Prior's Umborne itself lay in a narrow troughlike valley, which opened out beyond it into a broad vale, pastoral and well timbered, with Moreford visible on its far side; farther away, a line of downland hid the sea.

"Lovely, isn't it?" said Mark Raynham.

"What I can see of it, yes. I'm rather shortsighted. But Sir Archibald Blick provided me with a map, so I know more or less where to look for everything."

"He would," commented the vicar dryly. He stabbed at the foreground with his stick. " 'Below me, there, is the village, and looks how quiet and small! And yet bubbles o'er like a city, with gossip, scandal, and spite.' "

"That's *Maud*, isn't it?" Deep down in Nigel's mind something twitched, and was still again, like a premonition. "Things are getting worse?"

"Yes, I suppose so." The vicar sighed, giving Nigel a strange look, friendly yet watchful. "Yesterday I was to marry a young chap called Ottery; works for Templeton, down there." He pointed at the big farm below them. "They found him with his head in a bucket. Just after breakfast. He'd tried to drown himself."

"*What*? In a bucket of water? But—"

"I know, I know. It's grotesque, macabre—any of those words you like. But it's what happened. Luckily, his best man, who found him, learned artificial respiration in the navy. Just managed to pull him round. If he'd arrived a few minutes later—"

"But I shouldn't have thought it was possible to drown oneself like that. Surely, in the death agony, the thing'd get tipped over? Involuntarily?"

"Well, nobody held his head down in the bucket, if that's what you're thinking. There were no signs of a struggle at all. His mother, who lives with him, heard nothing. She says he got a letter after breakfast—Templeton had given him the day off—and went out of the cottage without a word to her, in his decent black wedding suit. She heard him filling a bucket. He took it round behind the outdoor earth closet, out of sight. He removed his coat, folded it up tidily and laid it on the ground beside him. Then he knelt down in front of the bucket, put his head in it, and held it there. Oh yes, and he'd taken the flower out of his buttonhole—torn it up into shreds—scattered them round him." The vicar's voice shook a little, and he combed his right hand fiercely through his hair.

"And the letter?" Nigel prompted.

"Said some nasty things about his girl. Things I happen to know are true. Gave chapter and verse. She's a flighty creature—or rather she used to be. I suppose young Ottery had suspected it, brooded about it, never talked to anyone. You know how reticent village lads are in that way. The tragedy is that Flora had gone straight since they started walking out; she's thoroughly in love with him. Perhaps it'll turn out a good thing in the end."

Mark Raynham shook himself, like a dog coming out of water.

"D'you know the West Country?" he asked abruptly.

"I used to live not so far from here, before the war, when my wife was alive."

"Then you'll know what the people are like. Genial and gentle, obstinate and a bit shy underneath; suspicious and fatalistic. The real peasants. Slow to catch fire, and hard to put out. Passions don't run high, but they run devilish deep. You'd be surprised."

Mark Raynham touched with his little finger an early cowslip which stood modestly in the grass beside him.

"I'm afraid of what'll happen if they find out who's been writing these letters. They'll lynch him. Or her."

There was silence between them. A lark trilled endlessly overhead. A car hooted at the village crossroads. Turkeys, ducks, hens and dogs in Templeton's farmyard suddenly started a pandemonium of noise, like an orchestra tuning up.

"Why did you say, 'I suppose so,' when I asked if things were getting worse here?" said Nigel.

The vicar gave his hearty, apologetic laugh. "Oh, I dunno. Silly thing to say, really. But I'd sometimes wondered if these people wouldn't be the better for a good stirring up. And now they're getting it."

"Yourself included."

"Ah, yes. Now we're coming to it." The vicar jerked up his head, as if to take a blow full in the face. He was gazing straight at Nigel, but he didn't seem to be seeing him. "You want to know about that letter. My wife ran away with another man while I was at the war. The old, old story." As if rebuking himself for his bitterness, he said gently: "Poor girl, it was too difficult for her. I'd been reported missing, in the Western Desert. She was a beautiful woman."

"Was?"

"She got killed later, by a flying bomb." For a moment Mark Raynham's face had an utterly ravaged look—a look of scorched earth. "You know, I thought I'd got over it all very nicely. But when this letter came—well, it made me realize I loved her still. That was the awful part of it; not what the writer called her, and not the fact that it was true. Yes, I'm afraid it was. She did have other men, afterward. It all came out." The vicar added, with a sort of shy pedantry, like a child pronouncing a new, difficult word, "She was very highly sexed, you see."

" 'It all came out'? Do you mean it was in the papers?"

"Oh, no. But when I got back to England, out of the prison camp, I came into possession of her letters, among other things—letters these men had written her. I spent a happy afternoon reading them, I remember: couldn't stop myself: human nature is really very queer."

"Then you destroyed them, I imagine?"

Mark Raynham nodded.

"Have you ever told anyone else about this? We must try to discover how the information could have got to Prior's Umborne."

"Only one person. An old friend of mine. I wrote to him in strict confidence soon after I'd come down here to work, in 1946."

"Who knows about the anonymous letter itself?"

"Only the Moreford police know what it said—unless they told our village bobby, and I'm sure they didn't. The Inspector is a sympathetic chap."

"And there's nobody in the village you could possibly connect with—"

"No, my wife was in London when all this happened. Hardly any of our villagers have so much as been in London."

"What about the gentry? The Blicks? The Chantmerles?"

Mark Raynham looked genuinely shocked. "My dear chap, you surely can't suspect people like them! I don't mean they're all saints; but they've got better things to do than—"

"I suspect nobody, and everybody. Celandine Chantmerle, for instance. She's a cripple, I'm told. Plenty of time on her hands. Plenty of reason to turn sour on humanity."

The vicar's Homeric laugh rang out again. "Wait till you meet her, then you'll see why I can't help laughing. She's a heart of gold. Wonderfully sympathetic. Of course she's difficult at times—a bit imperious—every beautiful woman is, if she has brains and temperament. But everyone adores her and—"

He broke off abruptly, and a slow flush came over his face.

"—and confides in her, you were going to say?" murmured Nigel, smiling at him.

"Oh, nonsense, nonsense. A lot of people confide in *me*, but you don't suspect me of writing poison-pen letters. Or do you?"

"Writing one to yourself?"

"Well, don't they often do that? To avert suspicion? Or is it something neurotic makes them do it—split mind?"

Nigel gazed at the vicar noncommittally. "Would you call the other Chantmerle sister neurotic? I've heard—"

"I must say, I've never been pumped so hard in my life. I take it Sir Archibald primed the pump?"

"He did seem rather down on Rosebay Chantmerle."

After a pause, the vicar said: "She's not had an easy time. All these years playing second fiddle and unpaid nurse to her sister. She's a sulky sort of girl. Full of repressions, I dare say. Never got much change out of her myself. But anonymous letters—no."

"You sound very certain of that."

"I am. You don't write those sorts of things when you're in love. She and Charles Blick have been about together a lot these last few weeks."

"And is he in love with her?"

"He's constantly up at the Little Manor. Opinion in the village seems about equally divided as to which of the sisters he is courting," said the vicar dryly. "Let's move on, shall we?"

They returned to the track and went on up till it ended in an old quarry cut from the northern face of the hill. The side of the quarry was a sheer drop of about a hundred feet. Yellowish water lay in its bottom, and the air seemed suddenly cold as Nigel leaned over the strands of wire which ran on rough stakes along the edge. The yellow water stared up at him from the pit, like a saurian eye. Shivering a little, he turned his back on it. He was now facing a short stretch of turf, thickly planted with daffodils, beyond which lay a plantation. Through this plantation ran a turf drive, leading to the Little Manor, two hundred yards away. Patches of celandines and windflowers glimmered among the trees.

It was a still afternoon, but some current of air created by the quarry or the hillside's configuration made the daffodils twitch and shudder spasmodically, while in the wood one branch suddenly rubbed on another, with the sound of a man grinding his teeth in an uneasy sleep, and was silent again.

"An enchanting spot, isn't it?" said Mark Raynham.

"The grove of Avernus," Nigel found himself muttering. "A queer place to plant daffodils, I must say. Who can see them here?"

"Funny you should say that. The village people never come up here, though you'd think it was a most eligible nook for courting couples."

"Why can't the damned things stand still?" asked Nigel, as the daffodils suddenly shivered again. "I've never seen such a nervous lot of flowers."

The vicar gave his strenuous laugh. "You'd better complain about them to Miss Chantmerle. By the way, she's asked you to lunch tomorrow. It's her birthday, actually. I'm going, and you'll meet Charles Blick too."

As they skirted round the left-hand edge of the wood, Nigel asked idly: "Why do the villagers shun that place?"

"You'd better ask Joe Summers—he's the landlord of The Sweet Drop; lived all his life here. You'll find him a mine of information. Now, look; isn't it an exquisite house?"

They were passing through a field to the left of the

Little Manor. Solid and elegant, its gray stone glowing as if with the remembered sunshine of centuries, the Chantmerles' house looked southward over a terraced garden toward the Hall and the pastoral country beyond. The garden was not large, but packed and glowing with flowers and flowering shrubs, which set off the modest Quaker-gray of the house.

The vicar waved to a man mowing a grass path between the flower-beds.

"That's Herbert Petts. He does the gardening and odd jobs. They've a woman living in—Charity Cooper—quite a character, and a girl comes up from the village for rough cleaning."

"Can the elder sister get about at all?"

"She's got an electric invalid carriage."

Nigel filed mentally another question. How do they keep all this up when the father lost his money?

They came out on the road, to the left of the Little Manor drive, crossed it, and went through a gate along a field path. This path soon forked, the right-hand branch leading to the Hall, the left-hand taking them down into the village.

"Does Stanford Blick live alone there?" asked Nigel, pointing toward the beech grove which shrouded the Hall from sight.

"Most of the time. His brother keeps a sort of flat in the house, but he has to be at the works in Moreford all day, and some nights too. Hard-working chap, Charles is. The mother died years ago, and Sir Archibald does not favor us with his presence very often."

"He told me his elder son was a bit of a recluse."

"Well, that's one way of putting it. He's certainly a tearing eccentric. Pots of money; but they say the Hall is like a pigsty."

"You've never been in it?"

Mark Raynham grinned. "Stanford attended my first service here. Took against my sermon. We had a set-to afterward over a doctrinal point in it—all quite amiable, but as a consequence I've never been invited up there. Keep off theology if you meet him."

"It's a subject I seldom moot."

The field track brought them, past some allotments, onto the main road through the village. Like all West-Country villages at almost any time of any day, Prior's Umborne appeared to have been totally evacuated, as if it lay in the path of an invading army or the wake of some annihilating plague. The road through it was scoured of all signs of human or animal life, and dead silent but for the murmur of the stream which bordered one side of it, running in a stone conduit. From the windows of thatched cottages there peered no faces, only geraniums or cyclamens. So it startled like thunder from a clear sky when this picturesque trance was broken by a scream—the scream of a child in abject terror.

"Don't hit me! No! Please don't—"

"Are you going to tell us, or—"

"Let me go, Greta! I'll tell my Mum on you!"

There was the sound of a hard smack, and a bubbling wail from the child. The vicar went limping fast, round to the back of one of the cottages. Following close behind him, Nigel saw a girl of seven or eight struggling in the grip of a tall, fierce-eyed woman. Two other village women were leaning over the fence which separated the back gardens.

"Stop this at once!" Mark Raynham's voice cracked out like a sergeant major's. "Greta Smart, let go of her this instant! Now, Reeny, come over here. It's all right."

The child, a nasty red patch already showing on the

side of her face, stumbled toward him and clutched his coat.

"I done nothing! She hit me!"

All three women started talking at once, volubly. Mark Raynham appeared to ignore them altogether, as he stroked the little girl's hair and gradually quieted her convulsive trembling. Only when she had stopped crying did he look at the woman—a look of such sternness that he was transformed from the pleasant, easy-going fellow Nigel knew into a man of power, a militant, uncompromising Christian.

"Well, now, Greta, what's all this about?"

"Mrs. Warren here saw Reeny creepen down to the post office, late last night, with some letters."

"I wasn't then!"

"Oh, you little liar! I see you!"

"I was'n creepen." The little girl was nearly in tears again.

"That's enough. Run along home, Reeny. Tell your mother I'll be round to see her presently."

The vicar's ascetic face was pale as he turned upon the women.

"You've had a bad time, Greta. But that's no excuse for bullying children. Are you going to torment every child in the village whose mother sends her to post letters? You know what Christ said. Whatever you do to one of these little ones, you do to Him."

One of the women by the fence muttered: "And did'n 'E say an eye for an eye and a tooth for a tooth?"

"He did not. Go home and read your Bible. I'll have no more of this blasphemous nonsense from you." Mark Raynham lifted a finger to heaven, like a prophet in the full tide of denunciation. His tones held such conviction that the gesture seemed inevitable. "I tell you, God is watching you. Get this poison out of your hearts before it's too late. Cruelty is never right—it works out its own damnation."

"God wasn't watching when my brother killed 'eeself," said Greta Smart sullenly.

Mark Raynham laid his hands for a moment on her shoulders, making her look up at him. "You know that is not true. He is merciful, and one day you'll see it, whatever you feel now." There was a rough, tonic confidence in his voice, more effective than any arguing and commiseration. The woman's shoulders suddenly shook with sobbing. "Now I want you to come along with me presently and see Reeny's mother. Let's have it out in the open. We'll ask her about those letters, and I expect we'll find there's some quite simple explanation."

"Oh, I couldn't do that, Mr. Raynham."

"Of course you could, Greta. What are you afraid of? Being proved wrong? I'll call for you in half an hour." The vicar turned, and limped out into the street, saying, more to himself than to Nigel: "It's like a forest fire. Stamp it out in one place, and it starts up in another."

"You did a good job then."

"It's my work."

Nigel was impressed by Raynham's neither apologizing for his recent outburst nor depreciating it, now that he was alone with a sophisticated person; he had the simplicity of his convictions.

"They *would* pick on Reeny's mother. She used to be the village tart."

"You've reformed her?"

"I don't honestly know. I've tried."

"Reeny's illegitimate, then, I take it?"

"Yes. Not that that worries the village. If half what one heard was true, there's hardly a child here conceived in holy wedlock. There's even a legend that the austere Mrs. Durdle slipped up in her younger days. No, it's because Rosie Venn was quite unashamed about her goings-on that we draw aside our skirts from her," said the vicar in lowered tones.

They had reached the post office, a raw, red-brick building by the crossroads, its window displaying the usual multifarious articles, from hair nets to tinned salmon, which the village shop-*cum*-post-office provides; but they were arranged with unusual neatness, and the interior had been swept and garnished till it looked like something out of an Ideal Small Traders' exhibition.

"Do I say what you're here for?" Raynham whispered, as the jangling of the shop bell died away.

Nigel nodded. A woman of about fifty emerged from an inner room and stood behind the counter, the fingers of her large red hands splayed out upon it. Her narrow, upright figure seemed not so much corseted with whalebone as composed of it, and the same constriction showed in her brow: the dark hair, which might once have been beautiful, was drawn back so tightly into a knob that it almost gave one a headache to look at. The whole face had a strained, skimped, scraped expression, nor did it in the least relax when Mark Raynham said pleasantly: "Good afternoon, Mrs. Durdle. Lovely weather, isn't it?"

"What can I do for you, Mr. Raynham?"

"This is Mr. Strangeways. He's a private investigator. Sir Archibald Blick has asked him to come down and look into this little trouble we're having. You'll give him all the help he needs, won't you?"

The woman looked at them defensively. "I don't know, I'm sure. We've had the police in and out for days now. It isn't very nice."

"Just think of me as one more policeman," said Nigel briskly. "The Chief Constable will vouch for me, if you ring him up."

"Oh, well, if it's official-like, I suppose it's all right. I was worried what the head postmaster would say."

"We'll square it with him. But of course the police are looking after the technical side of it, so to speak. I'm more concerned with the human element—the people who've been getting these letters. I'd like to have a talk with your son some time."

Mrs. Durdle's adamantine face yielded momentarily to some mixed emotion, in which both apprehension and pride featured. Turning her head, she called out: "Daniel! Shop!"

There was the sound of feet descending stairs. Then a remarkable figure appeared. Nigel's first impression was of a caterpillar which had outgrown its strength. Daniel Durdle must have been quite six and a half feet tall; but he had a habitual stoop which made his body the shape of a question mark. The black serge suit he wore accentuated the whiteness of a roundish, pasty face, which was surmounted by bright auburn hair, hanging lank and thin about his temples. As he entered, the head on its long neck groped round toward the visitors, moving from side to side like that of a caterpillar rearing up from a leaf. He came to stand behind the counter, his mother making way for him. Nigel noticed that his hands were surprisingly delicate and well shaped, though the fingers were stained yellow.

"Good afternoon, Reverend," he said, in a sleek yet vibrant voice.

The vicar introduced Nigel and said his piece again. Nigel was conscious of Daniel Durdle's eyes upon him; but their expression was indecipherable, his glasses being so thick that he seemed to be peering out through a ship's portholes.

"We must give the gentleman every assistance, Mother."

"Whatever you say." Mrs. Durdle's mouth snapped shut, like one of the mousetraps hanging on a card from the shelf behind her. This thin-lipped, grudging mouth was the only feature she had in common with her son.

"Very kind of you," said Nigel. "Cigarette?"

"I don't smoke," replied Daniel.

"Ah, you work with chemicals, then? A hobby?"

The pebbly stare of Daniel's glasses fixed Nigel for a moment. It was impossible to tell whether he was disconcerted. "Oh, I see. My hands." He stretched out the stained fingers on the counter. "A proper Sherlock Holmes. Yes, I do an occasional job for Mr. Blick, up at the Hall, in my spare time."

Mrs. Durdle, bridling a little with gratification, began:

"My son used to—"

"Now, Mother, these gentlemen don't want you showing me off to them."

Mrs. Durdle folded her hands over her abdomen and was silent.

"I hope you'll have a pleasant stay in our humble village, sir—and a successful one, of course. Sin is rife here, as the Reverend knows, and we must stamp out the iniquity even though it bruises our heel."

"We must indeed," said Nigel equably. "And talking of heels—Achilles' heels, so to speak—I assume there's no truth in the anonymous communication you received."

"There is a truth of the letter, sir, but not of the spirit. I find it necessary to imbibe an occasional glass, for medicinal purposes. My health—"

"Precisely. But you're not a roaring alcoholic."

Mrs. Durdle's eyes closed in an expression of pained rebuke. Her son remarked, with a sort of unctuous playfulness: "The letter killeth, but the spirit giveth life."

"One of these letters has killed a man," said Nigel. "And there's been an attempted suicide as well. I think we had better keep off Scriptural allusions."

Daniel Durdle's glasses flashed as he turned his head. "I hope I have not offended your susceptibilities, sir. You are a believer?"

"I'm a believer in people not writing poisonous letters to their neighbors," Nigel said. "Perhaps I could have a talk with you tomorrow morning."

An appointment was made. Nigel and the vicar withdrew. As they walked up to the vicarage, to fetch Nigel's baggage to the inn, he said: "What an extraordinary chap."

"He does rather give me the creeps," said the vicar.

"How old is he?"

"Thirty-one; thirty-two."

"You know, I felt that in some obscure way he was laughing at me. There's something derisive behind that deferential manner of his. Yes, I think I shall find him quite interesting. Who did you say his father was?"

"I said there's a legend that it wasn't the late lamented Mr. Durdle."

For once the vicar seemed evasive. Nigel affected not to notice it.

"Well, *I'd* say he was a gentleman's son—a by-blow of the village aristocracy. I wonder did Sir Archibald Blick ever misconduct himself with Mrs. Durdle."

And I wonder, Nigel added to himself, is Mark Raynham's laughter a sign of relief—that I picked the wrong father for Daniel Durdle.

3. The Innkeeper's Story

A few minutes with Joe Summers, the landlord of The Sweet Drop, was enough to assure Nigel that here he had an inexhaustible spring of gossip. Joe, a man of over sixty now, had kept the pub for the last thirty years. Indeed, he had never left Prior's Umborne except to serve in the First World War, relics of which period survived in the photographs of Sergeants' Messes hung on the walls of the parlor where he and Nigel were drinking tea.

"I suppose the village has changed a great deal since you first remember it," said Nigel.

"You've put your finger on it," replied Joe weightily. "And not by no means for the better. 'Change and decay in all around I see,' if you understand me, sir. Not that I'm against progress, mind you. Why, only last year I put a wireless set in the private bar. No one ever switches it on, for sure—they comes here for a bit of peace and quiet. But you've got to move with the times."

He took a copious draught of tea, sucking the last drops appreciatively out of his Kitchener mustache.

"The factory in Moreford must make a lot of difference," Nigel remarked.

"Well, now, it creates employment, yes. But look at it another way, and what do you see?"

Nigel offered no views.

"You see dissatisfaction," Joe went on. "Stands to reason. The wages our village lads—and lasses, too—can get in the factory tempts them off the land. Them that stays on the land, which is where they ought to be, are restless, knowing they could get better money in Moreford. And them as goes into the factory, why, after a bit Moreford isn't good enough for them, and they start pining to be in London or some such."

"You don't approve of the younger generation becoming more independent?"

Joe Summers had the landlord's acquired characteristic of deference to the customer's opinion.

"Now, don't get me wrong, sir. Independence is a very good thing in its way. But take India." He proffered Nigel the continent on the palm of a large hand. "You must give people independence gradual like, else it chokes 'em. We clears out of India, bag and baggage, all of a sudden; and what happens? The natives start up massacring each other. Take another case. Prior's Umborne. They're what you might call a backward lot here too. My contention is, they wasn't ripe for independence, if you take my meaning. That factory of Mr. Blick's has gone to their heads. So we get trouble."

"Anonymous letters, for instance?"

"In my job," pronounced Joe with all the evasiveness of an oracle, "you learn to be tactful. I may have my ideas, but I keep them to myself. Mum's the word, like the third monkey said. Gossip today is grief tomorrow. Johnny Smart now—they're saying he got into trouble during the war, and it caught up with him. I'm not expressing any opinion on that, though he was a foreigner, poor b——. What I do say is, these anonymous letters are a symptom, not the disease itself."

The landlord paused only to pour himself another mug of treacle-colored tea.

"The old order changeth," he resumed, "giving place to new. That's the root of the trouble, sir."

"I suppose you knew Mr. Chantmerle well?"

"You've said it. Now he was a gentleman. We always thought of him as the Squire, long after Sir Archibald came to the Hall. Not that I've anything against Sir Archibald, mind you—not personally. It's the principle of the thing. To my way of thinking, landlords ought to live on their property."

"But his elder son lives here, doesn't he?"

"Mr. Stanford?" said the landlord, temporarily deflected. "Ah, he's a queer card, if ever there was one. He's brainy as they come, mind you; but you never know what he'll be up to next. Soon after he come to live here permanent—that'd be in 1932 or thereabouts—he took a fancy to start a bus service between here and Moreford; said the regular service was too slow. So what does he do? Damn me if he doesn't buy a bus, and square the authorities—the Blicks 've got influence all right—and drive it himself! It didn't last long, of course."

"He got tired of the new toy?"

" 'Twasn't that. Not on your life, sir. What happened was he scared the passengers into fits. Drove that old bus so lickety-split, he had the old women squawking all the way into Moreford. Turned out he'd been a racing-car driver at one time. No, Mr. Stanford isn't cut out to be Squire, though he's a good customer of mine."

"Still, you've always got Miss Chantmerle. I believe she's the real power in the village, isn't she?"

Joe Summers gave Nigel a portentous look. "Miss Celandine is a great little lady, and I don't care who hears me say it. She's too good for this place. But now, wait a moment"—he tapped the table oratorically—"this is where we come back to my contention. In the old days, I'll lay there was hardly a man, woman or child in the village didn't go to her with their troubles. Why, she used to hold court up at the Manor, almost like a queen, you might say. But it's different now. Since the war and the evacuees and now this factory have unsettled the village, things are changed. The younger generation don't look up to her, not like they used to. They goes their own way. And, of course, we have a stronger parson now—more active-like."

"Mr. Raynham seems an excellent man."

"He's straight enough; though he does put some people's backs up. Be the better for what our old parson used to call a helpmeet."

"He's a bachelor, is he, or a widower?"

"Never been married, not to my knowledge. Do you mind if I put on a pipe, sir?"

"Go ahead."

Joe Summers ruminatively began to fill a heavy briar. "Mr. Chantmerle was a great pipe-smoker. Soothed his nerves, he used to say. He was a sad loss to the village, no two ways about it. And Miss Celandine—she's never quite got over it, I reckon. He and she were inseparable. The mother died, you know, when Miss Rosebay was born. Mr. Chantmerle and Miss Celandine went everywhere together—walking, riding, bicycling."

"She's not always been a cripple, then?"

"Bless you, no. It happened when her father killed himself. May have been coming on for some time before, but we didn't see no signs of it. If you ask me, she wore herself out nursing him—that was after the crash, when the poor old gentleman went a bit queer in the head. And then, in her weakened condition, she was fair game for one of them dirty bacilluses, see? Of course it was finding him dead put the cap on it. Our old doctor said it was a tumor of the spine she had, so I believe."

"It was she who found the body, you mean?"

"Yes. And so happen, it was me who found *her*. I'll never forget it. Thought there was two dead 'uns down in the quarry."

"The quarry? Not that one beyond the wood, just over the hill from the Little Manor?"

"The very same, sir."

It was Nigel's experience that in each of his cases there was a moment when the drama took on a third dimension and became fully alive for him, as when on the stage the entrance of a character, the delivery of a key line, or it may be only a single consummate gesture, a moment of stillness or a change in the lighting, grips the spectator so that he is no longer a spectator but a participant deeply involved with the tragedy enacted before him. Such a moment was this. The problem which had brought him to Prior's Umborne suddenly transformed itself, at the mention of the quarry, from an abstract, diagrammatic proposition into something full-bodied and real. Nigel felt, with the force of an infallible intuition, that the daffodils he had seen shivering on the quarry's brink had been planted there in memory of her father by Celandine Chantmerle. From the account Joe Summers now gave of that day twenty-one years back, Nigel's imagination constructed and colored the scene. . . .

When Celandine took up her father's breakfast that summer morning in 1930, she found his bed empty. She was then a girl of twenty, on edge with the strain of nursing him during the weeks of illness which had followed the financial crash. Edric Chantmerle had fallen into a melancholiac condition, but latterly seemed to be picking up a little. However, when the girl could find him nowhere in house or garden, fearing he might have lost his memory and wandered farther off, she telephoned to the doctor and the village constable, then set off to look for him herself.

In the meantime Joe Summers, taking his wonted constitutional between breakfast and opening time, happened to be walking up the track by which Nigel and the vicar had climbed the hill this afternoon. He was almost at the top when he heard a woman moaning. He ran toward the sound, and looking down into the quarry, saw the bodies of Celandine Chantmerle and her father. It had been a dry month, so there was little water in the quarry bottom. But Celandine was unconscious now, and Joe at first thought they were both dead. However, he scrambled down the precipitous face of the quarry, splashed out to where the bodies lay, and seeing that Edric Chantmerle's neck was broken, began lifting the girl out of the water. As he did so, she recovered consciousness.

"My legs won't work," was the first thing she said. Then presently: "I saw him lying here. I climbed down. Tried to drag him out of the water. But something's gone wrong with my legs. He's dead, isn't he?" She burst into a wild fit of sobbing, hysterically crying out: "They've killed him! They've killed him! I knew it would happen!"

Joe Summers's shouts for help brought the gardener from the Little Manor. Unfortunately they brought Rosebay too, a girl of eight then. Joe remembered her small face, shocked into blank expressionlessness ("She didn't seem able to take in what had happened," was how he put it), gazing solemnly down at them from the edge of the quarry as they prepared ropes to haul up her sister and her father's body.

After this, Celandine was gravely ill for some weeks. Rosebay was sent away to stay with relatives. Sir Archibald Blick, who was at the Hall with his son Charles for a holiday, had engaged nurses to look after Celandine. At the inquest on Edric, they brought in a verdict of "suicide while the balance of his mind was disturbed."

"It was a bad summer for Miss Celandine. Lost everything, she did. But she always had pluck. It'd have killed many another woman," said Joe Summers now. There was a faraway, sentimental look in Joe's eye which prompted Nigel to say:

"Her father, her health and the family money. Did she lose anything else?"

"Funny you should ask that, sir. The summer I'm talking of, Miss Celandine and Mr. Charles were very thick. They was thrown together, as you might say, their families being the only gentry in the parish, except for our old vicar. We all thought they was going to make a match of it. Charles Blick was on holiday from Cambridge University, and they went about together a lot, particularly when Sir Archibald wasn't here—he only came down for week ends. Pretty as a picture she was, with her golden hair and blue eyes and winsome ways."

Joe sighed sentimentally, and fell into a sort of reminiscent stupor.

"But, after she became paralyzed—?"

"Ah, that's the long and the short of it. Mind *you*, I never held with the folk who swore Mr. Charles had behaved bad to her. I said to them: 'Look,' I said, 'human nature isn't a matter of black or white. We don't know what may have happened between them.' Maybe she sent him away when she knew she could never make him a proper wife. Maybe they'd never clicked at all, if you'll excuse the expression, sir."

"No judgment without full evidence?"

"Eh? Ah, yes, I get you. That's right. Of course, it looked bad, his going off like he did. But there was wheels within wheels in that quarter."

The landlord paused to relight his pipe. Nigel gave what he felt to be a grossly exaggerated representation of a listener who is all ears.

Lowering his voice, Joe Summers said: "My old woman's sister happened to be working up at the Hall just then. I remember her telling us she'd overheard Mr. Charles telling his father that Miss Celandine wouldn't take no money from the Blicks. I should explain, this was when she was recovering from her illness, and the old doctor thought she was fit for the operation on her tumor. It'd be an expensive operation, and of course she couldn't afford it herself, not after the crash."

"But why shouldn't she accept money from the Blicks, if Charles and she—?"

"That's exactly what we asked ourselves at the time. And I'll tell you my theory. Putting two and two together, I came to this conclusion: Miss Celandine must have quarreled with Mr. Charles and broke it off, either soon before her father's death or after it. So she wasn't going to be beholden to him for money. Too proud to take it from the Blicks. But wait a minute." Joe held up a huge forefinger. "Where do we go from there? Mr. Charles did at least offer to get the money for her operation; so he couldn't 've been wholly bad and heartless, could he now?"

"No. It might have been conscience money, though."

"I don't rightly get your meaning, sir."

"Well, if it was Charles who'd broken it off, because of her having become a cripple, he'd be feeling rather a heel, wouldn't he, and he might try to salve his guilty conscience with a cash payment."

"You may be right," said Joe dubiously. "But I can't quite see Charles Blick letting her down like that. Don't believe it'd be in his nature."

"Was there any other reason why Miss Chantmerle should have come to hate the Blicks? Who was she talking about when you rescued her and she said: 'They've killed him'?"

"Oh, I don't reckon she meant anyone particular. Maybe the gang of politicians who started the slump and lost Mr. Chantmerle his money. She was proper dazed, anyway—didn't know what she was saying."

"Yes, but in that state of mind she'd be liable to put the blame on the handiest person. And Sir Archibald, I'm told, was her father's financial adviser."

"That's news to me, sir. You'd hardly credit it! Why, I thought Sir Archibald was one of these what-they-call financial wizards."

"Even experts can slip up."

"Too true they can. I recall—hey, hey, look, it's just on six. I must go and open up. Make yourself at home, sir. My missus'll put on the grub at eight."

Quarter of an hour later Nigel went into the public bar. It held only one occupant, who was eating out of a packet of crisps at the elm table, his back to the window. This individual—his face was in shadow, but he seemed to be a workman of some kind—raised a perfunctory hand to Nigel's "Good evening," and went on devouring crisps. Presently he said, in a surprisingly cultured voice: "Do you want a drink?"

"Yes. Where's the landlord?"

"What'll you have?"

"A pint of bitter. But—"

The individual laid a finger to the side of his nose, went behind the bar, and drew Nigel a pint.

"Thanks very much."

"That'll be one and twopence. And I'll have a gin and peppermint with you, if I may. Another half-crown. Much obliged."

As this unorthodox person mixed his drink, Nigel studied him with fascination. He looked like a cross between a defrocked priest and a leprechaun. Short and tubby, he wore a stained mackintosh open over a dark, lay-reader's kind of suit. His nails were filthy; so were his cloth cap and the muffler round his neck. He had a roundish, mobile face, with bad teeth but remarkable eyes—brown, lustrous, a permanent twinkle in them.

"Cheers, old fellow," this stranger said. "First I've had today—on you. Down the hatch." His voice was a rich baritone, slightly hoarse and drawling, and sounded as if at any moment it might break into a fat chuckle.

"Mine host," he said, resuming his seat by the window, "has just nipped over to the garage for some paraffin. I love oil lamps—don't you? The best period is the Birmingham 1860 standard. Quite unquestionably. Ah, brasswork was brasswork in those days." He emptied the bag of crisps into his mouth.

Nigel could think of no conversational follow-up to this. None, however, proved necessary, for the stranger rose abruptly to go.

"Must get back to my rural slum. Ta-ta."

Halfway to the door, he snapped his fingers, turned round and, advancing within a few inches of Nigel, remarked: "I say, old top, are you by any chance Strangeways?"

"Yes, I am."

"How lucky. Might have missed you. Come along up to my shack tonight, eh? About nine P.M. I have my feed at eight. Up past the church. A white gate. You can't miss it." He gave Nigel a theatrically conspiratorial look, and muttered huskily: "I've got some things to show you: you might be interested in them. Well, cheeribye for now."

Only when the door had shut did Nigel, bemused by the stranger's personality, realize that he did not know his name.

4. The Squire's Hobbies

He still did not know it when, at nine o'clock, he went out to find the white gate beyond the church. As soon as Joe had returned, the village constable came in, wanting a private talk with Nigel. Then there was the enormous meal laid on by Mrs. Summers. And after it, when Nigel put his head in at the bar, he saw a crowd of villagers taking up all Joe's attention.

P. C. Clotworthy turned out no more promising than Sir Archibald had predicted. Slow of speech, and slower of thought, he was evidently torn between professional suspicion of the amateur and compelled respect for the Londoner who had arrived under Sir Archibald's aegis. However, by showing a somewhat fulsome deference to the constable's official status, and by inquiring after his garden, Nigel contrived to break the ice a little.

Obtaining information from P. C. Clotworthy was a thing which required patience rather than finesse. He had to issue himself a permit, as it were, signed in triplicate, before answering each of Nigel's questions. This slow-motion dialogue did, however, produce a few facts. There had been the inevitable difficulty with the postal authorities over interception and examination of letters at the Prior's Umborne post office. The police had obtained the requisite authority from the P.O. Divisional Headquarters, after some delay, yesterday morning—too late to have stopped the letter which made Templeton's cowman attempt suicide. The cowman was recovering, but still refused to let his girl visit him. No anonymous letters had come to the post office since police surveillance started—none, that is, unless the writer had altered his habit of addressing the envelopes in capital letters, for the police were not as yet checking those addressed in ordinary script. Clotworthy had worked round the whole parish, inquiring at each house whether an anonymous letter had been received, and warning the householder that, if he did receive one, it should be taken at once to the police. The result, so far, was meager. Although Clotworthy had fair reason to believe that quite a few more letters must have gone out with the first batch from the poison pen, only farmer Templeton and a girl who worked as typist in Charles Blick's factory office acknowledged having received one. Templeton said he had torn up his letter, and he was extremely evasive about its contents. The Moreford Inspector had finally coaxed him into admitting that it accused him—"all damned lies, mind you"—of falsifying his returns. The typist had a nervous breakdown, and the doctor refused to allow her to be questioned yet. She had not destroyed her letter: it was "very unsavory," said Clotworthy, handing Nigel a copy, and blushing brick-red. Perusing it, Nigel thought the epithet an understatement; this letter was abominable, and frightening too.

As to fingerprints, none had been found on the letters or envelopes except those of the recipient, the postman, and the postmistress or her son, who sometimes helped her with the sorting. As far as could be checked, they had all arrived by the morning delivery: and they all had the Prior's Umborne postmark. They had, therefore, been posted some time between 3 P.M., when the box was emptied for the afternoon delivery, and eight in the morning. The stationery offered no hopeful lead either, being of a cheap brand obtainable at the village store, and in several Moreford shops. The police were trying to compile a list of all in the neighborhood who had bought such stationery, but they did not expect much from this routine. John Smart's past history looked the most promising line of investigation. He had come to Prior's Umborne not long after the end of the war, bringing his widowed sister with him, having answered an advertisement for a job as chauffeur-handyman at the Hall. He had offered an army discharge book by way of references, and Stanford Blick had been content with that. Smart's other sister, a highly respectable woman, was married to a veterinary surgeon who lived in Umborne Magna. Smart had proved so trustworthy and such an excellent mechanic that, when the works at Moreford opened, Charles Blick persuaded his brother to let him take the man onto its staff. Smart was extremely unwilling at first to change over; but he finally consented, and was soon promoted to foreman. His sister Greta, questioned by the police after his suicide, said she believed he'd been employed at some Midlands factory before joining up in 1941; but both sisters had been out of touch with their brother for some time, and he never spoke about it when they came together again. They had an old mother, who lived in an almshouse in Nottinghamshire. Police inquiries had elicited little information from her, except that she thought her son had been working on aircraft at that period. So far, inquiries from Midland firms who made aircraft during the war had turned up no employee answering to John Smart's description. Inspector Randall was now investigating the histories of the hands at the Moreford works, in case any of them could have been in contact with Smart in 1940.

It was clear that Smart must have done something pretty bad that year. Otherwise, the threat of exposure would not have driven him to suicide. On the other hand, he was by all accounts a decent, normal, trustworthy man. This, thought Nigel, seemed to point toward some nonprofessional crime—homicide in the heat of passion, for instance, or sabotage undertaken from honest if misguided political motives—for which he might have been suspected, but which had not been proved against him. Smart's reluctance to go into the Moreford works could well be interpreted as the reaction of a man who did not wish to revive memories of something that had happened in a similar milieu.

These were futile speculations until further evidence came to light. But the crucial point, thought Nigel, as he sauntered up the road toward the church, was the apparent omniscience of the poison pen. His letters had not been mere scurrilous abuse; they had gone unerringly to the victim's weakest spot, and at least two of them uncovered secrets which the victims had successfully kept dark for years from the Prior's Umborne gossips. How could one and the same person have been in a position to know what John Smart had done in 1940, when he worked in the Midlands, and what the vicar's wife was doing in London a year or two later? Even Joe Summers had had no knowledge of the vicar's ever being married, and Joe was a compendium of village gossip.

Turning over this problem in his mind, Nigel walked past the church and the tall stone gateposts of the Hall drive. It was dark now. A white owl slid like a phantom over the hedge to his right. But neither to right nor left could Nigel discover the "shack" with the white gate to which his eccentric acquaintance of the public bar had directed him. Indeed, after walking a quarter of a mile farther and finding only an outlying farm and a bungalow, Nigel began to wonder if he hadn't dreamed the man and his invitation. Turning back, he presently came again to the Hall entrance. The gateposts—stone pillars surmounted by heraldic-looking birds—attracted his attention. The gate itself he had not noticed before, because it was lying open. It was a white gate, he now saw. And a wild notion came to him that the individual he had met in The Sweet Drop must have been Stanford Blick himself.

He walked up the winding, tree-lined drive, which opened out into a rectangle of gravel in front of the house. Not a light was to be seen in its elaborate Jacobean facade. Nigel stood there for a minute, contemplating it. Then he rang the bell, and waited another minute. No one came to the door. On an impulse, he found his way round to the back of the house, which frowned down upon him with what he felt was a disapproving hauteur. As if his footsteps had touched off a mine, a fiendish clamor of dogs, yapping, snarling, baying, suddenly exploded nearby. There was a chink of light in the window of one of the outbuildings. Then the curtains were drawn open, and the face of Nigel's scruffy acquaintance looked out. Nigel moved toward this window; but before he had crossed the courtyard, the man emerged, calling out cheerily:

"I say, I absolutely forgot. Oh, lor' what a bloomer! Do forgive me. Have you been here long?"

"That's perfectly all right. Only just arrived. Afraid I'm late. I couldn't find your house at first." Nigel added, feeling a little awkward: "This *is* your house, is it? I mean—"

The man's mouth fell open in comical dismay, and he wrung his hands.

"My dear old fellow, what must you think of me! I should have introduced myself. My name is Stanford Blick. And I am domiciled here, really and truly." He took Nigel affectionately under the elbow. "Come along in. I do hate dogs, don't you?" The barking had started again, and he had to shout above the din. "I got interested in a job I was doing in my workshop, and quite forgot you were coming."

As they reached the back door, Nigel caught out of the tail of his eye a figure flitting away from the building on the far side of the courtyard. It was like an instantaneous exposure. The light from the window gave one glimpse of reddish hair; the face was averted, and the dark figure had a stooping, scurrying gait. The next instant, the shutters of the night closed upon it, and it was gone. So quickly did this happen that Nigel could not even be sure if the figure was a man or a woman. But the hair had seemed more abundant than a man's, and Nigel smiled to himself, remembering Stanford's "I got interested in a job I was doing in my workshop." Stanford had been opening the back door at that moment, oblivious to his other visitor's exit.

He now strode through the passages, throwing on electric switches with the lavishness of a magnifico scattering coins to the mob, and led Nigel into a large room at the front of the house.

"D'you know," he said confidentially, "I was so absorbed, I quite forgot my grub. The servants are in

Moreford, at the cinema"—he pronounced it "kin*e*ma" —"so I'll just see what's in the larder. Make yourself at home. Are you interested in trams? You'll find some in that wellington."

No doubt, thought Nigel, he's gone to tell the lady that the coast is clear and she can leg it for home. But he'll find the lady has vanished. Nigel looked round the room. Immense, superbly proportioned, with medallions on its greenish walls and elaborate moldings on the ceiling, it struck one first, however, as a mausoleum of its owner's dead hobbies. There seemed enough furniture in it, good, bad and indifferent, to stock three houses. On the long mantelpiece was arrayed an army of Etruscan figures. By the door stood a tall, exquisite porcelain urn, with an umbrella stuck in it, while a lighted niche nearby displayed, not an ikon, but a mug inscribed "Present from Clacton." The pictures on the walls, no less than the ceramics, revealed an indiscriminate acquisitiveness of which a jackdaw might have been ashamed. There were cases, with trays full of carefully numbered seashells; monstrosities of brass, from Birmingham via Benares; revolting pieces of pseudochinoiserie; a magnificent radiogram; a litter of dog baskets on the Aubusson carpet; and there was the wellington to which Stanford Blick had directed him.

Nigel opened one of its drawers, which was crammed with albums. The albums were filled with photographs, postcards, illustrations from trade magazines and press cuttings, all on the subject of trams. It appeared that there were, or had been, more trams in the world than Nigel cared to contemplate. The other drawers contained a mass of contributions to the same unalluring subject.

"Fascinating, aren't they?" came Stanford's enthusiastic, chuckling voice. "I've got just on three quarters of a million pictures of trams. You'll find the rest upstairs, if you're interested." He waved his left hand vaguely toward the ceiling; his right held some bread, cheese and onions on a newspaper. Spreading the newspaper on an elegant inlaid marble table, he began to eat. "The tram used to be my vehicle for meditation. It provides the perfect symbolism for the problem of free will and necessity. Have you met the vicar yet?"

Nigel admitted guardedly that he had, realizing they were on the edge of a doctrinal minefield.

"Not at all a sound fellow. I caught him out in a flagrant heresy in the very first sermon he gave here. Still, he's a Cambridge man, and one must make allowances. My brother hasn't had one of these letters yet, has he?"

"I don't think so." Nigel was learning to follow his host's free-associational method of talk: the link word here, no doubt, was Cambridge.

Stanford Blick champed an onion with his blackened teeth.

"How's the sleuth getting on? 'Sleuth,' you know, is a word probably of Icelandic derivation, originally meaning the trail of a beast followed by the hunter."

"Very suitable in the present context."

"Oh, the letters are all beastly, are they? Really beastly?" Stanford cocked a relishing eye at Nigel.

"Most of them."

"Funny the chap hasn't had a go at Charles yet. He seems to be picking on the village nobs mostly."

Nigel opened his mouth, then shut it again. Stanford, with startling alacrity, swooped on the unspoken remark.

"That's perfectly all right, old bean. I know who's been getting them because Daniel Durdle lends me a hand in the workshop sometimes. Queer fellow, Durdlepots—d'you know, he really does believe in the doctrine of predestination."

"He's a skilled mechanic, is he? How did he learn?"

"During the war, I believe. I took him on when John Smart went into my brother's factory."

"What about Smart now?" asked Nigel. "What was his guilty secret?"

"Oh, that's obvious, I should have thought. Have a glass of port, won't you? It's rather delish. Grandpop laid it down."

Stanford Blick fetched a decanter and glasses from a cupboard.

"Cheerio," he said, tossing back his port like beer, and smacking his lips. "Where were we? Oh, yes, poor old Smart. He'd been a Commie, you know."

"Had he indeed? Did he tell you?"

"No. But I took up communism myself once. And one old Stalinist can always recognize another. Little turns of phrase, and so on. Like lapsed Catholics."

"But you don't commit suicide because you've once been a Party member."

"Charles, or Pop, would have slung him out on his ear if they'd known."

"He could have got another job easily enough, a skilled man like him."

"Not if it came out that he'd been an active under-cover Commie during the war, and done something really naughty."

Nigel sat up. Here was something right in line with his own speculations.

"But who could have known?" he muttered. "Did you notice, was there anyone in the village Smart particularly tried to avoid?"

"Not specially. He kept to himself, as they say."

"You said that Durdle learned his trade during the war. Where was he then?"

"Factory. Somewhere up in the North, I believe."

"And where were you?"

Stanford Blick chuckled, wagging a forefinger good-humoredly at Nigel.

"Quite right, old sport! You keep at it! I was a boffin of sorts. Place near London. So hush-hush that I didn't know what I was doing myself, half the time. No, you'd better concentrate on Durdlepots. The mystery man of Prior's Umborne."

"Why do you call him that?"

"Because his past is shrouded in mystery," Stanford replied in his husky, confidential voice.

"His past?"

"His provenance. Very fishy. Now, if I was looking for a poison-pen writer in this village, I'd give one look at Mother Durdle and call it a day. Wheeoo, what a monster!"

"Yes, I've seen her. She is rather forbidding. But—"

"Which reminds me. I must show you my own Valentine. Come along upstairs."

"What? D'you mean you've had an anonymous letter too? But you must tell the police."

"I've saved it up for you, old top. Don't fuss."

Nigel followed his host up the main stairway. It was a handsome flight, with carved oak balustrade. The steps had been built wide enough for six people to go abreast; but at present they housed a considerable section of Stanford Blick's library, books being piled high on either side of each tread. They entered a room on the first floor.

"My den," said Stanford complacently. "How do you like it?"

Nigel was unable to answer immediately, since the room was in pitch darkness. His host lit a few of the oil lamps—no doubt of the Birmingham 1860 vintage—which stood everywhere. The light revealed a somewhat cheerless apartment, one wall lined with filing cabinets, another with crudely-colored religious posters depicting, in strip-cartoon form, profusely illustrated by references to Biblical texts, such subjects as "The Straight and Narrow Way or the Flowery Path?" Four office desks formed a hollow square in the middle of this room.

Stanford Blick sat down on one of the four swivel chairs, and rummaged in a drawer.

"Now, where did I put the dratted thing? I like to have four desks, so I can move from one job to another without getting them mixed up. Ah, here we are."

He fished a sheet of paper from under a heap of blueprints.

"What do you make of that? Came two days ago."

Handing the letter to Nigel, he gave him the look of an animal trainer testing out a new pupil—a look of dubiety masked by interest and encouragement. Nigel was by no means unaware how his host had been putting him through the hoops for the last half hour. He had a strong feeling, too, that Stanford's indiscretions were—sometimes, at any rate—very nicely calculated. The letter said:

Does Charlie know about your goings-on with his redheaded bitch?

"I make nothing of it at all," answered Nigel, rather disingenuously. "Perhaps you could enlarge on it."

Stanford Blick could hardly wait to do so. Bouncing

up and down in his chair, he said: "Old Charles has chummed up with Miss Chantmerle lately. Glorious girl. Spiffing head of hair—just like a copper warming pan. Well, you see, there are certain awkwardnesses about it; and Miss Chantmerle being an old buddy of mine, she comes now and then to cough up her troubles. Jolly smart of the chap to have spotted it, don't you think?" he added enthusiastically.

"You mean you meet in secret?"

Stanford Blick tapped the side of his nose, looking more than ever like a disreputable leprechaun.

"It has to be a bit hush-hush. Family difficulties, etc."

"I gathered your father didn't altogether approve of Rosebay Chantmerle—we *are* talking about her, I presume, not her sister?"

Stanford's eyes opened comically wide. "But of course. Good lord! Did you think I've been forgathering with the Ice Queen?"

"You don't like the elder sister?"

"Oh, I think she's perfect," was Stanford's reply: "a perfect masterpiece. Now, before you go, you must come and look at my Susie. I've got her on the bench."

Nigel pocketed the letter, which his host appeared to have entirely forgotten about, and followed him downstairs. They went out at the back again, crossed the courtyard, and entered the block of outbuildings. The lighted window by which Nigel had glimpsed Stanford's other visitor proved to be part of a large workshop, equipped with every facility, as far as Nigel could judge, which the mechanically-minded could desire, and in contrast with the Hall itself a model of cleanliness and order. For all that, he thought, it was a curious place to choose for an assignation with a lady.

"Have you any ideas on the writer of this letter?" he

asked. "Who might have discovered about your meetings with Miss Chantmerle? Does she come to the Hall to see you?"

"Generally. Sometimes in here. At night, of course. I'm convinced the servants couldn't have found out. Somebody must be spying on us, though."

Stanford's tone was distrait and uninterested. Here, in his workshop, he seemed a different man, a dilettante no longer. His attention was concentrated upon a large, elaborate engine, its metalwork gleaming, rigged on a bench before him.

Nigel was pondering the question—why should so unconventional a character have imposed such secrecy upon his meetings with Rosebay Chantmerle? Why did her emotional difficulties have to be discussed at night, with the servants out? His thoughts were interrupted by Stanford, who had been fiddling with the engine and now turned to him, a professional glint in his eye.

"Isn't she a beauty? I'll just give her a run. She's quite quiet."

He made a final adjustment, and pressed a button. The engine exploded into life with the deafening roar of a Spitfire, shaking the bench as if any moment it would take off and zoom through the workshop roof. Stanford's mouth was moving with immense animation; no doubt he was pouring out technicalities, but in this fiendish din Nigel could not hear a word he was saying. Now Stanford had reduced the volume a little and was listening to the engine, head cocked and a worried frown on his forehead, like a conductor who suspects a wrong note in a full orchestral passage he is rehearsing. At last he switched off the ignition.

"Damn those noisy brutes," he said, as a clamor of dogs, driven hysterical by the engine's din, became audible. "It's not right yet. I can't get that timing perfect. Never mind, old girl"—he slapped the shining cylinder block affectionately—"we'll fix you up."

"It must be an expensive hobby, all this."

"So-so. But it's not a hobby." A fanatical gleam appeared in Stanford's eyes. "I'm out to produce a world-beater. Do better than poor old B.R.M., you know. Pop can't see it; but there's money in a thing like this, as well as prestige."

Nigel thought it was time to take his leave. Having wished Stanford good night, he stepped out into the yard. He had only gone a few paces, however, before he heard his name called. Stanford was at the door, distractedly smacking his high, domed forehead.

"I knew I'd forgotten something. Should you have any *other* ideas about Durdlepots, keep them under your hat at lunch tomorrow, like a good sport, will you? *Verb. sap.* What the ear don't hear, the heart won't grieve for."

Nigel was pondering these enigmatic words as he walked back to the village. He had decided to take the other way—a footpath which led to the Little Manor and, just beyond the plantation north of the Hall, met the track going down from the Little Manor to the village. He had almost reached the intersection when he heard footsteps slurring on the grass. On an impulse, he froze still by the gap in the hedge he had been approaching. It was dark. But not so dark that he could not recognize, as it passed on the path from the Chantmerles' house to the village, the tall, stooping figure of Daniel Durdle. It moved with a sliding gait, as if on wheels or a caterpillar track, and unnaturally fast, it seemed: then the hedge gap framed nothing but the night's darkness again.

5. The Plymouth Brother's Father

At ten o'clock the next morning, Nigel walked along to the post office. After a hard frost, Prior's Umborne sparkled in the sunshine. Today there were a few people to be seen; but they stood in a knot by the crossroads, and Nigel's "good morning" was met with silence and averted eyes, not the usual cheerful West-Country greeting for a stranger. Prior's Umborne was a poisoned village, no doubt about that. Nigel found himself quoting, "Where each man walks with his head in a cloud of poisonous flies." The cordial sunlight, the clean brisk air seemed a mockery. He felt a spurt of anger against the unknown who had done such havoc—this maniac with a hypodermic syringe in his pocket. Or was it, not madness, but a coldly-calculated move in some game whose goal could not yet be seen?

The bell jangled as Nigel stepped into the post office. Mrs. Durdle, rigid behind the counter, squeezed out a quarter inch of smile for him.

"Daniel is waiting for you in the parlor," she said. But Nigel showed no disposition to hurry to the appointment. He commented on the beauties of Prior's

Umborne, the neatness of the shop. Had Mrs. Durdle kept it for many years? Was she a native of the village? Her face stony with suspicion, the woman grudgingly admitted that she had lived here all her life, and had taken over the shop and post office from her husband when he died, just before the war.

"It must have been lonely for you during the war, with your son away."

"I made do. Others had to."

"Your son was working in the North, I believe?"

"Yes, up in Lancashire. He was on airplane engines—some special parts for them. Skilled work. He was always clever with his hands. They thought very well of him at the Grammar School. If he'd had his rights, he should have gone to College."

Once again Mrs. Durdle's curious defensive-aggressive pride in her son showed itself. Nigel remarked negligently: "I suppose he took after his father?"

If an iron bar could grow visibly more rigid, this is how Mrs. Durdle looked. A flush came over her sallow face, and she snapped: "What might you mean by that?"

"Well, he doesn't look very like you, does he? But I really meant his mechanical skill. And his brains. His father must have been a remarkable—"

"Daniel is as God made him," the woman formidably replied.

Nigel had noticed, when he came in, that the door between shop and parlor was open. He wondered how Daniel, no doubt listening in there, would receive this comment on his creation. He began asking Mrs. Durdle about the postal arrangements. She cleared the box and stamped the letters whenever there was a slack period in the shop; but the regulations bound her to clear it again fifteen minutes before the postal van was due, and yet again when the van arrived. Yes, her son sometimes did the clearing and stamping for her. If there were a great many letters in the final clearance, she was allowed to send them into Moreford unstamped, so that the van driver should not be kept waiting. But she was supposed to make sure that no letters posted here to Prior's Umborne addresses went in to Moreford first. On a rough average, the village post office handled between one hundred and three hundred letters a day, outgoing and incoming. No, neither she nor Daniel had particularly noticed the anonymous letters, even the second batch of them. A lot of the village people addressed their envelopes in capitals. It wasn't her business to go prying into correspondence.

"It's funny they should all have been posted here, isn't it? You'd think it'd be safer to post them, say, in Moreford. Unless, of course, the person who wrote them is somehow tied to this place—or is someone who would be particularly noticed posting letters in Moreford."

Mrs. Durdle's eyes were like sparks struck off flint, but she said nothing.

"I mean," went on Nigel, smiling at her with the greatest amiability, "it would look pretty queer, you or your son posting letters there, for instance—sort of coals to Newcastle."

"We've had all that with the police. It's downright wicked, making such suggestions. And, anyway, if somebody wanted a Moreford postmark on the letters, they don't need to go into Moreford for it," Mrs. Durdle added, on a note of dialectical triumph.

"Oh? How's that?"

"You just put them in the box at the other end of the village, opposite the New Inn. The mail van clears them from there and takes them direct to Moreford G.P.O."

The doorbell jangled, and a customer came in. At the same moment, Daniel Durdle's head appeared around the corner of the parlor door, with the blind, weaving motion which Nigel had noticed yesterday.

"Ah, Mr. Strangeways. I thought I heard your voice. Step this way, sir."

The little parlor was as crowded, scoured, meticulously tidy as the shop. Aspidistras and maidenhair ferns on the window sill gave it a greenish gloom. Daniel Durdle might have been a caterpillar shut up in a matchbox, with green stuff thoughtfully provided. Pointing Nigel to a black, shiny armchair, he curled himself down onto the sofa.

"Are your investigations bearing fruit, sir?"

"Almost too much. A positive fruit salad."

Daniel gave a polite laugh. "Well, that is good news. We shall all be rejoiced here when the evildoer is caught in his own snare."

"Will you? *All* of you? This person must have friends, relatives, someone who loves her—or him."

"You take me up too quickly, sir. It would be a grievous burden to bear, indeed, for those near and dear. Nevertheless—"

"Nevertheless, 'If thine eye offend thee, pluck it out'?"

The man's thick spectacles flashed as he lifted his head. His sleek voice took on resonance, a tone of authority.

"The Elect are not judged by the judgment of this world."

"You think the poison-pen writer is one of the Elect, do you?"

The thin mouth in the lard-white face quirked a little. "That is what *you* think, isn't it, sir? I heard what you said to my mother."

"I made no accusations against your mother. But if you ask what I think . . ." Nigel paused; he wanted to shake this man, so apparently impregnable behind his pebbly spectacles and his Scriptural phrases; but even more he wanted to make any sort of human contact with him. "If you ask what I think, I'll tell you. First, anyone living in a post office has special facilities for the sending of anonymous letters. Second, people who write them usually have some grudge against life. Third, such people often get it into their heads that they're divine instruments for the exposure and punishment of wickedness."

"We are all divine instruments," replied Durdle in a flat voice. Nigel made no comment, but allowed the silence to protract itself till the ticking of the grandfather clock sounded like a slow torture. Finally, Daniel Durdle leaned forward.

"What grudge against life should we have, Mother or I?"

"Well, with your abilities, you're cut out for something better than this"—Nigel gestured round the poky, ugly room. "And your mother—don't tell me she's a contented woman, *or* a resigned one. And don't tell me, either," he added, "that you're happy in the humble estate to which God has called you."

"Happy! That's the cant of the unregenerate," said Daniel contemptuously.

"Is that your father?" Nigel asked, gazing at a large, framed photograph on the wall behind Daniel's head, which jerked sideways, as if trying to avoid the words.

"Yes. Yes, that's Dad. Why do you ask?"

"I'm interested," replied Nigel, getting up to scrutinize the picture more closely. "Extraordinary."

"I don't see anything extraordinary in—"

"Oh, please forgive me. I didn't mean that. It's a good

face. Generous. No, I was thinking about something else: the anonymous letter you got."

"I don't follow you."

"It's rather difficult. You mustn't take offense. One of the things I've heard since coming down here is that you are not Mr. Durdle's son. No, wait a minute! It's just silly village gossip, no doubt. But why didn't the anonymous writer put that in his letter, instead of some nonsense about strong liquor? It'd have been much more wounding, much more his style."

Daniel's delicate, stained fingers were writhing in his lap. Insulated behind those thick lenses, there must be some look of naked emotion, Nigel was sure; but was it grief, shame, indignation, or sheer vindictive hatred? He went on quickly: "There's another thing I wanted to ask you. Don't you think it very strange that Miss Chantmerle hasn't received a letter?"

Durdle uncoiled himself, and towered stooping over Nigel.

"Get out! Get out! I've had about enough from you!" He was trembling all over, his face twisting uncontrollably.

"No, not yet. Why should that question upset you so?"

"Why should I answer your questions at all? Who do you think you are, poking your nose into our affairs?"

"Is Miss Chantmerle your affair?"

Daniel Durdle's mouth set in an obstinate line, the image of his mother's. He would not reply.

"Are you protecting somebody else?" Nigel persisted. Daniel's face was turned away, like a stubborn child's. Nigel's pale-blue eyes scrutinized him with merciless curiosity. "Well, then, I'll be going. I shall see you again."

Daniel turned his head, where he stood by the mantelpiece. Nigel was startled to see a covert, arrogant, childish smile on his face.

"You know you can't do anything about it," said the man.

"It's difficult to convict poison pens, if that's what you mean. But one can give them a thorough good fright, and hope they won't do it again. Good-by."

Back at the inn, Nigel took out a sheet of paper. His memory was phenomenal, but he liked to set out its results and clarify his mind in writing. After half an hour, the paper read as follows:

The Letters

(i) All except the vicar's and J. Smart's (and possibly Templeton's?) based on gossip and/or observation. How was information obtained about vicar's wife and Smart's past? Answer surely obvious; but verify with vicar's friend. And police must find out if Smart's mother ever got a letter from him. Also, police should work from other end—all cases of suspected sabotage in 1940.

(ii) The second letter box, opposite New Inn. This surely clinches it.

(iii) Why no letter to Chantmerles? Or Charles Blick? Verify.

(iv) *Motive*: *(a)* bloody-mindedness; *(b)* madness—sex and/or religion; *(c)* sabotage of Moreford factory—foreman and secretary out of action: work suffering, according to Sir A.

Interesting, if irrelevant

(i) Sir A's unveiled hints.

(ii) Source of Chantmerles' money: financing of Stanford's experiments.

(iii) Rosebay's "difficulties."

(iv) Stanford's relationship with R. Also his parting remark.
(v) Daniel's walk last night.
(vi) Mark Raynham's mixture of indiscretion and reticence.

The answer to one of his questions was forthcoming sooner than Nigel expected. Just after midday, the landlord put his head in at the parlor and said:

"There's a lady come to see you, sir. Miss Rosebay."

Nigel's first impression of the younger Chantmerle sister was that her father, who gave his children such far-fetched names, had chosen better than he knew. Her hair was a rich bay-red color, luxuriant and glossy. It seemed darker now, in the dim little parlor, than it had looked by the light of Stanford's workshop window; but there was no mistaking the hurried, slouching, apologetic gait which he had seen for a moment last night. The woman came rapidly in, half tripping over the mat at the door.

"I'm awfully sorry," she said.

"It's the mat's fault. You mustn't apologize to it."

"What? Oh, yes. Stupid of me." She smiled uncertainly. "Am I disturbing you? I thought I'd—but I expect you're busy."

"Not a bit. Come and sit down."

She made a plunge for a chair, dropped her bag, said "Sorry," picked it up and held it tightly to her.

"This is like the beginning of a Sherlock Holmes story," said Nigel, smiling at the girl. "A young woman is announced, and appears 'in a state of high agitation.' Don't tell me you're being pursued by a sinister gentleman with the little finger of his left hand missing!"

Rosebay Chantmerle took a grip on herself, like a

stammerer counting up to five before he speaks; then said: "I've come to fetch you for lunch. It's my sister's birthday."

"It's very kind of you. But you needn't have bothered. I know the way."

"Well, actually there was something else too. Stanford said I ought to show you—I do hope you don't mind?"

As she fumbled in her bag, Nigel studied the downturned face. It was white, freckled, the bone good, the mouth untidily made up with a disastrously wrong shade of lipstick. Her body, hunched over the handbag, looked narrower, thinner than it was. She doesn't give herself a chance, thought Nigel. Or perhaps she's never been allowed to. But surely Charles . . .

"We got this letter on April 7," Rosebay began, as if repeating a lesson. "It was addressed to my sister, but I took it. Mark Raynham rang me up the moment he'd got his, and the postman doesn't reach us till ten minutes later, so I was waiting for it."

"Very thoughtful of the vicar. But why should he suppose—?"

"Oh, it was just in case other anonymous letters were on their way, you know."

"So the idea was that you should intercept it?"

"Of course, when I saw what it said, I didn't tell Mark we'd had one. I mean, it's sort of a family secret."

"A secret you want to keep from your sister?"

"That's awfully clever of you to guess."

There was something pathetic in the way she said it, as if she'd read that men should always be flattered, but had had only too few opportunities for practicing the precept. Her green eyes gazed eagerly at Nigel, as she held out the letter.

"The secret being," said Nigel, "that your father had an illegitimate son, about thirty years ago? Daniel Durdle?"

"My God! How did you—who told you that?" Her voice had suddenly become sharp and aggressive.

"The vicar gave part of it away—no, quite unintentionally. And there's the color of his hair. And his hands. And his brains. And some other things. But d'you mean to say your sister doesn't know about this?"

"I've always—I kept it from her. She idolized father. It would have been a terrible shock."

"You've 'always' kept it from her. How long have you known?"

The girl's face lost all its rather harassed animation. She now looked absurdly sullen and mutinous, her full lower lip sticking out.

"Well, aren't you going to read it?" She thrust the letter at him, with one of her ungainly movements.

"If you like."

The letter said:

Your dear noble Dad a bastard had. So R.I.P. the dirty old rip.

"H'm. Breaking into verse. And what am I to do about this?"

Rosebay's tone was positively scolding now. "Don't be silly. Find out who wrote it, of course. Doesn't it help—I mean, the letter itself?"

"But, don't you see? I've got to find out how *you* knew about Durdle if you're going to help me find out how the writer of this thing knew it," said Nigel patiently.

"I suppose that means you think I wrote it," she said, jutting out her lip at him.

"It doesn't mean anything of the sort. Durdle was blackmailing you, I imagine. When did it start?"

"Imagine away, if it makes you happy."

"I can't think why you should want to conceal it from me. What's the sense, now you've shown me the letter?"

"Oh, very well," muttered the girl ungraciously. She had risen, and was pacing across the parlor with her queer, loping stride. Suddenly she stopped dead, dramatically, crying: "Isn't it obvious? Nobody likes showing themselves up. All right, I was feeble, cowardly. I should have told him where to get off. But I'm no good. I'm frightened of him. That's why he picked on me. Dinny would have stood up to him."

"Your sister? You did it to protect her, though. You shouldn't blame yourself for that."

"Protect!" exclaimed Rosebay bitterly, throwing herself back in her chair.

"When did it start?"

"About six months ago."

"Why then? Why not six years ago?"

"Perhaps he hadn't found out, himself, till then."

"Can you remember anything happening about that time—anything which might have made him boil over?"

Rosebay was chewing her thumb in a childish, intent way. "Oh, lord! Yes! I never thought of that! The meeting."

"The meeting?"

"Yes. There was a village meeting. About Charles's factory. I don't expect you know how petty the people in villages can be. There was opposition to a scheme Charles had for night shifts—the work's frightfully urgent—which would have meant people sometimes having to work on till six o'clock on Sunday mornings. Of course, it was voluntary, and overtime pay and all that. Durdle led the opposition. He's always been anti the factory. But he took a line about profaning the Sabbath. He's jolly eloquent, you know; and he got the meeting on his side. But then Dinny got up—I mean, she spoke from her electric carriage. She made such fun of Durdle's speech that even the Plyms began to snigger. It was all done quite nicely—you know—not sneering at him personally or offending religious susceptibilities—sort of gently showing him up, and stressing the rearmament emergency. But the fact is that, in spite of looking such a freak, Durdle is riddled with vanity."

"So I've noticed."

"Well, don't you think being deflated in public like that might have sort of turned him spiteful against us?"

"I can't imagine anything more likely. So then he started to blackmail you. But what proof did he give you of being your half-brother?"

Daniel had shown the girl a letter written to his mother by Edric Chantmerle. It urged her to marry Albert Durdle, who had been courting her, as soon as possible. The letter implied quite unmistakably that she should allow Albert to believe that the child she was carrying was his.

"You see why I tried to keep it from Dinny. It wasn't so much that father had had an illegitimate child. It was this letter he wrote—panicky and mean; and fobbing the child off on someone else. You see, Dinny has lived on her illusions about him." Rosebay's voice became bitter. "He was God to her. Nobody else came anywhere."

"So you paid him money. How much?"

"I've given him two lots of fifty pounds so far."

"The devil you have! That's a lot of money."

"Oh, I don't mind about the money. It's—it's . . . He

frightens me so," the girl wailed, and was suddenly broken with ugly, hard sobs, her face a picture of utter despair. Nigel saw the small, white face looking over the edge of the quarry twenty years ago.

"I'm afraid . . . he's . . . mad," Rosebay sobbed out. And presently, when she had got control of herself: "Don't pay any attention to what I say. I'm sorry for making a fool of myself."

"Where did you get the money from?" asked Nigel gently.

"My savings."

"You know it's puzzled me how you and your sister manage. Your father lost all his money, I thought."

"*He* thought so. Not all, it turned out." Rosebay gave a queer, slantwise look at the door. Then, lowering her voice, said: "Oh, you might as well know. But you must promise not to breathe a word to my sister. We live on charity. Stanford and Charles fixed it up somehow between them, when father died—so as to look as if something had been saved from the wreck. It's their money really: or their father's, I suppose. Anyway, it comes through solicitors. Dinny would never have taken a penny from the Blicks, knowingly."

"I see. So that's what you have your secret confabulations about with Stanford?"

The girl started violently, knocking her bag off the arm of the chair. "What? Who told you?"

"He did. But not what they were about, of course."

"Really, Stanford is impossible," she breathed to herself, with a faint smile which Nigel found rather enigmatic.

"Was Daniel Durdle fetching back some hush money from you last night? I saw him walking down from your direction, about eleven o'clock."

"Last night? No. How extraordinary! What could he have been doing? From our house, you say?"

"Just taking the air, then, I presume. Does anyone else know about this blackmail?"

The girl looked discomposed. After a brief hesitation, she said in a flurried way: "Well, actually, I told Stanford. Lately."

"Not his brother?"

"Charles? No." For the first time, Rosebay Chantmerle looked the woman of twenty-nine she was, not a nervous, uncertain girl. "Charles has far too much on his hands for me to bother him with things like that," she said firmly. "Perhaps we'd better move along now."

"And what was Stanford's advice?"

"Oh, he was for telling the police. But it's all very well; Dinny'd be bound to hear about it. And then—"

"Somebody ought to start a society for the protection of *you*, for a change," said Nigel lightly.

Her face took on again its mutinous-child look. "Oh, *I* don't matter." She rose from her chair. "Don't tell my sister we've been talking all this time. I've just come to fetch you after doing the shopping."

6. The Beauty's Birthday

Nigel's memories of Celandine Chantmerle were always to be mixed up, garlanded as it were, with daffodils. There had been those clumps shivering in the chill wind on the brink of the quarry. And now, as Rosebay led the way onto the mossed stone steps at the back of the house, he saw her sister, framed for a moment by the open French windows, out in the garden beyond, with daffodils like golden fountains spurting all round her. The sunshine, which enhanced the fine gold of her hair, discovered on her face few marks of age or suffering. She was exquisitely made up: but she had that Botticellian purity of feature which can only be refined, not coarsened, by the passing years. Sitting there, with the blossoms foaming and flouncing about her, she seemed an eternal Primavera. You did not have to ignore politely the wheeled chair, the rug over her knees, for wherever she sat, she was enthroned.

Nigel was aware of her body swaying gracefully forward, the fluttering hand, a dancing look from the periwinkle blue eyes, a voice bubbling and tinkling like a fountain.

"Isn't it lovely out here? I'm so glad you could come. It makes my birthday. 'My heart is like a water-chute.' What an absurdly expressive line that is! Now let me introduce you. The vicar you know. And this is Charles Blick."

A dark, grave man, in his early forties, rose from the deck chair beside her—a taller, spruce, dependable version of Stanford, with the same deep brown eyes as his brother, but a worried, abstracted look in them at present.

"How d'you do," he said. "Very good of you to come down. Rather an unpleasant assignment for you, I'm afraid."

"Oh, Charles, you *are* a silly boy," cried Celandine. "I'm sure Mr. Strangeways adores delving into dark secrets. I should. Like having the run of somebody else's attics, as a child. D'you remember how we used to explore the attics at the Hall?"

"Stanford's turned the whole place into a gigantic lumber room now. You wouldn't recognize it."

"I wish he'd disgorge some of it for my jumble sale," said Mark Raynham.

"Oh, your jumble sales!" Celandine lifted her hands gaily. "All the most horrible objects in the village drifting round from hand to hand, year after year. The circulation of the bloody."

The vicar laughed. "I must admit they create a lot of bad blood. The last one turned into a sort of smash-and-grab raid."

"But for rousing naked passions," said Celandine, "there's nothing to compare with a good, all-in, village whist drive."

"Except perhaps a poison-pen writer."

There was an instant gulf of silence, over which they

looked at Rosebay Chantmerle, standing apart by the tray of drinks. She seemed to have shrunk into herself, thought Nigel, like a shadow at high noon.

"Bay, *darling!* Don't spoil my birthday." Celandine smiled enchantingly at her sister, who winced a little, narrowing her eyes as if against an intolerable radiance.

"Doesn't anyone want a drink?" she said.

Charles Blick made as if to move to her side, but instead took out his cigarette case and offered it to Celandine and Nigel.

"You'd better let Mark pour them out," said Celandine. She turned to Nigel. "Bay is accident-prone. Bottles reel at a glance from her."

"Oh, nonsense, Dinny," said Charles.

"But it's a sign of a generous, impulsive nature. I wish *I* knocked everything over."

"You bowl us all over," said the vicar, with his rough, ringing laugh.

"Really, Mark! Stop being a hearty curate out of *Punch,* and give Mr. Strangeways a drink."

Looking back on the scene afterward—Celandine Chantmerle holding court among the flowers and blossoms—Nigel was to rack his mind in vain for any hint about the appalling thing which shortly befell. As he chatted with his hostess, he could still catch faint signals from the human problems around him.

Intercepting a glance from Rosebay to Charles Blick, he could wonder idly if it was an S.O.S. or just one more manifestation of her self-distrust and nervous instability. Then Charles, that solid, dependable man—what was it that gave his eyes their haunted look? Was it trouble at the works? or some unlayable ghost out of the past? or being somehow the center of tension between the two sisters? As for Mark Raynham, there was no doubt where his heart lay; he was not a subtle man; his tone, when he spoke to Celandine, betrayed him.

But it was part of Celandine's quality that human problems withdrew to a respectful distance from her presence. She did not beglamour you into ignoring them, or wave the wand of her enchantment to make them disappear. It was just that, through her, you seemed to be seeing them in perspective, neither blurred nor unnaturally remote, as if she nicely adjusted the range finder of your mental eyes.

"A perfect masterpiece," Stanford Blick had called her. "A heart of gold . . . Wonderfully sympathetic . . . Of course, she's difficult at times—a bit imperious," the vicar had naïvely said. Stanford's was the sardonic view, the tribute perhaps of a man who deliberately resisted her charm. "Difficult at times" she certainly could be. Only just now there had been a little brush of temperament. Rosebay had brought her a Martini.

"No, darling, I want a Dubonnet."

"But you always like Martini best. I got it specially for you. And actually the Dubonnet has run out."

"Oh, and on my birthday too! Can't I have what I like on my birthday? No, sweetie, I really don't fancy Martini. Bring me gin and tonic—anything else."

Celandine was giving a quite conscious imitation of the spoiled beauty. Her manner conveyed, "This is what I'd be like if I was the fretful, capricious creature which I'm entitled to be." Her touch was light as feathers; but, seeing Rosebay turn away, flushed with mortification, Nigel thought that feathers, if there were enough of them, could suffocate.

When the maid, Charity Cooper, had announced lunch, Celandine wheeled her chair round to the front door. The vicar lifted her out of it and carried her into the dining room. Her body was small, light, delicate as a figurine; and she contrived to make the process seem the most natural thing in the world, not the spectacle of a helpless cripple.

"You may put the bundle down there," she said, pointing to a chair at the head of the table, her blue eyes dancing at Mark Raynham. "Parcels!" she exclaimed, looking at a side table stacked with them. "I'll never get over the thrill of opening parcels, if I live to a hundred. You sit here, Mr. Strangeways. Charles here. Mark, next to Charles. That's right."

Presently she turned to Nigel. "This is a time-honored ceremony. When we were children, my father always kept the presents for after lunch. The word 'tenterhooks' will be found written on my heart. Yes, that's him up there." She indicated a portrait at which Nigel had been glancing—a handsome, delicate-featured man with a wispy blond mustache.

"I read some of his essays the other day. He wrote beautifully."

"I'm *so* glad you liked them." Her eyes seemed to burn a deeper blue. "I wish you'd known him. He was the most wonderful man I've ever known. Charles, will you deal with the wine?"

She had a pretty, proprietorial way of addressing Charles Blick. Well, they are old friends, thought Nigel; there was an understanding between them once. Perhaps there is again. But then, why should Charles be so silent, so little at ease?

They drank to Celandine Chantmerle's health. Mark Raynham made a pleasant, ingenuous little speech, his looks saying a great deal more than his words—so much more that, when he sat down, there was a moment of rather awkward silence, in which a metallic sound made itself heard. Rosebay's hand, trembling violently on the table, was making the knife beside it knock against a spoon. She put her hand hurriedly into her lap.

"Well, Strangeways, have you had any luck yet?" asked Charles Blick.

"About the letters? Yes, I know who wrote them, I think. But it's not going to be easy to prove."

"Already?" Celandine's eyes opened wide. "You must be formidable. I'm not quite sure I like you as a birthday guest," she went on, with a ravishing smile, "reading the darkest secrets of our souls like an open book."

"Don't be absurd, Dinny. You haven't any dark secrets," said Rosebay in a rush of words.

A queer look, half-serious, half-teasing, swept over the beauty's face like a cloud shadow across a golden cornfield. "Haven't I? There's someone I'd gladly have murdered once. Perhaps I would still, if I had the chance. Is that dark enough?"

The vicar laughed, as if some tension had been broken. "Oh, we've all had someone we'd like to kill. That's nothing to boast about."

"But you'd be much too sporting to do it, wouldn't you—except in fair fight." There was a slight edge upon Celandine's voice. She turned to Nigel, saying gaily: "I do hope it's not Mark you're going to arrest."

"My dear girl, what are you talking about?" said Charles.

"The anonymous letters." She gave the vicar a mischievous look. "After all, with his confessional he must have wonderful opportunities. I'm glad I don't go to confession."

Charles and Rosebay blurted out together: "Really, Dinny, that's going too far."

"But Mark had one of the letters himself."

"Poison pens always write one to themselves, don't they, Mr. Strangeways? What *was* your letter about, Mark, anyway? I'm sure you've lived a blameless life."

"Dark secrets," replied the vicar, the look of pain on his haggard face contradicting his light tone. He added, gently and firmly: "And I don't, as it happens, use the confessional to write letters driving people to suicide."

Celandine stretched a hand toward him. "Silly. I was only joking. My birthday's gone to my tongue. Forgive?"

When lunch was over, the men moved the parcel-laden side table over to their hostess. She fell upon the presents with childlike glee, tearing open the wrappings impatiently and commenting upon the contents with a child's lack of inhibition. They were all gathered round her. So infectious was her pleasure that Nigel felt as if it was his own birthday.

"What's this? . . . Oh, Mark, you shouldn't. But it's the most exquisite thing," cried Celandine, opening a case with a miniature inside it. . . . "Charles? From you? Aquamarines! Oh, you are an angel! Just *look* at this pendant. Like flowers of blue ice . . . Now, hold tight, everybody. This is from the Women's Institute, I warn you. They've been doing raffia work, and I anticipate the worst." She bent her head over the frightful object, her shoulders rippling with laughter. "No, it's beyond my worst nightmares. Bless them, poor loves. . . . Oh, Bay, darling, how sweet of you. It's just what I wanted, you clever thing. . . . Now what? From *Stanford!* This is unheard of." She drew out of its wrappings an elaborate construction of shells enclosed by a glass dome. "He must have made it himself. You see? It's a sort of mausoleum. Rather weird and *réussi,* isn't it? Absolutely typical. But, Charles—fancy your brother marking the occasion! . . . What a heavy parcel!

Goodness, these are rather splendid, aren't they? But whoever sent them?"

She took out of a stout cardboard box a pair of binoculars, and raised them to her eyes. "I can't see anything. Charles, you're in the light." As he moved aside, she directed the binoculars toward a window.

"I still can't focus. . . . This screw's awfully stiff," she said, her middle finger on the range finder.

"Here, let me try it," said Rosebay, brusquely taking the glasses from her sister's hands. Holding the binoculars a little way from her head, to get a better purchase, she put thumb and index finger on the screw.

That same instant, Charles Blick suddenly reached out as if to snatch the binoculars from her. But, before he could touch them, there was a click, the binoculars jerked like a small, furious animal in the girl's hands, and fell to the floor.

Charles snatched back his own hand, as if he had been stung, and looked stupidly at the blood beginning to ooze from it.

With a hoarse, choked scream, Rosebay bent down, picked up the binoculars and held them in front of her sister's face. Two needles projected from the end where the eyepieces should have been.

Charles Blick was at Rosebay's side. "Oh, darling, you might have been blinded," he cried out to her in a voice distraught with horror. "Are you all right, love?"

"It was Celandine the damned thing . . ." began the vicar. But Celandine Chantmerle had somehow clawed herself to her feet and was leaning on the table she gripped, a look of utter incredulity on the Primavera face, the blue eyes angry as bruises, the mouth warped downward to one side. Then she fell forward on the table, and slid to the floor.

Mark Raynham carried her to the bedroom on the ground floor, followed by Rosebay. While they were out, Charles muttered, more to himself than Nigel: "My God, what a fiendish thing! I—it's absolutely incredible." He stared at the bloodstained handkerchief he'd loosely tied round his hand. "I had a sort of premonition something was wrong. That's why I tried to snatch—they'd have killed her, wouldn't they?"

"Killed or blinded. Not very cozy. Go and ring up the Moreford police at once, like a good chap."

The floor was littered with paper, string, packings. Nigel suddenly realized his mouth was bone-dry, as if he'd had a near miss by a bomb. He gulped a glass of water, then knelt down amid the debris.

When Charles Blick returned, he found Nigel holding a half sheet of paper in one hand, in the other the cardboard box.

"Read this," said Nigel. "No, don't touch it. I found it under the tissue paper in the box."

Charles's face turned sick as he looked. In capital letters, on that piece of cheap stationery, were the words:

Read this now, Bright Eyes, if you can.

Charles Blick poured himself out some whisky from the sideboard, and tossed it back neat. "Did that contraption come by post?"

"By hand, apparently. No postmark. Name and address in capitals, as with the anonymous letters," said Nigel, holding up the brown paper.

"Good God, it's the same joker, is it?"

"Possibly. Possibly not. No, use this handkerchief if you want to look at them," Nigel said quickly, as Charles stooped to pick up the binoculars. "Not but what the prints'd be smeared by now, if your joker left any."

Charles Blick gingerly touched the range finder and the projecting needles. "Damned neat little job by somebody. Faked up so that the screw released two springs, presumably, with these needles on the end. Eyepieces removed and plastic substituted, the needle points lying flush with holes bored in the plastic."

"Yes, quite a precision-tool job."

"What the devil do you mean by that?" Charles's mouth went thin and hard as his father's.

"Exactly what I say. Only a highly-skilled man, with specialized tools, could have done it."

"If you really think I could do a thing like that to Rosebay—"

"I never suggested you did. And you're forgetting—the binoculars were sent to her sister."

"Sorry. I spoke out of turn. It's shaken me up. If that screw hadn't been a bit stiff to move . . ." Charles whistled, turning up his eyes. "The needles struck like a damned cobra."

"Which reminds me. Go and disinfect that puncture at once. No, do as I tell you. We can't take any risks."

"Oh, draw it mild. *Poisoned* needles? That's Borgia stuff."

"And ask the maid to—oh, it's you." Rosebay had entered the room, to say that her sister wanted to see Charles. Nigel could almost hear the unspoken question in Charles's eyes as he turned to the girl. She gave a barely perceptible shrug.

"No, I'm sorry, but I damn well can't." Charles Blick muttered it to himself, in a voice so strained that the vicar, now standing in the doorway, gazed at him with consternation. The next moment he was brushed aside by Charles, who lunged out of the room and out of the house. Nigel saw him hurrying past the windows, in full flight from whatever it was that had driven him forth.

"What on earth—?" began Mark Raynham.

"Please go back to Miss Chantmerle," said Nigel. "She mustn't be alone."

"She doesn't want *me*." Mark's expression was nakedly sad. "I think Bay had better go up again."

"No, I've got to talk to Bay at once. Send up the maid. Now," said Nigel slowly and gently, when the vicar had gone out, "sit down and tell me just how this parcel got here."

Rosebay's green eyes regarded him mistrustfully, but she obeyed. "It must have been left on the ledge outside the front door. I just brought it in with the other parcels."

She seemed to have herself remarkably well under control, though she twisted a handkerchief, and her eyes kept swiveling back to the binoculars which Charles had left on the table. Nigel's questions elicited the following information: the village postman quite often left parcels outside on the ledge, instead of waiting for the front door to be opened. This morning Rosebay had gone out from breakfast, on hearing his knock, and taken three off the ledge. She had noticed that one of them was unusually heavy for its size, but not that it had no postmark. She put all three on the side table in the dining room, together with those which had arrived previously, all ready for the birthday lunch.

"And did you notice it there last night, when you came back from the Hall?"

"Came back? Oh, no. No, I didn't."

"Or hear anyone moving about outside during the night, or early morning?"

"No. But—"

"But?"

"Well, you said you saw Daniel Durdle walking away from here last night."

Nigel gazed at her noncommittally, saying nothing.

"I mean, it does seem queer, doesn't it?"

"Yes. But wouldn't it be queerer still for Durdle to want your sister dead?"

"I'm sorry, I don't quite—"

"You'd have no need to pay him any more blackmail money. You were paying to protect her, not yourself."

"Oh, I see." The girl's eyes flinched away from Nigel, then returned to him. "Well, as a matter of fact—I didn't tell you this morning, but last time I paid him I said I wasn't going to pay any more."

"You've not had much practice, have you?" murmured Nigel.

"Practice?"

"In lying."

Rosebay Chantmerle went up like a battery of rockets. Pacing the room, with that louch, loping stride, her red hair blazing, her self-distrust forgotten, she gave Nigel a thorough dressing-down for his rudeness, his impertinent curiosity, insensitiveness, etc., etc. She might be a bad liar, he thought, but she had the makings of a superb actress. He had the impression that this outburst was a relief to her—that she was giving vent to some smoldering chagrin which had nothing to do with his own provocative remark. As she flung round at the door, to give him a last fine angry glance, he was reminded of Charles Blick's exit, so notably less dignified. Was the girl's deep chagrin due to Charles's having somehow failed her? He had cut a poorish figure, certainly, skittering out of the house rather than going up to see Celandine. The domestic "difficulties" Stanford had mentioned were not chiefly centered upon Daniel Durdle, Nigel now realized. However, the arrival of Inspector Randall and a police sergeant prevented him from prolonging these speculations.

Randall was a clean-shaven, pink-faced man, with a farmer's deliberation of speech and the shrewd, steady gaze of his own profession. Nigel took to him at once. When he had given a full account of the happenings after lunch and his other observations, the Inspector eyed him meditatively for a few moments, then said:

"So it looks like this. A skilled man, with access to the right tools. Probably someone in the neighborhood, since this boobytrap"—he poked a finger at the binoculars—"was delivered by hand. First job—jot this down, Harry—trace the field glasses. Won't be so easy, as the chap has filed off the trademark and serial numbers; and I don't reckon he'll have left prints for us. The box and wrapping paper won't help much; it looks like an egg box with the compartments removed. Buy 'em anywhere. Well, then, the obvious places where the job could have been done are Mr. Stanford Blick's workshop and the Moreford factory. Take the former. Job done by Mr. Blick or Durdle. Durdle seen walking down from this direction last night. He has the skill, and the run of Mr. Blick's workshop. He has a grudge against Miss Chantmerle. But, as you say, sir, why kill the goose that laid the golden eggs for 'n? Suppose Mr. Blick did the job. He has no motive we know of, but never mind. He gives it to Durdle or Miss Rosebay to deliver, or delivers it himself. Can't rightly see him and Durdle in a conspiracy together. The servants at the Hall would have got back from the flicks at Moreford soon after you left the Hall last night. Find out from them if

Mr. Stanford was at home when they returned, or did the dogs bark later that night, signifying that he'd gone for a liddle walk."

Inspector Randall gave Nigel a sly, humorous smile. "Am I doing all right so far?"

"A masterly analysis."

"Miss Rosebay, then. She was up at the Hall last night. She's on very friendly terms with Mr. Stanford. Maybe she's got good reason for wanting to kill her sister. She's in a nervy state during lunch. Well, now, 'tes all very pretty. But first, why adopt such an outlandish method? I can imagine Mr. Stanford thinking it up—he has some comical notions—but not Miss Rosebay. But would Mr. Stanford go those lengths for a woman who's in love with somebody else? Suppose he did. Say it was a plot between them. Then why the hell should Miss Rosebay snatch the glasses away from her sister just at the critical moment?"

"She might have lost her nerve."

The Inspector pulled dubiously at his lower lip. "I suppose that's possible. What about the other line? Mr. Charles had the means and the skill. He's been working late at the factory. We'll check up on his movements last night. Say he planted the binoculars. He sees Miss Rosebay take them from her sister and put them to her own eyes. So he tries to knock them out of her hands. Why should he, unless he *knew* they were deadly?"

"He said he had 'a sort of premonition that something was wrong.' "

"Very convenient. No, I don't like theorizing so early, but Charles Blick fits the facts best at present."

"Motive?"

"He's in love with Miss Rosebay. Her sister's creating difficulties—perhaps she wants Mr. Charles for herself and is determined not to let Rosebay have him."

"That's pretty thin, you know. But if it *is* true, it opens another possibility. Suppose Celandine wants to get rid of her sister, hates her for having snatched her old love. She has an accomplice, X, to doctor the glasses and address them to her, which turns suspicion right away from herself. She opens the parcel, tries to focus the glasses—"

"But you say Miss Rosebay *snatched* them from her."

"That was my impression. But things happened very fast. You must remember everyone falls over backward to anticipate Celandine's lightest wish. She could bank on that. When she says plaintively, 'This screw's awfully stiff,' and perhaps gives her sister an appealing glance, it'd be second nature for Rosebay to take the glasses from her. And it's natural to put glasses to your eyes when adjusting the range finder."

The Inspector eyed him doubtfully. "Ye-es, I suppose that's possible. Well, I must go and see Miss Celandine. The usual routine. Does she know of anyone who might wish to do her an injury? Blah, blah. It's going to be a bothersome business."

"There's one little thing bothers me particularly."

"Oh, yes?"

"I'd have thought a chap who had the skill to rig up this Grand Guignol device would have been able to make it foolproof. Why was the screw so stiff?"

7. The Manager's Misgivings

Inspector Randall's interview with Celandine Chantmerle was short and unproductive. As he put it to Nigel afterward, she was "a bit mazed still but plucky enough." She couldn't quite credit that an attempt had been made on her life, didn't believe she had any enemies ("Thoughtful look at the back of her eyes just then, though," said Randall), tended to dismiss it all as a practical joke. She had asked where Charles was, and what success the Inspector had had over the anonymous letters. "But she didn't really seem much interested in what I was saying. Acted as though her mind was on something else," the Inspector summed it up.

Randall had then interviewed the maid, Charity Cooper. She was rather deaf, and had heard nothing untoward in the night. Miss Rosebay had locked the front door at about nine-twenty, when she came in from her walk, and told Charity she could go to bed. The maid swore that Rosebay had no parcel with her when she came in; but this meant nothing, the Inspector considered, for she could easily have left it on the ledge before entering. Herbert Petts, the gardener, thought he remembered seeing a parcel there, early this morning, before the postman came.

Nigel in the meanwhile was talking to the young Moreford doctor, whom the vicar had sent for. He was evidently a bit disgruntled at having been summoned for a mere case of fainting. Miss Chantmerle had only become a patient of his a couple of years ago.

"I've given her a sedative. She's back in the drawing room—insisted on it. Had a bit of a shock, I gather. Wouldn't tell me what it was. The vicar was cagey too."

Nigel enlightened him. The doctor whistled: "What a filthy trick! On top of these anonymous letters, too. You've got a case of morbid pathology loose in Prior's Umborne all right."

"What's wrong with Miss Chantmerle? Hysterical paralysis?"

"I should say so. My predecessor diagnosed a tumor of the spine at the time. Suggested an operation, I believe; but she wouldn't have one. Don't think they'd have found it. The shock of finding her father dead, plus mental and physical exhaustion after weeks of nursing him, plus a hereditary predisposition to nervous disease—the old boy went off his rocker, you know—they would be more than enough to do the trick."

"She really is a cripple, though?"

The doctor gave him a piercing look. "What's on your mind? Think she's been posting these letters herself?"

"No, but I'd like the possibility eliminated."

"Well, for all practical purposes you can eliminate it. The body speaks for you. You're helpless because you want to be helpless. That's the truth of hysterical paralysis. And Miss Chantmerle has made a very good thing out of it. Why should she want to recover?"

"People do, don't they, from this condition?"

"Sometimes. Lourdes has cured such cases. Violent spiritual experience? Faith? We doctors don't know all the answers, believe me."

"You can have a cure long after the thing has set in?"

"Years after. Any time. There's little or no muscular wasting, you see. The machine's out of practice, of course, but it's all ready to start again. Just the spark needed. Which is what Miss Chantmerle hasn't got. If she had, she'd have been walking years ago. But she's created a pattern of life out of her disability, which is highly satisfactory to her. I tell you, the proof of the pudding's in the eating. If she wanted to walk, she'd walk. If she doesn't walk, it means she can't walk."

"Have any of her friends or relations consulted you?"

"Yes, her sister did when I took over the practice. But I couldn't tell her any more than I've told you." . . .

Inspector Randall, with his fresh face, his plodding walk and the appraising eye he cast upon the pasture grass as they took the field path down to the Hall, looked more than ever a farmer.

"I wouldn't mind settling down here when I get my pension. Pretty little place. Do a bit of market gardening. I'd like to get the taste of crime out of my mouth."

"These poison-pen letters have a particularly nasty taste. Have you got any further with them?" asked Nigel.

The Inspector told him that the Special Branch at Scotland Yard, at his request, were looking into the records of sabotage cases in 1940, to see if anyone answering to John Smart's description had been convicted or suspected.

"There's another thing I'd suggest," said Nigel. "Get the Notts police to ask Smart's mother if she had a letter from him, probably soon after getting his job at the Hall, making some reference to what happened in 1940."

The Inspector gave Nigel his innocent, crafty, countryman's smile.

"I've done that already. Seems our minds are working on the same line."

"It seems Sir Archibald's wasting his money sending me down here."

Randall made him an ironic little bow. "He's got money to burn. Don't you worry about that, sir. And I reckon Mr. Stanford's burning it up for him fast enough," he added, as the roar of the racing-car engine suddenly burst out from the Hall ahead, shaking the rooks out of their trees.

Stanford wiped his hands on a piece of oily waste when he saw them entering the workshop. His brown eyes sparkled at them.

"I've got it! I've really got the answer this time, boys! Oh, you sweet thing!" He patted the cylinder block affectionately. "Come and let's have a drink on it."

The weird figure of Daniel Durdle elongated itself from a bench at the far end of the workshop.

"Come on, Durdlepots," cried his employer enthusiastically. "Pluck off that Blue Ribbon and have a small cider-and-water!"

"I'm sorry, Mr. Blick, but I'm here on official business," said the Inspector. He took the binoculars from the cardboard box he was carrying, and held them out, lying on his handkerchief, on the palms of his hands. "Do you recognize these, sir?"

"What make are they?" Stanford expelled a breath through his blackened stumpy teeth. "Oh, lor'! Look at those needles. Naughty, naughty."

"You haven't answered my question, sir." The

Inspector was looking coolly at Stanford like a farmer appraising fat stock.

"My dear old top, give me time. I don't *think* they're mine. There are several pairs about the place somewhere. I took up bird-watching once. But these'd be too high-powered for that, wouldn't they?"

"I must ask you to check them presently. I want to know if a pair is missing. Would you have any objection to my men searching your workshop when they arrive? I can obtain a warrant, of course, but—"

"Only too delighted," said Stanford, in an absurdly social tone. "Durdlepots, what have you been up to? Making infernal machines when my back was turned. Fie upon you."

Daniel Durdle, who was stooping over the binoculars as if fascinated, gave a deferential giggle which sounded quite horrible in Nigel's ears.

Inspector Randall's West-Country voice burred slower still.

"Infernal machine. Ye-es. The person it was sent to was lucky not to be blinded by it."

"I know. But Celandine *is* lucky."

Randall gazed at him with great deliberation, then said lazily: "I never mentioned Miss Chantmerle, sir, did I?"

"No, indeed." Stanford's tone was affable. "But Chas told me all about it. How is Celandine? No serious after-effects, I hope? Poor Chas started all his rivets. But women are tougher."

"I understand she is none the worse for her experience."

"But none the better, either?"

Daniel Durdle uttered another of his infelicitous giggles.

"What do you mean by that, sir?" Randall's blue eyes were opened wide.

"Oh, but surely you must see. A woman who's spoiled all her life—brisk, fond lackeys to fetch and carry—the moral effect of discovering that somebody hated her enough to try and puncture those bright eyes of hers—I should have thought it would be most salutary."

Nigel was far from being a queasy person, but that word "puncture" gave him an unpleasant qualm.

The Inspector, apparently unmoved, shooed Durdle out of the workshop, telling him to wait till sent for. His questions to Stanford Blick, however, produced no positive evidence. Durdle was quite often alone in the workshop for considerable periods; but Stanford had never seen signs of his having done other work than what he was employed for. "But you know, old sport," Stanford commented, "anyone who was doing a job like this would clean up jolly carefully. I can't imagine your chaps finding fragments of vulcanite or plastic."

When Stanford had gone to rout up the pairs of binoculars which were lying about in the Hall, Inspector Randall called Daniel Durdle in again.

"I want a full account of your movements last night, from nine o'clock onward."

The man's eyes groped round, behind those porthole spectacles.

"Movements? I was at home, searching the Scriptures."

"All night, from nine o'clock?"

"I've said so."

The Inspector gave him a long, wide-eyed stare. "So how did Mr. Strangeways see you walking down from the Little Manor, about eleven?"

Durdle's neck seemed to grow longer as his head

turned slantwise from them, averting the sick smile which betrayed him.

"He bears false witness."

"Oh, nonsense," exclaimed Nigel. "You know perfectly well you were there. You can't evade it by mouthing sanctimonious jargon."

The thick spectacles flashed at him malevolently.

"I was about the Lord's business."

"Leaving these binoculars for Miss Chantmerle's birthday?" asked Randall.

"No." An arrogant, martyred expression was on the man's face, as if he suffered these questions for a Cause quite beyond the questioner's understanding.

"You had an appointment with Miss Rosebay Chantmerle?" asked Nigel.

Daniel refused to answer. Beads of sweat appeared beneath the lank red hair on his forehead.

"How much did she give you this time?" Nigel persisted. "We know you've been blackmailing her."

"If the woman says that, she lies," Daniel violently jerked out. "Ye shall be persecuted for righteousness' sake."

Inspector Randall was imperturbable. "I just want a straight answer. Did you visit the Little Manor last night, and if so, why? . . . Oh, well, if you won't answer, I'll put my own construction upon it. I shall be seeing you again. Good afternoon."

Durdle was evidently disconcerted by this abrupt dismissal. The dazed glare of his spectacles followed them as they crossed the courtyard.

"The plot thickens," said the Inspector, with an ironic smile.

A few minutes with the servants were enough to establish that none of them could positively identify the binoculars, that Mr. Stanford had been at home when they returned last night, shortly after Nigel's departure, and that he had not gone out later—or at any rate, the dogs had not barked, except just after midnight, when Mr. Charles returned.

Stanford Blick now appeared, dangling a collection of field glasses. "I *think* these are the full muster," he said doubtfully; "but things do accumulate here: there might have been another pair. Oh lor', more bobbies."

A police car drew up outside the windows. Inspector Randall gave them instructions for searching the workshop, then he and Nigel went to interview Charles Blick. Charles's flat, on the second floor, was the antithesis of the rest of the house: neat, sparely furnished, ordinary, the room where he sat writing gave no clue to his personality, except for a shelf full of scientific textbooks and a few athletic trophies—silver cups on the mantelpiece, faded football and cricket caps hung on the corners of pictures.

Laying a piece of blotting paper over the letter he was writing, Charles rose to greet them. The afternoon sun showed up the lines of worry on his face. His expression was polite but preoccupied. Nigel remembered the note of impatience, of faint contempt in Sir Archibald's voice when he had mentioned this son. Charles was a plodder, one might have assumed; a nonentity who only just made the grade; at any rate, a disappointment to his father. And a father like Sir Archibald would have no compunction about sacking a son who failed to maintain his standards of efficiency. That would be enough to account for his permanently worried look. But Nigel fancied there was more behind it than this—some deep-seated guilt, was it, which had made Charles run just now from the Chantmerles' house as if pursued by Furies?

Inspector Randall, hands planted on knees and leaning forward affably, seemed in no hurry to get to the point. He was asking about the work at the Moreford factory—to what extent it had been hampered by the loss of a foreman and of Charles's secretary. Charles said that it had been necessary for him to work late most nights recently. In his own office? Chiefly, but he went round the works at least once every night, to keep an eye on the late shift. And last night? He had left the factory at 11:45 P.M. and got to the Hall shortly after midnight. Nigel did a lightning calculation: Charles Blick would have had time, if he had come fast from Moreford, to drive up to the Little Manor, deposit the binoculars and return to the Hall. But this would have entailed driving through the village, and up past Templeton's farm, which would surely have been too risky at that time of night. On the other hand, if he had left his car somewhere at the southern end of the village, apart from the danger of someone noticing an empty car, Charles could never have walked to the Little Manor and back in the time available.

"You'd never seen these binoculars before?" the Inspector was asking.

"Not to my knowledge."

"My trouble," continued the Inspector comfortably, "my trouble is that there only seem two places hereabouts where a tricky little job like this could be done."

"I quite appreciate that. But frankly, you know, I can't see how anyone could have done it at the works. No unauthorized person is allowed in, of course; and his workmates would spot it at once if a chap was fiddling with a pair of binoculars on the bench. No, it just isn't conceivable."

"Is there no special room—no sort of experimental place, apart from the main workshops?"

"Oh yes. But it's private. We keep it locked. Only the works manager and myself have keys. Nobody could go in there without our permission; besides, a hand would soon be missed from his bench if he had somehow got into the experimental room without authorization."

Charles Blick was being singularly obtuse, thought Nigel. He even divulged, without apparent misgivings, that the only access to the experimental room was through his own office.

"I must ask your permission, sir, to let my men search it," said Inspector Randall.

"That puts me in rather an awkward position." Charles at last was looking disconcerted. "You see, we've got a top-secret job set up there. I don't know if my father—"

"Oh, come now, sir. My men are entirely trustworthy."

"I don't doubt it, but—"

"If you like, I will do the search myself, and in your presence."

"I—but look here, what's the point? You can't imagine that the works manager or I have time to waste fixing up a filthy practical joke like this?"

Inspector Randall gave him his long, meditative gaze. "Practical, yes. But do you call it a joke?"

For the first time, the distrait look was entirely gone from Charles's dark eyes. "I *see*. So you really do. Now look, Inspector, I've known Miss Chantmerle nearly all my life. She's an old friend. You can't surely suspect—"

"Miss Chantmerle is a victim of hysterical paralysis," Nigel broke in unexpectedly.

"What on earth has that to do with it?"

"It's one of the salient features of this illness that its victims become extremely obstructive."

"Obstructive?" Charles Blick's voice was like a bit of frayed thread. His dark eyes rested on Nigel with a dazed expression. He rose abruptly, went to the mantelpiece, lit a cigarette; then, turning to Randall, said: "When d'you want to search the works? Today?"

"As soon as we've finished here, if possible, sir."

"I'll give you a chit to Franks, the works manager. He'll let you have every facility, the experimental room included; but don't bring a horde of police in there, like a good chap."

"Much obliged to you, sir. It'll save time, not having to get a warrant. I'll keep in touch. You'll be here till tomorrow morning?"

"Probably."

When Inspector Randall had departed, with the chit and the field glasses, Nigel remarked: "Now you've got rid of him so neatly, what do you want to tell me?"

Having made his decision to co-operate with the police, Charles Blick seemed a different man. He said firmly: "I want you to enlarge on that word 'obstructive.' What's in your mind? But first, are you working for my father or the police?"

"Both. I hope. Your father only engaged me to look into the anonymous letters, of course. But it's still just possible they tie up with the binoculars."

"Well, then?"

Nigel walked over to the window seat and looked out upon the shadows lengthening over the lawn and the pastoral country beyond, the golden evening of a day which had given him the nastiest experience of his life.

"This isn't at all jolly," he said broodingly at last. "But I'd better go through with it. Let's take a hypothetical case. Suppose you had fallen in love with Rosebay. Suppose Celandine loves you and believes her love reciprocated. You *suspect* that Celandine cherishes false hopes about you—there was an attachment between you many years ago, perhaps, and she has misunderstood your recent visits to the house, to see her sister, as evidence that you wish to revive this old attachment. You *know* that she will put every possible obstacle in the way of your marrying Rosebay, once it comes out that this is your real intention. So, possibly with Rosebay's collusion, but probably without it, you prepare the field glasses. It may be you intend to get rid of the obstructive Celandine altogether, maybe only to give her a fright—one must remember that the screw releasing the needles was extremely stiff. How about that for a hypothesis?"

Charles Blick was silent for a very long time. At last, with an expression curiously like relief on his face, he said: "It's quite plausible. And some of it is true. Celandine and I were—well, very close, twenty years ago. I am fond of Bay now. And I'm afraid, yes, Celandine may have misinterpreted my visits. But I can assure you of one thing—she had no inkling of the state of affairs between Bay and me. We'd kept it absolutely dark."

"Because you're afraid of her? You, personally, I mean."

"Afraid *for* her. Well, perhaps a little afraid of her too—of what she might do."

"That's very honest," said Nigel. "You consider Celandine a vindictive character, *capable de tout*."

"Oh, no, no. Rubbish," Charles replied, much too fast. "I was merely saying—"

"And if she *had* got wind of your feeling for Rosebay, she's capable of getting someone to rig up the binoculars, and of handing them to her sister after lunch, to make sure Rosebay shouldn't have you, or to frighten her off you?"

"The whole thing's ridiculous. People just don't—it's sheer bad melodrama," said Charles angrily.

"Melodramatic. But not ridiculous. Rosebay is very highly-strung. A fright like that might easily have sent her over the edge. Then you'd not have married her. Or your father would have put his foot down against it. History repeating itself."

Charles Blick flushed deeply. "I fail to see what—"

"Twenty years ago, when Celandine became a cripple, your engagement, understanding, whatever it was, was broken off. Quite possibly against your will. But broken off it was. That's what I mean."

"If you can seriously imagine that Celandine would do such a horrible thing to Bay, as a sort of poetic justice, you must be—"

"I don't. Why did you run out of the house after it happened?"

Charles Blick flushed again. His face was tortured and desperate, but he tried to keep himself under control.

"I don't care to discuss that," he said stiffly.

"Well, I'll tell you. You couldn't face Celandine because you knew you'd given yourself away. When that infernal machine went off, you cried out to Rosebay: 'Darling, you might have been blinded,' and 'Are you all right, love?' No, wait a minute! Don't you see? If that was the first inkling Celandine had of your feeling for Rosebay, it lets her out. She couldn't have been responsible for the binoculars."

"Yes," said Charles, almost inaudibly.

"And if it wasn't she, or you, who had them prepared, the only person left is Rosebay."

"But it's fantastic. How on earth—?"

"Rosebay has a motive—to get rid of the obstacle in the way of her marrying you. She's been very thick with your brother lately. He's quite capable of rigging the field glasses."

"Stanford? But that's simply grotesque. Look here, we're normal people, not fiends. I know Stanford's a bit eccentric, but—"

"Well then, it's not you or Celandine or Rosebay or Stanford, singly, or in any combination. What about Daniel Durdle?"

Charles's relief was as pathetically obvious as his attempt to conceal it. "Durdle? He's a nasty bit of work; but what motive could he possibly have? He just doesn't tie up with the Chantmerles."

"He apparently hates Celandine, and he's been blackmailing her sister. That's something of a tie-up."

Nigel could have no doubt, from Charles's shocked, incredulous expression, that this was news to him.

"Blackmailing Bay? Are you making this up?"

"It's nothing to her discredit—that I can assure you."

"But why didn't she tell me?" said Charles to himself painfully. "Why is she so secretive?"

"Because it's a family secret," Nigel replied. He did not add that Rosebay had discussed it with Stanford.

"Not a secret from you, apparently." Charles's inflection was that of a sulky adolescent. Nigel smiled at him.

"She only didn't tell you because she thought you had quite enough worries on your hands."

"Oh God, these protective women! Sorry, but I'm really fed up with all this. Daniel Durdle, you were saying?"

"He's a possibility. But I shouldn't put your shirt on him, if I were you."

Charles Blick paced about the room, biting his nails. At last he stopped, and came out abruptly with "Look here, what'll they do to the person who—?"

"Charge of attempted murder, I presume."

"The whole thing's a nightmare," said Charles slowly. "I just can't take it in. Dinny's birthday party. Everyone so happy and on top of the world. Sun shining. And those field glasses waiting to go off, like a trembler fuse. Christ!"

"Somebody at the party couldn't have been altogether imbued with the birthday spirit."

Charles Blick gave a sudden, impish little grin, which reminded Nigel of Stanford. "Perhaps it was Mark."

"I don't somehow think the vicar would wish Celandine any harm."

Charles seemed very faintly put out. Still a trace of jealousy over Celandine? wondered Nigel.

"Of course not. I was only joking. Mark's a first-rate chap." After a pause, Charles went on naïvely, the hagridden look in his eyes again. "I've got a beastly feeling in my stomach. Sort of premonition. Like what made me try and snatch the glasses from Bay." He glanced at the puncture on his hand. "I must be getting psychic. Oh, damn it to hell, there couldn't be anything *worse* to happen—not after today."

He seemed to be appealing for reassurance, but Nigel remained silent.

"I wish to God I didn't have to be at the works all the time. Look here, you've got to look after—" his voice trailed away.

"Look after? Rosebay? Celandine?"

"Oh, both of them, of course," Charles jerked out with a sort of struggling, strangulating misery.

That look was still in his eyes when Nigel said good-by a minute later. It was a look, Nigel interpreted, of apprehension and inescapable guilt.

8. The Poison Pen's Mistakes

Nigel was meditating on the subject of Charles Blick while he walked back to the Little Manor. Stanford had intercepted him, as he was leaving the Hall, with a telephone message from Celandine Chantmerle, asking to see him at once. Charles, thought Nigel, is an average chap with an outsize conscience. Whatever might be the truth about that parting between him and Celandine twenty years ago, he had never really got free of her—perhaps never wished to. He had somehow arranged for the Chantmerles to have an income which enabled them to live on at the Little Manor. Nigel felt sure that Charles had been the moving spirit in this, even if Stanford had made the practical arrangements; and Charles had seen to it that Celandine was kept ignorant of the source of this income. He was as conscientious in private affairs as in his management of the factory. And now, when he had fallen in love with Rosebay, his conscience about her sister made a coward of him. For fear of hurting Celandine, or because the old attachment had never been quite broken, he could not bring his feeling for Rosebay out in the open. It was this moral cowardice, so dramatically illustrated by his running out of the house after he had given himself away to Celandine, which accounted for some at least of Rosebay's unhappiness and uncertainty.

Charles was torn between the two women—that was certain. And a man so divided, whose conscience is perpetually working overtime, is liable to crack. Psychologically, thought Nigel, the Charles who drove himself so mercilessly was more likely to have done the binoculars job than the erratic, self-indulgent Stanford. The binoculars could easily be a symbol of his unconscious revolt against the woman who obsessed him. He might have already become a split personality, deadly dangerous to himself and those around him. Did he suspect this himself? Was that why he had implored Nigel to "look after" the Chantmerles?

Yet, at the back of Nigel's mind, there was a nagging conviction that something had been said just now at the Hall which provided a clue to the binoculars episode. He strained to put his finger on it, but it eluded him like quicksilver.

Celandine was sitting in her drawing room, with Mark Raynham beside her. She seemed untouched by her experience, unless it had given her eyes a brighter sparkle, her whole personality an air of vibrant excitement.

"I'm just telling Mark he really mustn't fuss about me. I'm perfectly all right," she said, resting her hand lightly for a moment on the vicar's.

"She's hopeless," Mark said. "She ought to be in bed. I've seen too many cases of delayed shock in the war."

"Well, I'm not *going* to bed, till my bedtime." The exquisite Botticelli face turned to Nigel. "We've not had a proper talk yet, Mr. Strangeways. I can't wait to hear about these anonymous letters. Didn't you say at lunch you knew who'd written them?"

"Yes, I think I do."

"Celandine, ought you really to—?"

"Oh, Mark, don't be so maddening. I'm not a Sèvres shepherdess. Are the police going to make an arrest soon?"

"No. There are several points to clear up. And we've no real proof yet. By the way, Vicar, you can help—I'd like a word with you presently."

"How mysterious we are," laughed Celandine. "All this male freemasonry. Protecting the little woman from life's harsh realities."

"You've always been protected, and so you should be," said the vicar, with that rough forthrightness of his which Nigel found extremely sympathetic. "If I could lay my hands on the man who sent you those—"

Celandine's laughter bubbled up like a crystal spring. "Mark, you're straight out of the *Idylls of the King*. *Sans peur et sans reproche*. But you must stop breathing fire about a silly little trick—"

"Celandine will talk as if she'd been sent a jolly practical joke, calculated to set the whole table in a roar."

"I don't want to talk about it at all. It's Bay I'm worried about, Mr. Strangeways. I wish you'd have a talk with her and find out what's the matter. She's closed up like a clam, and whenever she comes into the room—well, she stares at me so oddly."

"Nonsense, my dear. You're imagining things. And after all, she had quite a turn too, you must remember."

"It's not nonsense," Celandine replied patiently. "Bay being like this, and Charles not coming to see me—it makes me feel as if I was in an isolation hospital. What's wrong with them?"

Mark Raynham gave Nigel a quick, appealing glance, which Celandine intercepted with the ease of a bird snapping up a fly.

"Don't be absurd, Mark," she said gently. "I've known them both all my life. I'm very fond of them both. Do you really think I don't use my eyes?"

Nigel opened his mouth to speak, then thought better of it. If Celandine, knowing about Charles and Rosebay, took this attitude, there was nothing more to be said. Mark Raynham's reaction was very different. His craggy face transfigured by a dawning hope, he said ingenuously: "So you don't *mind*, Celandine? I'd always thought you—I mean—"

"Charles and I were engaged once. I broke it off after my father's death. *Et ça c'est tout.*" Celandine looked meditatively at the vicar. "The real problem is my sister, Mr. Strangeways. She's looked after me for so long, and it ought to have been the other way round. Invalids are very selfish. I'm afraid it's not been good for her, feeling tied to me like this."

"Oh, Bay's all right. You needn't worry about her," said the vicar.

"But I do, Mark. She had a bad nervous breakdown a few years ago, before you came to the parish. And I couldn't help feeling responsible. She's so good-hearted, underneath. I tried to persuade her to take a holiday afterward, but she wouldn't leave me. So you see, Mr. Strangeways, this is where you could help." Celandine made a charming gesture of appeal; her eyes were darker, cornflower blue in the evening light that washed the room. "Someone from outside might do more than any of us." She stretched her hand to Nigel in a gesture queenly yet intimate. "I know we can all rely on you." As Nigel rose to go, she added: "And don't forget to tell me when the anonymous-letter business is going to blow up. You'd better go along with Mr. Strangeways, Mark—he wants to talk to you."

"Wonderful woman, isn't she?" said the vicar, limping along beside Nigel down the hill.

"Very remarkable, yes."

"You know, it's a great load off my mind, what she said about Charles. I'd thought she was still a bit taken up with him." The vicar began to whistle cheerfully.

When they reached the vicarage, Nigel asked him if he could get in touch immediately with the friend to whom he had written about his wife. Mark Raynham put through a long-distance call to London. The friend confirmed that he had never breathed a word to anyone on the subject of Mark's letter.

The next morning, having made an appointment with Inspector Randall, Nigel took a hired car in to Moreford. The Inspector had news for him. The Special Branch had turned up information that John Smart had been involved in a serious case of sabotage in 1940. Though nothing could be proved against him, the Security Officer of the factory where he was working had had every reason to suspect him of complicity, as an undercover activist, with the two men who were arrested for the crime. John Smart was sacked, and kept under observation. But shortly afterward, when Russia came into the war, he joined up, and his army record had been excellent. Furthermore, the Nottinghamshire police had interviewed Smart's old mother again, and persuaded her to admit that, soon after coming to Prior's Umborne, her son had written her a letter saying, in effect, that he believed he had now lived down the 1940 episode, had changed his political opinions and would be able to make a fresh start.

"That just about clinches it," said Nigel.

"I reckon so. But which of them? They're a pretty pair. D'you think they might both be in it?"

"No. The poison pen always works alone, surely. Going to be damned difficult to prove, though."

"I'd say the woman was the weak spot. Might break her down. She struck me as nervy as a cat. If she's not in it herself, she's scared that her nearest and dearest has been up to mischief."

"Yes, I got that impression, too. But I'm glad I don't have the job of softening her up."

Inspector Randall gave Nigel his slow, crafty, countryman's smile. "You'd best earn Sir Archibald's money. Tell me how you got onto it. Up-to-date psychological theories, eh?"

"Psychological grandmothers! It was all plain as pie, as soon as it was established that two of the poison-pen letters were based on information that no one else in the village could possibly possess."

"Ah." The Inspector nodded sapiently.

"No one we're concerned with, except for the vicar and his friend, and Smart and his mother, knew the secrets. But these secrets had been referred to in *letters* from Raynham and Smart to their confidantes—letters sent from Prior's Umborne. Letters go through a post office. Therefore, the only person who could have discovered the secret was somebody in the post office. Somebody who had an obscene, or malevolent, or dotty curiosity about the affairs of newcomers to the village, and steamed open their letters. I told Daniel Durdle that anyone living in a post office has special facilities for the writing of anonymous letters. I hope it shook him. They've stopped, anyway."

"You'd say it was him, not Mother Durdle?"

"Yes. The letters had an artistic touch which I don't believe she'd be capable of. Daniel gets it from his father, I imagine—from the late essayist, Edric Chantmerle."

"Eh? What's that?"

"Yes. He's a by-blow. It accounts for his hatred of the Chantmerle sisters—jealousy that they've got the things which his Chantmerle blood entitled him to. It's also what he was blackmailing Rosebay over; but we'll come to that in a minute. It accounts for a great deal of his warped personality. The proof of how bitterly he feels about it is in the letter he wrote to himself, of course. Why accuse yourself of alcoholism when you could write a nice juicy letter about bastardy? Only possible answer: because the latter is still too sore a subject. And conversely, if anyone else had written the letters, he'd have brought up against Daniel the old village rumor about his illegitimacy, not a feeble accusation of imbibing strong liquors. Daniel isn't clever enough by half."

Nigel paused to light another cigarette. "Then there's the clue of the other post box."

"But the other post box was never used. Yes, and there lies the clue," said the Inspector, poker-faced.

"Have you country bobbies nothing better to do than recline, with your feet on the table, reading Sherlock Holmes?"

"Oh, we're master minds down this way. As you were going to say, it's significant that all the anonymous letters had Prior's Umborne postmarks. If any had been posted in the other village box, they'd have gone straight into Moreford and been stamped there. Why weren't any of them posted in that other box? Because it's just opposite the New Inn and even at night there'd be a risk of being observed posting letters there—a risk, that's to say, if you were Daniel Durdle, or Mrs. D. It'd look very peculiar—someone who lives at the post office putting letters into a box at the other end of the village."

Nigel and the Inspector eyed each other with some gratification. "We're a couple of pretty clever chaps, I suspect," said the former.

"It was elementary. If Durdle had only stuck to information he got through gossip or snooping, like he used in all the other letters, it'd have been just another case of 'the police are baffled.' "

"Well, there's no use your crying over his spilt milk. What do we do next?"

"Can I rope him in over this alleged blackmail? I'd like to know more about that," said Randall.

Nigel told him everything Rosebay had said. Evidently, unless she had received and kept some letters from Daniel demanding money, or was prepared to co-operate with the police into trapping him over a further demand, no immediate steps could be taken against Durdle.

"And I doubt if she would co-operate. It would be difficult for her to do so without the substance of the blackmail coming out in public, and that's just what she doesn't want—her sister to learn about their father's disgrace." Nigel took from his wallet the anonymous letter to Celandine Chantmerle which her sister had intercepted, and passed it to the Inspector.

"I wonder could this link up with the attempt on Miss Chantmerle's life," he said.

"How so?"

"Rosebay had been paying Daniel to keep quiet about Edric Chantmerle. In this letter, however, he blows the gaff. Therefore, Rosebay must have already told him she was not going to pay any more. Therefore, when he walked up to the Little Manor the night before last—"

"If he did."

"If he did, it could not have been to receive another payment. Therefore, it *might* have been to deposit the field glasses."

"Yes, that's a point. And why should he lie about his walk if he hadn't been up to something shady?"

"On the other hand," said Nigel, "when I was talking to Rosebay after lunch yesterday, she did rather draw my attention to Durdle; and also, she said that, last time she'd paid him, which was some little time ago, she'd told him she wasn't going to pay any more; but I was quite convinced she was lying about this. Which rather confuses the issue. And why should she lie, anyway?"

Inspector Randall's eyes, fixed upon Nigel, had become almost dreamy. "Oh, well, if we're just having a knock-up with theories, I could give you one for that. Rosebay is behind the binoculars business. She makes an appointment with Durdle for that night, promising him another installment of hush money. He goes up to the Little Manor, or wherever the rendezvous was, nearby, but finds nobody there. Rosebay has maneuvered him under the suspicion of having gone up to deposit the binoculars. And very neat too. He can't tell us what he went there for, without admitting to his blackmail racket."

"Yes. It sounds plausible enough," said Nigel. "And it gets us round the difficulty of Durdle having done the field glasses job. Why should he want Celandine killed when it paid him, via Rosebay, for her to be alive? But I can't see Rosebay being all that clever."

"She must have had an accomplice, anyway, to doctor

the glasses. And I reckon it must have been one of the Blicks."

"Any luck with them yet—the glasses, I mean?"

"Sent them up to the scientific chummies at the Yard, together with assorted sweepings from Mr. Stanford's workshop and the experimental room at the factory here. I like other folk doing the work for me. Then I can just sit and think."

"Very proper. Been having any nice thoughts lately?"

"I'll tell you one thing I've been thinking. This business of the field glasses—it doesn't make sense. Can you imagine any dafter way of trying to kill a person?"

"It's certainly far-fetched."

"But not original, in this case. The Yard rang me just now to say they'd got a pair of binoculars in the Black Museum. Sent to a girl who'd been demobbed from one of the Services—quiet girl who'd never had any enemies, as far as they could discover. Sender was never traced. Whole thing a senseless mystery. These field glasses were doctored in a much more rudimentary way than ours, but they had needles all right. So, of course, I asked if any of our suspects had visited the Black Museum." The Inspector paused aggravatingly.

"Well?"

"The answer was in the negative. But, by a funny coincidence your employer was taken round a year or two ago."

"My employer?"

"Yes. The great Sir Archibald Blick."

Nigel was trying to digest this bit of information as he strolled round Moreford. It was the kind of country town which goes into a coma between its weekly markets. In the market square a few rural characters hung about by the cattle pens, exchanging desultory conversation, and at long intervals shifting their weight momentously from one leg to the other. An exanimate group of village housewives stood at the bus stop, in the patient attitudes of the dead awaiting Charon's ferry. A policeman on point duty looked unhopefully for some traffic to direct. The streets smelt of dung, faintly laced with petrol fumes. Nigel walked downhill toward the station, by which his car was parked.

On his right was the raw, red-bricked factory building. Beyond the railway line, the town shredded off into green fields. The sun, stepping out from behind billowy April clouds, struck a glint from the railway metals. Like quicksilver. And instantly Nigel's mind fastened upon the thing that had been eluding him: a phrase of Stanford Blick's: "Somebody hated her enough to try and puncture those bright eyes of hers." The note that came with the binoculars had said: "Read this now, Bright Eyes, if you can." No, thought Nigel, that could too easily be a coincidence. He made an impatient gesture, as if flinging an undersized fish back into the water, which drew some loudly and frankly expressed doubts as to his sanity from a group of children sitting on the railings. Nigel rat-tat-tatted an imaginary tommy-gun at them, with such verisimilitude that one startled boy fell backward off the railings, while the rest followed his progress dumbly, eyes and mouths wide opened.

There was something Stanford had said, though. Nigel groped his way back through their last conversation at the Hall, till he came to it. Yes, that was really an extremely odd thing to say, even allowing for Stanford's oddity. He fished his driver out of the Railway Arms Bar. The glimmering of an idea, bizarre yet rational, had come to him.

Nigel directed the driver to take him to the Hall. By

force of habit he walked round to the workshop at the back. The usual demoniac shindy from the compound of dogs greeted his arrival. He put his head in at the workshop door, but the place was empty.

As he closed the door again, he became aware of a shadow, elongating itself with a chilling swiftness over the courtyard and running along the wall in front of him. Turning, he found himself face to face with Daniel Durdle.

"I would like a word with you, Mr. Strangeways."

"By all means. In here?"

The man shook his head, and led the way through the plantation into a paddock to the north of the house. They were not far from the hedge gap where Nigel had seen him hurrying past two nights ago.

"We shan't be overheard here," said Daniel. He was wearing a black suit and hat—the garments, no doubt, in which he walked to the Gospel Hall on Sundays. They emphasized the dead whiteness of his face and hands. Standing there, in the lush April grass under the April sky, he looked like something out of another world—out of no human world—a figure summoned up from the vasty deep where nightmares breed. Nigel did not find it difficult to imagine why Rosebay Chantmerle was terrified of her half-brother.

"You made an accusation against me yesterday," said Daniel, "in front of a witness. A slanderous accusation."

"Yes."

" 'The tongue can no man tame; it is an unruly evil.' "

"Yes, and so is the pen," said Nigel equably.

"Nevertheless, I warn you to bridle your tongue. The Lord has given me authority in this place." Daniel Durdle suddenly pointed his finger in a comminatory gesture. "I say unto you, beware! We shall not suffer the stranger within our gates to set a pitfall for the Elect."

The extraordinary thing, thought Nigel, is that behind this rigmarole there is a formidable power. The man was possessed, if only by the delusion of his own sanctification. One could imagine that resonant voice and eerie personality whipping up superstitious villagers to a witch-hunt.

"If any man stands in my way, I will crush him as I crush this flower." Daniel ground a buttercup into the earth beneath his heel.

"Oh, come, the poor flower hadn't done you any harm."

"Nature is evil," exclaimed Durdle with singular intensity. "Its beauties are the snares of the Adversary."

"Is this what you wanted to talk to me about?"

"I am to warn you, also, against the woman Rosebay Chantmerle."

"Do you suggest she was lying when she told me you had blackmailed her?"

"I did but seek my own portion."

"Oh, I see. Your father's money. But it isn't. Edric Chantmerle was pretty well broke when he died. Surely you know that?"

"Not my father's money?" Daniel exclaimed, in evident surprise.

"You've just been bleeding a girl of her own savings, by using threats. And you have the contemptible hypocrisy to call that 'the Lord's business.' "

Durdle's lank-haired head, under the black hat, wriggled on the long neck. There was still foam at the corners of his mouth; but he looked like a man on the defensive now, not a minor prophet in the full tide of denunciation. He said sullenly: "I did not employ the monies for the lusts of the flesh."

"I'm quite prepared to believe that you donated it all to your chapel, and kidded yourself you were spoiling the Egyptians. But it remains blackmail. You've used this money to buy yourself greater power in your own community. Vindictiveness, and lust for power—those are your ruling motives. And they've led you into more than blackmail, as you damn well know." Nigel's pale-blue eyes gazed freezingly at Durdle.

"I am innocent of the attempt upon Miss Chantmerle," said Durdle, licking his lips.

"That's not what I was referring to. But what proof can you give me?"

Durdle came out with a scurry of words. He had gone up to the Little Manor that night, he swore, in response to a note from Rosebay Chantmerle. He had destroyed the note—not unnaturally, for it mentioned a further payment of hush money. Rosebay had failed to turn up at the rendezvous on the edge of the little wood behind the house, and after waiting for twenty minutes, Daniel had returned home.

If this statement was true, it bore out the Inspector's theory only too convincingly. But Durdle might well be lying.

"That's no proof of anything. How do I know you're not making it up to save your own skin?"

"Ask the woman Rosebay." Durdle's spectacles dully glinted, as with a blindworm writhing he pushed his head closer to Nigel's. "And ask her this too. What did she mean by 'It hasn't worked'?"

"What *are* you talking about?"

Durdle's mouth was set in a complacent, gloating expression, which Nigel found inexpressibly repugnant.

"Just now, while I was in Mr. Blick's workshop, the telephone rang. He has an extension there, you know.

I happened to be standing close beside him. 'Hallo, Bay,' he said. And I heard her voice say, before he could warn her: 'Stanford, it hasn't worked.' How do you like that, *Mister* Detective Strangeways?"

The note of triumph in the man's voice was obscene.

"I'll look into it." Nigel went on hotly: "You've warned me to bridle my tongue, and you've warned me against Miss Rosebay Chantmerle. Now it's my turn to issue a warning. And I'm telling you that, when the village discovers who wrote those poison-pen letters, there'll be a lynching."

Nigel turned on his heel and walked away through the sunlit paddock, leaving the tall, black figure of Daniel Durdle motionless and silent, like some weird African ju-ju, in the flowering grass. Nigel was already regretting those words, spoken at the heat of the moment. He was to regret them a great deal more, before many days had passed.

9. The Sister's Discovery

Stanford Blick was in his "den," a quart flagon of cider and a plate of bread and cheese beside him, when Nigel entered.

"Hallo, old top. Hot on the trail? You look rather hot and bothered, I must say. Have a drop of auntie's ruin."

He poured some cider into a tooth-glass which he had found, after some searching, in a drawer of the desk.

"Yes," said Nigel; "I've just been talking to Durdle."

"And what did the dear fellow have to say?"

"Among other things, he warned me against Rosebay and told me of a telephone conversation he overheard this morning."

Stanford carefully brushed some crumbs off the drawing board in front of him, then turned his beaming brown eyes on Nigel.

"Aha!" he chuckled. "Mad scientist unmasked, eh?"

"What did she mean by 'It hasn't worked'?"

"Not what you think," replied Stanford, gleefully rubbing his grubby hands together.

"And what do you think I think?"

"How jolly this is! Just like one of those horrible games on the Light Program. *You* think she was referring to the lark with the field glasses—telling her accomplice that the dastardly engine had failed to puncture her sister's blue orbs." He waved aside Nigel's protest. "To which I reply: (a) little Bay wouldn't have rung up, a day after the event, to tell me something she must've known I knew, and (b) she'd hardly have bawled it out on the old blower without first making sure that the second murderer was alone."

He took another huge mouthful of bread and cheese.

"What was she talking about, then?" Nigel pursued.

Stanford was only too ready to explain. Rosebay had come over to the Hall before dinner yesterday. She wanted to see Charles, but Charles was out for a walk. So she talked to Stanford instead. She was in a state about Charles's indecision, his refusal to come clean with Celandine over his love for Rosebay. Stanford had advised her that she should confront Charles, when he called at the Little Manor next morning to inquire after Celandine on his way to Moreford, and tell him he must make a choice or she could not go on seeing him. Since Celandine had been so little affected by the field glasses, her health could surely stand the minor shock of learning that Charles wanted to marry her sister.

"It wouldn't have been a shock," said Nigel. "She made that clear enough to Mark Raynham and myself yesterday."

"Well, Bay and Charles were not to know that. Bay only saw her sister at dinner, then she had to go out to a village do. And Charles didn't see Dinny this morning—just left a message for her. Anyway, he didn't give a positive reaction to Bay's ultimatum. That's what she meant when she said our little scheme hadn't worked."

Stanford's spaniel-brown eyes sat up and begged. The story may be true, thought Nigel; and if it isn't, there'll be enough truth in it to fit any facts I can check.

"You're an impossible lot round here," he said. "Rosebay pays through the nose for her sister's peace of mind. Charles is so riddled with conscience over Celandine that he's driving himself into a nervous breakdown. And you—where do you come in? Are you another of the Friends of Celandine Society? I expect it was you who arranged about the Chantmerles' income. Everyone falling over themselves to protect Celandine from the faintest draught of reality. Why?"

Stanford watched him soberly. The quizzical note was gone from his voice when he spoke. "Some of us *have* a guilty conscience about her. And Bay does it because she's Bay. That's a good girl, you know."

"Does your father know it?"

The little leprechaun of a man shrugged, then laid his finger to the side of his nose. "You must enlighten him. He'd never believe *us*."

"I'm paid to investigate anonymous letters, not to straighten out family problems. Which reminds me, it's time I sent him a report."

"Pop? No need, old scout. He's coming tomorrow for the week end."

"Is he? Why?"

"Oh, just to give Chas a pep talk, and tell me I mustn't waste any more of the Blick fortune on playing with motor cars, I expect. An austere man, Pop."

Soon after, Nigel took his leave. He walked down the tree-lined drive and came out through the stone gateposts into the road. Here he turned right, wanting a little walk before going back to The Sweet Drop for lunch. As he moved along, deep in thought, he heard a whirring noise close behind him. For a petrifying instant, he thought he was about to be transfixed by an arrow. Then, before he could look round or jump aside, Celandine Chantmerle's electric invalid carriage caught him up.

"That's a remarkably quiet conveyance of yours. I never heard you till you were right behind me."

"I'm just taking my morning constitutional." Celandine smiled ravishingly at him. "And thank God for someone who doesn't tell me I ought to be in bed."

"Certainly not. You look as fresh as Primavera."

"What a sweet thing to say, Nigel. May I call you Nigel? I feel as if you were an old family friend already."

"I'd love you to. We've hardly met properly yet, but I seem to know you quite well. Mark Raynham and Joe Summers and everyone have been so full of your praises."

"You've made quite an impression on the village, I can tell you. It's not every day they have a detective gentleman from London in their midst. I saw some children imitating your walk just now. There's fame for you."

They went half a mile along the undulating road, Nigel walking beside the electric carriage. Then Celandine steered it into a copse, where Nigel lifted her out and they sat on a rug beneath the whispering trees, among wildflowers, primroses and bluebell shoots.

"My father often came here," she said. "He knew every inch of the country as a blind man knows his own room. You've never seen the spring till you've met it in Dorset, he used to say. When he was in France, in the 1914 war, my mother used to send him the first of each spring flower she found, pressed, in her letters."

Celandine stretched her arms above her head, sighing. Some small animal rustled through the undergrowth, and a wood pigeon exploded out of a tree overhead.

"So peaceful," she said. "On a day like this, I just can't take anything very seriously, from poison-pen letters to atom bombs! D'you think I'm terribly selfish?"

"I think you're very sensible. What's the use of brooding about things one can't remedy?"

"But I *am* a selfish woman. I've been spoiled and cosseted and generally had my character ruined by kindness, ever since." She gestured at her helpless legs, spread out straight and woodenly in front of her like a doll's.

"You'll be able to walk again, perhaps, one day. It does happen."

"Mark tells me I only need faith. Take up thy bed and walk. Well, faith is something I haven't got. Not that kind, anyway. So I go on being a decorative burden all round. However, possibly they also serve who only sit and are waited on."

Nigel laughed. "You don't strike me as in need of any bracing sermons about self-help."

"Oh, I put up a front. Anything to ward off the well-meant arrows of pity." Her profile held for a moment the purity and hardness of an Artemis. "Pity! I've watched it corroding everyone round me—Bay, Charles, Mark. That's why I've turned myself into a little stainless-steel marvel. Sheer self-defense." Her expression changed. "Bay ought to go away for a bit. She's started dreaming again."

"Oh?"

"Last night she dreamed she heard footsteps in my father's room. He used to get up and move about sometimes, at night, during his last illness. She was a little girl then, and slept in the room beneath, and it frightened her. When she had a breakdown a few years ago, it started with the same dreams."

"You mean, they caused the breakdown?"

"Oh, no. That was overwork. We had no staff for the last year or two of the war, and she had to do all the work. She's always been a bit nervy, you know, since she saw—saw my father's body in the quarry. It didn't do either of us any good, as you may imagine."

"Do you think she inherited some sort of mental instability from him?"

"Good gracious, no!" Celandine replied very quickly. "He was as sane as you or me, till the thing happened that killed him." Her eyes, cornflower blue in the shadow of the copse, regarded Nigel curiously. "You've not got it into your head that *she* might have had anything to do with these letters?"

"No, no. She couldn't have written them."

"You quite alarmed me for a moment. But I do wish you'd see her, and persuade her to take a little holiday. We've got relations she could go to. And I can manage perfectly all right by myself, though she'll never believe it, bless her heart."

"I'll come up this afternoon."

"You *are* good and kind. Now dump me back in my machine. It's nearly lunchtime. . . ."

"Your sister thinks you ought to go away for a holiday."

"Oh? Why?" said Rosebay Chantmerle ungraciously.

They were sitting in her room that afternoon—a small room on the first floor, facing west, furnished with a miscellany of objects which had been put there, Nigel suspected, not by Rosebay's taste, but because they were unwanted in the other rooms. Her tastes, or her phantasies, could best be seen in the bookshelf beside the divan-bed, filled with volumes about the theater and the ballet, and in a few signed press photographs of minor theatrical celebrities pasted on the wall above a cramped-looking imitation-oak bureau. There was something pathetic, little-girlish about the room. It was a haunted room, too—haunted by the fettered ambitions of the fiery, sullen creature who now said to Nigel again, impatiently:

"Well? Why?"

"She told me you need a change—been having bad dreams. Is that so? I'm sorry."

"Oh, dreams! I've always had them."

"Why not turn them into realities?" said Nigel, catching her meaning and glancing at the bookshelf. "Why not go away altogether?"

"That's just what a man *would* say. As if one could pick up and go at any minute. Besides, I'm too old now."

Rosebay was looking out of the window, seeing something far beyond the treetops outside. There was a little pause.

"Well, what about the bad dream? Last night?" asked Nigel.

"Oh, it was the usual. Father's room was above this—a long room converted out of the attics. I used to hear him walking up and down the length of it—I was very small then—that time when he was ill. Sort of slurring footsteps. He'd struggled out of bed. I still dream I'm hearing them sometimes."

"You're sure it was a dream last night?"

Rosebay's green eyes opened wide, as she turned abruptly from the window. "Sure? Whatever do you mean? Of course it was a dream. You're not suggesting it was his ghost, are you?"

"What time did you have this dream?"

The girl gave him one of her angry, challenging looks. "Do you think I've made it all up?"

"No. And I don't believe in ghosts, either."

Rosebay's expression changed. A faint apprehension dawned in her eyes. Gesturing brusquely, as if to sweep it away, she said: "Twenty to two. I remember howling and whinnying in my nightmare, like I do. I woke myself up, just at the point where I was dreaming that father's door was opening and his footsteps coming downstairs. I looked at my watch, and it was twenty to two. Then I heard Dinny calling out to ask if I was all right: she sleeps in the room beneath this one, you see. So it couldn't have been a ghost."

"It's a recurrent dream? Always exactly the same?"

"Yes. No—it's the first time I've dreamed that horrible bit at the end." Rosebay shuddered reminiscently. "But if Dinny thinks I'm in for another nervous breakdown, she's just being silly."

"You'd been overworking, that time?"

"Yes."

"Nothing else to it?" asked Nigel gently.

"No. What else should there be?" said Rosebay, with an aggressive inflection.

"Did you tell Charles about it this morning?"

"Of course not. Why should I? I had other things to talk to him about. Private things . . . Oh, well, I don't mind telling you. We've been sort of engaged, secretly. And I told him it was about time we came out into the open."

So that's that, thought Nigel. He said: "Why did you keep it secret? You're both old enough to make your own decisions."

"You do ask a lot of questions. Surely you can see that for yourself. Charles is not a very strong character. He was worried there'd be opposition from his beastly old father. And I was worried about the effect on Dinny."

"Your sister seems to be bearing up very well."

"Bearing up? But—"

"She gave Mark Raynham and myself a pretty broad hint that she knows about you and Charles."

The girl swung away from him suddenly, as if to hide some betraying expression. The light from the window struck upon her smoldering red hair and the habitual stoop of her shoulders, hunched by the life-long expectation, thought Nigel, of a blow about to fall.

"She doesn't mind?"

Nigel barely caught the girl's incredulous whisper, which had not been meant for his ears.

"I think you ought to go away," he found himself saying. "It might clarify things for Charles—and make him see that he must make up his mind. And I don't like you looking so unhappy."

Rosebay turned to him again, nervously fingering the blind cord, a wondering look in her eyes.

"*You* don't like? Why should you mind?" Her mouth quivered and she buried her face in her hands. "Oh God, if you knew how lonely I've been all my life! . . . And whose fault is it? Nobody's but my own. I'm a coward. That's why I don't go away. And I've never learned how to get on with people, so I make everyone feel awkward. Now you know. I can't even believe Charles loves me. It's—" Her voice choked on a childish sob, and she was in tears.

There was little Nigel could say. He put his hands on the girl's thin shoulders, which shook convulsively as if some engine too powerful for her body was at work within it. She gave him a forlorn, appealing look, her eyes brilliant with tears, which made him suddenly angry with everyone—Celandine, Charles, Sir Archibald, even himself.

"I'll have a talk with Charles," he said. "Don't cry any more."

"You don't really trust me, do you?" she asked presently.

"How can I? You haven't told me everything."

"No. But I can't. Not yet . . ."

The next twenty-four hours dragged slowly. Nigel felt the case was out of his hands. He would make his report to Sir Archibald, and go. Inspector Randall could look about for more definite evidence against Daniel Durdle. The affair of the field glasses would probably remain an unsolved mystery. Nigel was by now pretty certain that he knew who had been behind it, and why. But he saw little hope of proving his theory, unless one of his suspects broke down, or had been careless enough to leave evidence which the scientific laboratories at Scotland Yard could interpret. He said something of this to the vicar, at dinner that night.

"You seem to take it all very calmly," said Mark Raynham. "Or have you thrown up the sponge?"

"Randall will look after it. He's an efficient chap. You must give the police time."

"Time! But, my dear fellow, I'm desperately worried about Celandine. Suppose another attempt is made on her life?"

"It won't be," said Nigel dogmatically.

"Well, let's hope you're right. I'd never forgive myself if—"

"You needn't worry about Celandine. It's her sister who wants help."

"I don't happen to be in love with her sister," replied the vicar flatly. "She's Charles's job."

But Charles Blick, when Nigel had a brief interview

with him the next morning, showed at his least satisfactory. His father was coming straight to the factory off the London train, in a couple of hours' time, and Charles was evidently preoccupied with the visit.

"I'm afraid he'll give me a rocket for letting Randall into the experimental room," he said, glancing rather shamefacedly at Nigel.

"That's not my affair. And I suppose Rosebay Chantmerle isn't my business either. But you've no right to keep her on a string like this."

Charles's manner became very cold. "As you say, it isn't your business. You just don't know enough about it to tell me what I ought and oughtn't to do."

"I know enough about it to tell you that the girl is heading for another breakdown. If you're interested."

"That's damned offensive! Who the hell are you to—"

"I'm an outsider. And I never asked to be dragged into all your family affairs. But I don't like seeing human beings suffering unnecessarily. Celandine won't die if you marry Rosebay: in fact, she says she knows about you and her sister."

"Knows? I dare say. But does she accept it?"

"So all you've got to do is stand up to your father. Or, if you still can't choose between the past and the present, make a clean break with them both."

"That sort of advice is easy enough to give," said Charles wearily. "I've been giving it to myself for some time. But I don't seem able to take it. . . . Look here, who did send Celandine those binoculars?"

Nigel regarded him steadily for a few minutes. "That ought to make no difference to you," he said at last. "I must be going. Will you tell your father I'd like to see him sometime today?"

The summons from Sir Archibald arrived at 3:30 that

afternoon. Nigel walked up to the Hall and was shown into the room where he had his first long conversation with Stanford Blick. Sir Archibald's dapper, city-clad figure looked like just one more oddity added to the anomalous collection of objects there. He had, however, created a small oasis for himself in the middle of the room—a long table with chairs at either end, to one of which he directed Nigel.

"I was expecting a report from you," he rapped out.

"I heard you were coming down shortly, so I deferred it till we met."

"Well?"

Nigel gave him a full account of his investigation of the anonymous letters, and the conclusions he and Inspector Randall had reached. He was aware, throughout, of Sir Archibald's eyes, like beads of jet, fixed unwinking upon him. There was something disconcerting in Sir Archibald's attitude, too; he sat there, motionless as a lizard on a sunny wall, basking in some secret satisfaction which would soon enough be revealed to Nigel.

"So there's no doubt that Daniel Durdle was responsible. Randall may find it difficult to get enough evidence for prosecution. But the letters have stopped, anyway, and there won't be any more. Durdle has had a good fright."

Sir Archibald licked his lips, upon which a disagreeable smile had formed during Nigel's concluding remarks.

"There won't be any more letters? I'm afraid I must undeceive you. I've just had one by this afternoon's post."

"That's extremely odd," said Nigel, taking the envelope which Sir Archibald threw down on the table in front of him. "So Daniel Durdle has started up again?"

"The letter has a Moreford postmark. I have just contacted Inspector Randall, who tells me the police have been keeping this man Durdle under observation the last few days. Durdle was neither in Moreford yesterday, nor did he go anywhere near the other post box in Prior's Umborne," Sir Archibald said grimly. "What are your comments on that?"

"Obviously somebody else has started writing poison-pen letters."

The financier pursed his mouth. "That is not obvious to me at all. You are not prepared to admit the possibility that your pet theory is totally wrong?"

"Not until I have evidence to disprove it."

"I suggest you start looking for such evidence, then. You might read that letter, for instance."

Sir Archibald Blick was one of those men who seem to have been formed by the Creator for the sole and specialized purpose of riling their fellow creatures, thought Nigel, as he opened the letter. It was in capitals, on the same cheap stationery.

Charles Blick goes with Rosebay Chantmerle

it winningly announced.

"You've got off lightly," Nigel said, with a smile.

"I fail to understand you." Sir Archibald's voice was freezing.

"The other recipients were all told horrible home truths about themselves. But, of course, a man of your well-known integrity doesn't give a poison pen any purchase. Though I must say it's a bit strange that—"

"I would advise you not to adopt that tone with me." The financier was glaring at Nigel, who went on imperturbably: "A bit strange that the writer did not bring up the old story about your having ruined Edric Chantmerle."

Sir Archibald's eyes flickered: his mouth went thinner than ever. "I am not interested in whatever nonsense this creature *might* have written. Is it true about my son?"

"He's seen quite a lot of her lately."

"You know perfectly well what I mean. Has this young woman entangled him?"

"That's a question you had better ask him."

"I certainly shall. But I have the right to expect some co-operation from you, Strangeways."

Nigel's pale-blue eyes regarded Sir Archibald with an impassive, clinical gaze. He said: "I was employed to investigate anonymous letters, not to act as an engagement broker, or breaker."

"So he does want to marry her, eh?" said the financier, with the air of counsel trapping a witness into a damning admission.

"Well, he does and he doesn't."

"He most certainly won't. I shall see to that."

"Why are you so opposed to it?"

"There's bad blood in that family. It's an effete stock. The father was insane." The dapper little old man was positively trembling, Nigel noticed, with some irrepressible fury. "D'you know, her sister refuses to see me. I rang her up as soon as I got this letter. Refuses to see *me*! I shall go there this evening and *demand* an interview."

"I don't see how you can stop your son marrying Rosebay Chantmerle, if he really wants to."

"I can cut the purse strings. That'll bring them to their senses."

There was a pause, while Nigel digested this unpalatable remark. Then he said: "Are you sure you're right about the Chantmerles? After all, your elder son is on the eccentric side. But nobody would say the Blicks have bad blood, and refuse to let their daughter marry into your family for that reason."

Sir Archibald was excessively displeased. "If I understand what you are saying, it is both preposterous and impertinent."

"Not so very preposterous. I can even imagine people thinking *you* were a bit touched—the way you pour your money into these expensive hobbies of Stanford's."

"Is that what they're saying?" Sir Archibald came out with it involuntarily. His discomposure would have been comic in anyone but a financier, whose delicate balancings must rest upon an unshakable reputation for sanity. "Nonsense! Poppycock! I have financed certain experiments by my elder son. If the present one fails, or he exceeds his allocation, he'll very soon be hauled up short. I am not in the habit of throwing good money after bad."

"Oh, but it won't fail, Pop," said a voice from the doorway, and at once burst into song: "S-s-s-Susie's my favorite floosie, She's the g-g-g-g-girl that I adore."

Sir Archibald's face was a study of conflicting emotions, as he listened to Stanford. Outrage vied with grim amusement, parental partiality with a quite obvious alarm that Nigel's recent remarks should be so colorfully illustrated. However, his feelings soon canceled one another out, leaving his usual glacier expression in command.

"Now you've finished your work on the engine, you must sack this fellow Durdle. I intend to get him and his mother out of the post office, too, if the police don't do it. In fact, they'd better be run right out of the district. The fellow's a bad influence, all round. No better than a damned agitator, with all this religious tommyrot he talks."

"Pop talks just like a Tammany Hall boss, doesn't he?" said Stanford admiringly. "Big shot cleans up small-town corruption."

"The first thing I'm going to clean up is this house. Never seen such a pigsty."

"You've never seen it because you never come down here. Just an absentee landlord, that's you. And who else are you going to discipline, after you've liquidated old Durdlepots and pepped up brother Charles and fumigated the Hall? Let's see now. The vicar is jolly unsound—I suspect him of Arminianism. Better make him toe the line."

"Don't be ridiculous, Stanford, my boy. Not that I entirely approve of Raynham. I shall certainly have a word with him about this pacifist drivel of his that gets printed in the local press."

"Goody! Off with his head!" Stanford did an idiotic little war dance on the carpet. "Now who else shall we purge?"

"I don't think Mr. Strangeways need be brought into these private affairs of ours. The matter of the anonymous letters will be exercising all his powers for some little time yet, I rather fancy, judging by the results to date. . . ."

Sir Archibald was to be proved conspicuously wrong on both counts. Nor would his plans for the regeneration of Prior's Umborne be carried far. At nine o'clock the next morning, when Joe Summers brought in Nigel's breakfast, he announced: "Terrible doings up the hill, sir. Just heard. Sir Archibald's dead. Miss Rosebay found his corpse in the quarry."

PART TWO

10. There in the Ghastly Pit

Nigel swallowed a cup of tea, and walked quickly up the hill toward the quarry. It was a fine morning again, a haze over the distances, and scatters of bird song coming from hedge and copse. Ahead of him on the track Nigel could see villagers, mostly children, hurrying along as if already late for some gala event, among them the gangling black-clad figure of Daniel Durdle.

This was going to kick up an almighty dust, thought Nigel. Men of Sir Archibald Blick's eminence, or notoriety, cannot fall into quarries without setting up a gigantic ripple. Did he fall, or was he pushed? Sir Archibald was not the sort of man to trip up on the edge of a quarry; or, for the matter of that, to take nature rambles at night. One must assume it had happened late, otherwise his disappearance would have been reported before now. And only yesterday afternoon he had obligingly pointed out a group of potential murderers. How many of them had he interviewed? If all, there were at least five people with assorted motives for killing him. It was almost too pat. The anonymous letters and the affair of the binoculars would somehow fit in neatly too—if this was fiction; but real life is less tidy.

P. C. Clotworthy was shooing children away from the roped-off south face of the quarry, where men were rigging up a pulley. The children, pursued by raucous cries from their mothers, wandered round the quarry's edge, eating bread and jam or fighting one another or feinting to climb down into the pit below. Nigel could see a group of police busying themselves down there round a splayed-out figure, taking photographs and measurements, splashing through the shallow water in the center, looking for clues. It must have been very like this twenty years ago: the same drama, with a different cast.

As he made for the roped enclosure, Nigel passed Daniel Durdle, standing above the pit, his head blindly weaving as if to snuff the smell of blood. The man was muttering to himself: "This is the Lord's doing, and it is glorious in our eyes." That was going a bit far, thought Nigel, though one could not pretend that Sir Archibald had been a shining example of godliness or the human virtues.

Within the roped enclosure, to which Clotworthy admitted him only after a long, theatrically suspicious scrutiny, the daffodil clumps stood impassive. There was no wind today to shiver them, and they shone in triumphant glory, all but a few which lay drooping, broken-backed, the minor casualties, no doubt, of the morning's alarum. Perhaps Rosebay Chantmerle had trodden them down as she ran back to the Little Manor after seeing the body down there. The turf was pretty hard, but here and there Nigel noticed faint indentations—the wheel tracks of Celandine's electric carriage, he assumed. She would often come up here on a pilgrimage: there were vestiges of several sets of tracks, some fainter than others, none deeply grooved. Nigel now observed that some of the stricken daffodils lay in a straight line, as though a wheel had passed over one clump after another. A fantastic picture formed in his head—of Celandine transporting her old enemy's body to the quarry's edge, then tipping it over in a transport of poetic justice. No, not possible—their combined weights would have made one set of much deeper wheel tracks, he laboriously argued; then ridiculed himself for ever having entertained such a wild fantasy. Probably the fellow just committed suicide. That's even sillier—can you imagine Sir Archibald killing himself, under any circumstances? But, as far as Nigel could tell from examining the edge of the quarry below which the body lay, there were no signs of a struggle.

Nigel's thoughts seemed as unreal as the whole scene before him—the broken doll sprawled in the quarry; the children yelling to late arrivals: "Come *on,* do! It's a deader!" The figure of Daniel Durdle standing alone above the pit, like some high-executive fiend overseeing the ritual commotion of flashlights, measuring tapes and inquisition which was in process there. The village women and a few men, who were watching operations with all the placid absorption of Londoners staring at a road excavation, might have been the ranks of the Blessed, looking down in a primitive painting upon the antics of the damned.

Presently a car was heard approaching up the track, and a spruce figure strode upon the scene, whom P. C. Clotworthy saluted. Nigel introduced himself to Major Beale, the Chief Constable.

"Ah, yes. Heard you were down here. Sorry I've not looked you up before. This is a nasty business. What did he want to do it for, eh? Going to kick up a stink.

Look at all those damned ghouls sitting around! What a picnic!"

Vigorously wiping his mustache, which showed traces of breakfast egg, the Chief Constable strode to the quarry's edge and bellowed: "Randall! I'm coming down."

He turned to Nigel again, and said: "See you later. Tell Miss Chantmerle I'll be coming along." Then, with a brisk wave of the hand, he lowered himself, neat gray suit and all, over the lip of the quarry, climbing down with a boy's agility.

There was nothing Nigel could do here. He walked off down the narrow ride which led through the wood to the Little Manor. He was shown into the drawing room, where the two Chantmerle sisters sat, with Stanford Blick and Mark Raynham, in the becalmed, fatalistic attitudes which Nigel had so often seen among those nearly affected by a violent death.

He expressed his sympathy to Stanford. The man's mouth, turned down at one corner, quivered a little as he thanked Nigel.

"Funny thing," he added: "I'm beginning to realize I was fond of Pop. He wasn't such a bad stick, in spite of what people said. Just needed the right handling."

There was an awkward silence. None of the others was a person addicted to the conventional half truth. They had disliked the dead man, and could not bring themselves to pretend otherwise. Celandine Chantmerle turned away her beautiful head. Rosebay was picking feverishly at the braid of the sofa. The vicar, coughing dryly, broke the silence.

"Have the police discovered anything yet? How it happened, I mean?"

"I don't know," answered Nigel.

Their voices were muted, as if the body were in the room and the blinds drawn. It made it the more shocking when Rosebay harshly exclaimed: "Why are we all pretending? What are we waiting for?"

"The police, darling," said Celandine. "They have to interview each of us. You mustn't be so upset."

"I dread it. I shan't know what to say to them. Why did it have to be me who saw—saw the body?"

"It had to be someone, Bay," said Stanford, with remarkable gentleness. "They won't bully you. You just sit back and answer their questions. It'll be easy as pie."

Rosebay gave him a faint, distracted smile. "But what *can* I tell them? I don't know what happened. I just went out before breakfast, and I—I found him. I thought at first it was an old suit of clothes someone had thrown into the quarry. Oh, God! do you think he *was* thrown there? Murdered, I mean?"

"Really, Bay, you must pull yourself together," her sister said. "Of course he wasn't."

"Do we all want to talk about this?" asked Nigel. "I think it might be a good thing."

"Why not? Give us a bit of net practice before we go out into the middle," said the vicar. "But perhaps Stanford—"

"Don't mind me. Tell the truth and shame the Devil."

"Well, then, who saw Sir Archibald last?"

"He came up here after dinner," said Celandine. "I hadn't wanted to see him, but he—well, he more or less forced his way in. Sorry, Stanford, but there it is."

"What on earth did he want up here?" Rosebay's tone was embarrassing in its naked petulance.

"To discuss private matters."

Stanford gave a ghost of his old, impish smile. "This

is where the Detective-Inspector asks: 'Did he appear to be in an agitated state?' "

"Oh, he was agitated all right. The subject of our discussion could not have failed to upset him. But he gave no indications that he would later throw himself into the quarry," said Celandine. "To put it quite plainly, he was in a murderous rather than a suicidal frame of mind."

Mark Raynham gazed at her in consternation. "Oh, come, Celandine, surely you can't mean that?"

"Why can't she? I'm sure Sir Archibald would rather have seen me dead at his feet than married to his son. That's what you were talking to him about, Dinny, wasn't it?" Once again Rosebay's voice left a wake of uneasy silence behind it.

"I think we should stick to times," suggested Nigel. "When did he leave here?"

"About twenty past eleven." Celandine hesitated a moment. "He was not absolutely sober. He drank rather a lot of whisky here."

Stanford Blick was looking at Celandine, Nigel noticed, in a peculiar way—intently, puzzled, as if studying a new formula. He said: "Pop didn't walk over the edge, drink or no drink. He got back to the Hall about half past eleven."

"Did you see him return?" asked Nigel.

"The dogs barked. Everyone else was in by then. It must have been him."

"So you didn't actually see him."

"No. But Cook did. I asked her this morning, when I got the news. The dogs woke her. She looked out of the window—her room's at the back, over the courtyard—and she saw him letting himself in at the back door."

There was a silence, while they all digested this. Then Mark Raynham blurted out: "I say, that's rather queer, isn't it? If he was going to kill himself in the quarry, why should he go back to his house first?"

"He didn't kill himself," said Stanford grimly. "Nor did he go out again, apparently. That was the last time anyone heard the dogs barking."

"But it's impossible," said the vicar. "He must have gone out again. Damn it, he was found in the quarry."

"The dogs wouldn't bark if someone went quietly out of the front door and made a detour, would they?" asked Nigel.

Stanford frowned. "No. That's true. But why make such a detour, so as not to disturb the dogs, if you know you are taking your last walk?"

"Was your brother at home?"

"Yes. We both went to bed fairly early, soon after ten-thirty. Charles had to start early for the factory this morning."

"Well, it's all very mysterious," said Celandine; "but there must be some simple explanation."

If there was a simple explanation, it did not suggest itself to the group who were sitting in the Chief Constable's study that afternoon. The results of the autopsy on Sir Archibald's body had just come through. He had died between ten o'clock and midnight. His neck had been broken, and he had received head injuries, presumably in the fall from the quarry's edge. Traces of blood had been found on jutting parts of the quarry cliff which he had struck in falling; this suggested that he was still alive when he fell, and in conjunction with the absence of any signs of a struggle up above, argued for suicide or accident. Examination of the organs had revealed a large but not a lethal dose of sleeping powder.

This last was the fact which had put a worried frown on the Chief Constable's forehead. At first, it seemed to fit in with the theory of suicide. As Major Beale had said:

"Straightforward enough, isn't it? Blick was in a suicidal frame of mind. Couldn't quite face chucking himself over the edge in cold blood, though he'd been drinking heavily at Miss Chantmerle's, to nerve himself for it. Goes home. Takes a strong sleeping draught. Slips out again quickly, in case anyone comes up and tries to stop him. Walks round to the quarry. By the time he gets there, he's pretty well drugged and can throw himself off with a minimum of discomfort. How's that, Randall?"

"I don't altogether like it, sir," said the Inspector. "What reason had he to kill himself? We know that his financial position was sound. His health was good, for his age. He'd nothing on his mind except this business of his son and Miss Rosebay. He went up to the Little Manor to browbeat Miss Celandine into taking his side against those two marrying. She refused to do so, according to her own evidence—and there's no reason for disbelieving it. What'd we expect him to do next? Not fling himself into the quarry in a huff because she wouldn't co-operate. He wasn't that kind of man. If he was so set on stopping the marriage he'd make sure to stay alive."

"He'd go back to the Hall, and have it out with Charles straight off, eh?" said Major Beale keenly.

"Just so. He wasn't one who let the grass grow under his feet. Look what he'd done that afternoon all within a few hours of arriving—kicked up a shindy at the works, sent for Mr. Strangeways about the anonymous letter, given Stanford a rocket for overspending, interviewed Mr. Raynham and Daniel Durdle, and then gone up to see Miss Chantmerle. A busy day. Hopping mad, he was, all round. He needed a sleeping draught, I reckon. Question is, who gave it to him?" The Inspector turned to Nigel. "The housemaid at the Hall says there were no dirty glasses anywhere this morning."

"Your point being that a prospective suicide wouldn't bother to wash up the glass after he'd taken a sleeping draught?"

"I shouldn't think Sir Archibald had ever washed up a glass in his life," said the Chief Constable.

"And there's this too," Nigel put in. "Why go to all the business of throwing yourself into a quarry when you've got enough sleeping powder to kill yourself quietly at home?"

"Well," said the Chief Constable after a pause, "the team is skeptical about suicide. What about accident?"

"If he'd not been seen arriving home, and if the sleeping draught hadn't been found in him, it'd be just possible he might have shot out of the Little Manor, blind with rage, taken the wrong direction and walked over the edge. It was a darkish night. As it is—" The Inspector shrugged his shoulders.

"I agree. Accident is out, then," said Major Beale briskly. "Who did it, Randall, my son?"

The Inspector's mild, clever eyes rested for a moment on his superior. "One of the brothers, looks like. Plenty of motive there, what with the old man's money and his opposition to the marriage. They both say they didn't see him alive again after dinner, when he left the house. Suppose, when he came back, he went up to have it out with Charles; threatened to sack him and cut him off with a shilling if he married Miss Rosebay. Sir Archibald takes a sleeping draught, or Charles slips it into his drink, at some time while they're arguing. Nobody'd hear them—the servants' quarters are well away from the family rooms. Charles carries his father up to the quarry, asleep. Same would apply for Stanford. He stands to inherit the greater part of his father's fortune, so he told me. Sir Archibald weighed very light. Either of them could have carried him up there. What do you say, Mr. Strangeways?"

"They wouldn't have much margin of time. If midnight is the outside limit, as the doctors say, it'd all have to be done in half an hour—quarrel with father, sleeping draught to take effect; body to be carried the best part of a mile, allowing for a detour to avoid rousing those dogs again. It *could* be done, perhaps, but you'd have to stop and rest now and then, taking even a featherweight that distance. And wouldn't it be damned risky?"

"You're making investigations about any suspicious movements seen that night, Randall?" asked the Chief Constable.

"Yes, sir. It's our main line of inquiry at the moment."

"Durdle been taking any more nocturnal walks?" Nigel said.

"Funny you should mention that. I'd had a couple of men keeping an eye on him in relays. That's how we knew he couldn't have sent this last batch of anonymous letters. Neither he nor his mother stirred out of the house over the period when they must have been posted. So I took off the men. Couldn't spare 'em longer, anyway. Well, last night, Durdle goes and gets half croaked at the New Inn."

"Half croaked? He was attacked?"

"No, sir. It's our way of saying half-seas over, hereabouts. This was after his interview with Sir Archibald.

He left the pub at ten o'clock. He and his mother both swore at first that he got home five minutes later. But we have a witness who says he saw him returning to the village about eleven-thirty, along the road from the Hall. Confronted with this evidence, Durdle admitted he had not got home at ten-five: said he'd got a bit drunk, tried to walk it off—reckon he was afraid to go home to that mother of his till he'd sobered up—fallen into a ditch and gone to sleep for a bit. He'd been letting off steam about Sir Archibald at the New Inn, too."

"Well, he's out," said Major Beale. "That witness gives him a fair alibi. Unless you're suggesting he went back again to the Hall soon after eleven-thirty, and somehow inveigled Blick outside and murdered him."

"Oh no, he's not worth considering, sir, I agree."

"I wonder," said Nigel. The other two regarded him with some astonishment. "Let me see that deposition again—the cook's at the Hall. . . . Yes. Here we are. Woken by dogs' barking. Got out of bed. Went to window. Just got a glimpse of Sir Archibald below—thought he was walking a bit unsteady—wondered if he was ill."

"What are you getting at?"

"We've assumed it must have been Sir Archibald and the unsteady walk was the result of too much whisky at the Little Manor. Well, Durdle was drunk too, or had been. Suppose he met Sir Archibald leaving the Chantmerles'. Knocked him insensible—the body had head injuries. Threw him into the quarry. Suppose Durdle then tries to manufacture an alibi. He's no fool, mind you. He walks down to the Hall and pretends to let himself in. The cook sees him from above, foreshortened; she wouldn't expect it to be anyone but Sir Archibald, and she's dazed with sleep anyway. Durdle has a black suit and hat—we must find out if he was wearing them at the New Inn. Easiest thing on earth for the cook to mistake him for Sir A."

"I'll have another word with her," said Inspector Randall. "Find out if she actually heard him come into the house, how long she was at the window, and so on. You think he might have slipped off again while the dogs were still barking?"

The Chief Constable broke in impatiently, "But it won't do. It's an ingenious theory, but it falls down on the sleeping draught. When did Blick take it, if he never returned home?"

"He might have asked Miss Chantmerle for some."

"You'd think she'd have mentioned it, then, in her evidence."

"People forget things under stress. Was she asked about it, Randall?"

"No, Mr. Strangeways. We didn't know the findings of the autopsy when I interviewed her. I'll check up on that as well."

Nigel gazed at him abstractedly for a moment. Then he said, "And while we're on the subject of impersonations, I'd like to point out that there's somebody else who has dark clothes and hat, an unsteady walk, and a good reason for disliking the deceased . . . Mark Raynham."

11. A Gray Old Wolf, and a Lean

The Blick case rapidly graduated from a village sensation to a national calamity. Reporters and feature writers swarmed down upon Prior's Umborne, whose natives met the invasion with one eye upon the main chance, the other upon the never-staling rural pleasure of leading the townsman up the garden path. Free beer and untrammeled fantasy flowed in equal proportions. None proved more adept at the latter than Stanford Blick, who stuffed the more gullible newspapermen—and nobody is more innocently credulous than the hard-bitten newshound in search of a story—with enough pure milk of invention to have nurtured a dozen Munchausens. Reams of paper, hours of telephone time were expended upon the communication of human-interest stories and criminal theories only less fantastic than the solemn obituaries in which the national dailies and weeklies paid their tribute to the dead man's career.

Sir Archibald, it transpired, was not only "Mystery Financier Found Dead in Quarry" and "Millionaire Magnate Murdered?"; he had also been a steadying influence on the national economy, an apostle of eugenics, a sound churchman, a simple family man who liked nothing better than a quiet evening by his own fireside, a modest and likable personality though of austere convictions, a corrupt lackey of the Tory card-playing clique, and an Hon. D.C.L. of Cambridge University. No expense was spared, no cliché left unturned, to present to the British public a picture of the deceased which should accord with the newspaper proprietor's policy and the editor's notion of what his readers wanted.

The canonization of Sir Archibald Blick had hardly begun, and Superintendent Blount was still on his way down to Moreford, instructed by his Assistant Commissioner to take over the case, Major Beale having called in New Scotland Yard immediately after the conference recorded in the last chapter, when Nigel found himself sitting with Celandine Chantmerle and the vicar on the lawn of the Little Manor.

He had returned to the village with Inspector Randall, and been present at this second interview with the Hall cook. This good lady was not now prepared to swear that it was Sir Archibald whom she had seen below her window the night before last. She had seen little of the figure, indeed, being directly above it. But she retained the impression of a dark hat and suit, or overcoat, picked out for a moment as the figure moved in a stream of dimmish light cast through the curtains by a bulb in the kitchen—Sir Archibald had asked for this to be left on, in case he returned late. He had said he would come in by the back door, it being the nearest to the Little Manor, and would turn off the kitchen light himself. Two interesting points emerged here: the light was still burning next morning, and the cook had left the door locked, and found it locked next day. She could not be certain whether the man had actually entered the house. She could not have heard a key in the lock, or the door opening and shutting, because the dogs were creating such a din; and she had gone back to bed at once, so had not seen whatever movements the figure made after approaching the door. Her impression had been so slight and momentary that nothing could be built upon it, one way or the other; but she held firmly to her statement that the few steps she had seen it taking were queer-like. Yes, he might have been a little the worse for liquor—certainly seemed unsteady on his pins, she said. Did it look like the gait of a man who had been injured? Well, it might have been. Or a man with a limp? Not exactly like a limp; more like the way a toddler walks; still, it could have been a gammy leg—sort of unbalanced—but she just couldn't be sure.

The Inspector, after questioning the other maids, and Sir Archibald's valet, who were heavy sleepers and had not even been awakened by the dogs, went on with Nigel to the Little Manor. Celandine Chantmerle greeted them with her most enchanting smile, and suggested they should all go out into the garden. The vicar lifted her into her electric carriage, which stood outside the front door.

"I'm afraid you'll have to push me," she said. "The battery ran out yesterday, and it's not back from the garage yet."

"What a nuisance for you, Miss Chantmerle," said the Inspector, adroitly placing himself behind the carriage before the vicar could get there. "How long has it been out of action?"

"It packed up on me yesterday. I'd been for rather a long drive in the afternoon. Luckily I was nearly home when it gave out."

"You ought to keep spare batteries, Celandine," said Mark Raynham.

"I saw you'd been up to the quarry recently," the Inspector remarked to Miss Chantmerle.

Mark swung round on him with a stern expression. "You're not trying to bully Miss Chantmerle, I hope."

"Oh really, Mark, don't be so silly. You know I often go up there. I went yesterday, actually. I suppose you saw the wheel tracks, Inspector."

"That's so, ma'am."

"And measured the indentations, I suppose?" put in Nigel, playing up to Randall's little game.

"Indentations! Whatever's this?" cried Celandine gaily. "Am I under suspicion?"

"You see, ma'am, it's like this," said the Inspector in his ambling, amiable voice. "Suppose someone had wanted to convey a body up to the quarry, and had borrowed your carriage for the purpose, the combined weight of two people would have left deeper tracks than the ones you'd made yourself the same afternoon. Of course, as the conveyance was out of action, you tell me, the only way this person could have used it would be to push the body there in it. And that would leave impressions no deeper than you did, the late Sir Archibald being a man of light weight."

While, with his blandest expression, the Inspector was beginning this discourse, they had passed round the house into the garden, where Rosebay was weeding a bed nearby. Nigel noticed her figure stiffen, and a hand poised tensely with the little fork in its grasp, as she listened, stooping, to Randall's exposition. Then, seeing Nigel's eye upon her, she hastily dug the fork into a clump of leaves.

"Oh, do be careful, Bay!" her sister called out. "Don't

dig up my prize orange pansies!" Her voice was almost agonized; and when she turned to the Inspector again, her expression was more nearly flustered than Nigel could have imagined it. "Sorry, Mr. Randall, I'm a bit dotty about my flowers. You were saying?"

"But look here, Inspector," the vicar roughly interrupted. "What is the point of all this? Are you saying that Sir Archibald allowed someone to push him up to the quarry in this carriage? It doesn't make sense."

Randall's eyes rested upon him, with that unhurried, meditative gaze. "Not exactly that, sir. He was asleep, you see."

"*Asleep?* What on earth—"

"Shortly before his death, he was given, or he took, a strong sleeping draught. So it'd be easy to wheel him up to the quarry in Miss Chantmerle's conveyance—a good deal easier than carrying him. I'm told that the shed where you keep it is a little way from the house, ma'am, and seldom locked up."

"But I thought he'd gone home after he left here," said Celandine.

"He may not have reached home."

"But Stanford told us he did," Mark Raynham expostulated.

"What I'm interested in just now," said the Inspector, "is this sleeping draught. He didn't by any chance ask you to give him one, Miss Chantmerle, did he?"

"No. Though he could certainly have done with a sedative. I say, did *you* drop a powder in his whisky before you brought it in, Bay darling?"

Celandine's laughter was like fountains in spring. Her sister, standing beside her now, muttered sullenly, "Don't be so absurd, Dinny! Of course I didn't."

"He is dead, Celandine, remember." There was a

touch of the gentlest rebuke in Mark Raynham's voice.

Celandine, throwing up her beautiful face and gazing straight into his eyes, replied, "Which is no reason why Bay or I should suddenly turn into hypocrites and pretend it's a grievous affliction to us. We can safely leave that line to press and pulpit."

Mark's sallow, haggard face flushed, and he compressed his mouth. Inspector Randall, very faintly smiling, gave them a ruminative look all round, then asked permission for his men to examine the electric carriage and the shed where it was kept at night. Celandine was transferred to a deck chair, and the Inspector wheeled the carriage away. He himself was returning to Moreford, to interview Charles Blick. Rosebay edged off a minute or two later, and did not return. Nigel and the vicar drew up deck chairs near Celandine, who stretched out a repentant hand to the latter.

"I'm sorry, Mark. That was a horrid thing to say. But I cannot burst into tears over Sir Archibald—I can't even feel his death as a reality. He was a completely unreal figure to me; probably distorted in my mind because of what he did to my father, but unreal."

"Oh, I don't know," said Mark. "He had his good points, I dare say."

"A ghost can have good points, for all I know. But it's still unreal. And Sir A. lived in a world I just don't see as anything but a world of phantoms. What do you think, Nigel?"

"A world of abstractions? Ye-es. High finance must be a rarefied atmosphere to live in."

"Oh, it's more than that," she said, with an intensity that reminded Nigel of her sister's. "People like him see everything from such an extraordinary angle. Inhuman. Everything resolves itself into money, is translated into a code of money values. It's not a matter just of being obsessed with the need for money; any small shopkeeper, or housewife struggling to make ends meet, has that obsession. But his sort of operations had about as much in common with ordinary money problems as the higher mathematics with simple addition sums. And he was insulated from reality by the nature of his operations, and their magnitude. All secretaries and telephone calls and bits of paper. He hadn't the faintest idea of what ordinary people mean by personal relationships, any more than a chair-borne general at the base, living in a world of maps and strategy, knows what war means to the private soldier. Even bed had to be turned into an abstraction—all that nonsense about eugenics."

Celandine's face burned with an extraordinary animation. The air of excitement, which Nigel had felt in her after the birthday party, she now emanated more strongly than ever.

"He was absolutely set against Charles marrying your sister?"

"Yes. It wasn't a problem of two human beings for him—only a question of genes. I tried to talk him round, but it was like—like trying to break a hole in a safe with one's bare hands. He as good as told me that Bay is mentally unbalanced. Horrible!" Celandine's hands clenched tight in her lap, and her eyes grew darker.

"But I still don't see how he thought he could stop it," said Mark Raynham.

"Sanctions. Cut off the money. You've no idea, Mark, how ruthless he could be."

"But surely Charles could get another job, if he really wants to marry Bay?"

Celandine's mouth was set in a bitter line. "Cut off Charles's money, *and ours*. I suppose I'm madly unworldly. But I'd never suspected where our money came from. They told me, after my father's death, they'd saved some money from the wreck. Sir Archibald enlightened me. We'd been living all these years on his charity—his money, rather, for I've no doubt the charity was Stanford's, or Charles's. If Bay didn't give Charles up, he'd stop our supplies too. A very pretty ultimatum."

"Ultimatum!" exclaimed Mark hotly. "It was blackmail. What a vile thing to do!"

"He *is* dead, Mark, remember," she murmured ironically. "So Bay and I had a good motive, too, for wanting him out of the world, Nigel."

"Bay knew about this threat, did she?"

Celandine looked a little disconcerted. She said quickly, "No. She wasn't there, of course. I meant, if she'd known about his threat."

Nigel's eyes rested for a moment on the clump of leaves in which Rosebay's weeding fork was still stuck. He said: "It's rather lucky your electric carriage was out of action last night."

"Lucky? Yes, I suppose so."

"You're very fond of flowers. And particularly fond, I imagine, of the daffodils you planted up by the quarry?"

"Why, yes. But I don't see—"

"I noticed that one clump had been run over by a wheel. Very recently. I'm sure you'd never drive over those flowers yourself, if you could help it."

"What are you getting at?" asked Mark.

"Oh, it's obvious," Celandine said. "Either I did it accidentally, in the dark, or someone else was using the carriage. That's right, isn't it?"

Nigel nodded. "I'm telling you this because Randall

has cottoned onto it already—the likelihood of the carriage having been used, I mean. And anyway, they've called in Scotland Yard, and an old friend of mine, Superintendent Blount, is coming down. And Blount very seldom misses anything."

There was a taut silence. Mark and Celandine noticeably avoided each other's eyes. At last Mark said: "So there's no doubt, then? It must have been murder? They wouldn't send down a C.I.D. superintendent otherwise, would they?"

"Blick was a very important man. The combination of Blick and murder calls for Scotland Yard's best."

"Damn him," said Celandine, her voice pure and hard. "I'm sorry, Mark, but now he's going to ruin our lives for a second time. We were all so happy. Now everything's a nightmare again. Unreality. We shall all start looking at each other—wondering." . . .

Nigel rose to go. The vicar, taking up his stick and black hat from the grass, said good-by also. His craggy face had the look of one enduring torture; and as if some twist of the rack had wrung it from his lips, he exclaimed, while they walked down the drive together: "God forgive me, but I could have killed him myself."

Nigel made sympathetic noises, and the vicar came out with it all, his voice harsh and uneven. Sir Archibald, the evening of his death, had turned up at the vicarage. It was his day for ultimatums. He threatened to make trouble over Mark's antiwar sermons and articles. The sanctions he proposed to apply, in Mark's case, were very simple, deadly effective.

"He'd discovered about my wife, you see. Oh, he didn't threaten. That wasn't his way." The vicar's face had gone white. "He just let it be understood that he'd feel it his duty to communicate his knowledge. I could have strangled him. But how the devil did he find out?"

Nigel had little doubt about that. Sir Archibald had previously interviewed Daniel Durdle, who might well have tried to buy Blick's good will and do a bad turn to his own religious rival.

"So what did you say?"

"Told him to publish and be damned. Threw him out of the house. Then I began to realize what I'd let myself in for. He couldn't chuck me out of the living, but he could ruin my work here—make it impossible. I went up later to talk it over with Celandine."

"Did you indeed?"

Shortly after ten o'clock last night, the vicar had walked to the Little Manor. Seeing no lights in front, he went round the house intending to tap at the French windows if he saw Celandine in the drawing room. She was there all right, but so was Archibald Blick.

"So you went away again?"

"Actually I didn't. Not at once. I had a silly idea she might need my help. They hadn't heard me—I was walking on the grass. So I stood there for a little, listening and pretending to myself I wasn't listening—always the gentleman."

"What did you hear?"

"Only bits of what they said. The French windows weren't wide open. And Blick never shouted at people, least of all when he was in a fury. I could see him shaking, though. He said something I didn't quite catch about Durdle; and then, 'Charles marry into a family of poison-pen writers!' Celandine was staring at him, as if he'd taken leave of his senses. 'Are you daring to suggest that Bay—' she began. And he said something I couldn't make head or tail of: sounded like 'Your brother has two sisters.' Aeschylean stuff. Then he lowered his voice. Poor Celandine was looking so sick, I nearly rushed in. I suppose he was telling her about Durdle's being her father's illegitimate son. You know that, don't you?"

"Yes. Was that all you heard?"

The vicar nodded. "I sheered off then. Felt I wouldn't be able to control myself if I stayed any longer. I walked about for an hour or more, trying to calm down."

"Meet anyone?"

"No. I've only the haziest idea where I went, either." Mark Raynham grinned wryly. "So you see, I've a motive and no alibi."

Soon after this, the two parted company. Nigel decided to look for Rosebay, and the Hall seemed the likeliest place. He found his interest concentrating, after the vicar's disclosure, upon the dead man's visit to the Little Manor and his long session there with Celandine. Surely Rosebay, whose future depended upon that interview, must have listened in to some of it?

The girl, however, roundly denied this. She had stayed in her own room, she declared, all the time Sir Archibald was with her sister, except when she had heard the drawing-room bell ring, and gone downstairs to see what Celandine wanted. Celandine asked her to bring the whisky decanter and two glasses. This, she said, was not long before Blick had left the house—about ten past eleven, she thought. She had returned with the tray, poured out drinks for the other two, then retired to her room again.

Nigel studied her—the restless hands, the eyes that showed traces of recent tears, the voice which had that sandpaper timbre of the overdriven and exhausted. She kept glancing from him to Stanford Blick, who sat cross-legged on the sofa like some tutelary image, his face sleepy-looking yet alert.

"Where's Charles?" Nigel asked.

"We're expecting him back any moment. I believe old Randall is interviewing him at the works."

A blackbird let loose some bursts of melodious impromptu in the garden outside; then, like an artist perversely defacing his own work, ended with a chattering screech.

"Superintendent Blount is going to be very interested in the matter of those field glasses," said Nigel.

Rosebay's body, slouched on the window seat, grew suddenly tense.

"They've nothing to do with the case," Stanford sang in a vivacious baritone. "They've nothing to do with the case."

Rosebay was laughing, edgily, a bit too loud.

"It would save a lot of trouble if you two admitted you'd sent them," said Nigel.

A gulf of silence opened in the room.

"D'you really think I'd do that to my own sister? You must be mad!" exclaimed Rosebay, her green eyes flaring with anger. Stanford just sat there, beaming.

"I've always told this girl she ought to go on the stage," he remarked presently.

"Don't be a fool, Stanford. Do you realize Mr. Strangeways has accused us of—"

"Of sending the field glasses. O.K. Accusation noted. Calm down, old top. Now perhaps the eminent sleuth will enlarge upon our motives for the alleged felony. We pause for a reply."

Stanford paused, his leprechaun face alive with interest. Before the reply was forthcoming, however, they heard the sound of a car approaching up the drive. Rosebay waved frantically through the open window.

"It's Charles!" she cried.

"Relief of Mafeking," murmured Stanford. "In the nick of time. Lone motorist saves ugly situation."

The combination of Stanford Blick and this bizarre room, crowded with the memorials of his discarded hobbies and anomalous tastes, was a formidable one indeed. Nigel wondered what Blount would make of it—Blount, whose Pickwickian exterior camouflaged a mind as ruthlessly purposeful as a guided missile.

Charles Blick looked surprised at the warmth of Rosebay's reception. She flung herself into his arms when he entered the room, crying, "Oh, Charles, thank God you're back at last!"

He kissed her, rather abstractedly, then disengaged himself to go and pour out a drink.

"Phew! Thought I was never going to get away from Randall."

"Not arrested you yet, Charlie-boy?" said Stanford.

"Sorry you had to bear the brunt here, Stanford. When you rang up this morning and told me, we were starting to sort out a difficulty at the works. Took longer than I expected. Of course if I'd realized father had been—I mean, I assumed it was an accident. Look here, is nobody else drinking?"

It was evident to Nigel that Charles Blick had come perilously near the limit of endurance. The hand holding the glass, which he had refilled with a second shot of neat spirits, was trembling violently; there was an intermittent tic in his left eyelid; and his voice had the same roughened quality as Rosebay's. He kept glancing at the girl, and glancing away, with an expression both puzzled and impatient, as if he could not wait to get her alone so that he might ask some question of which only she had the answer.

"Well, what did the police say to you?"

"Oh, what you'd expect, Bay. Where was I last night between ten and twelve? Had I heard father return? Did he come up to my room? Had he previously discussed my marrying you? Did we keep sleeping drugs? Look here, Strangeways, is it really true? He *was* murdered?"

"Yes, I'm afraid so."

Charles Blick put his shaking hands over his face. "It's too much. On top of everything. I can't take it. I'm at the end of my tether," he said, almost inaudibly.

Rosebay was at his side in one swift movement, clasping his face strongly in to her shoulder, almost as if to smother the quivering lips.

"There, darling," she whispered passionately. "It's all right. I'm here. Don't worry. Don't talk any more. It's all over."

Stanford, with a little grimace at Nigel, slid out of the room. Nigel followed him, after a moment's hesitation. Turning round at the door, he saw Charles's head straining back against the girl's arms, the bewildered expression on his face again as he stared up at her, and caught Charles's low-voiced words: "What happened to you last night, Bay? Why didn't you come?"

Her eyes widened for an instant with a look of pure, numb terror, so it seemed to Nigel. Then she hugged Charles's head convulsively to her breast again, saying: "Hadn't you better go, Mr. Strangeways?"

Nigel went.

passed between Stanford and his father yesterday afternoon. If on the other hand—"

"Easy, now, easy." Blount put up a large hand. "Let's stick to those two laddies for a minute. I'm just a slow-witted policeman"—he ignored the rude word which Nigel interjected—"who's never read books about psychology. Now you tell me—what like are the Blick laddies?"

"As possible murderers? Stanford's an enthusiast rather than a fanatic; eccentric, but not lunatic, irresponsible; part of him hasn't grown up yet. Take the binoculars episode—you've heard about that?"

Blount nodded. Nigel gave his own theory of the motive and plan behind that extraordinary occurrence.

"Aye. Verra like. I'll have to work on the girl, Rosebay. She'd be the weaker link."

"Don't you be too sure. She's temperamental, and not very clever. But she's got plenty of loyalty and protectiveness. She'd just go dumb on you, if she grasped what you were driving at—the implication of what she and Stanford did."

"Loyalty to Stanford?"

"Yes. But it's loyalty to her sister I meant."

"I see. Ye-es," said Blount slowly. "Now for Charles Blick."

"Charles is a weakish character. Good-hearted up to a point; but he's always suffered from his father's attitude toward him—Sir Archibald treated him as a plodder, a born subordinate. Then there was this guilt of his about the broken engagement to Celandine Chantmerle. It rose up again recently when he fell in love with her sister, and prevented him taking action. He might easily have cracked up with the strain. He'd recently heard that Celandine gave him and Rosebay her blessing. So his father was the only obstacle. On paper, it's a strong enough motive."

"On paper. Just so."

"For all that, I wonder simply if Charles would have the *nerve* to kill his father. I doubt if he would, in hot blood, as it were. But you can never tell with these repressed, guilt-ridden characters; when they do break out, they're apt to go the limit and beyond."

"It wasn't precisely hot blood, though—not with the sleeping draught."

"That's certainly a point. Suppose his father returned that night, having failed to get Celandine on his side against the marriage. He'd quite likely go storming up to Charles's room, to have it out with him. But would he go equipped with a sleeping powder? It doesn't seem awfully plausible. On the other hand, if Charles was determined to get rid of his father, and somehow persuaded him to take a sleeping draught during the interview, you'd think he'd have given him an overdose and let him die quietly in his bed, not just enough to make him unconscious so that Charles could carry him up to the quarry."

Blount rang the bell and ordered drinks to be brought in. When the landlord had retired again, he said:

"What's your alternative, then?"

"That Blick was killed before eleven-thirty, and the murderer impersonated him—went back to the Hall, pretended to go in by the back door, etc. I'd put my money on that, at present. Sir Archibald had said he'd turn out the kitchen light when he got home, but it was still burning next day. I don't think he was the kind of man to forget a little thing like that, though he might have, being so worked up by then. And I feel pretty sure that Miss Chantmerle's electric carriage was used. There were its wheel tracks on the grass near the quarry next morning, and they'd run over a clump of daffodils. She planted them in memory of her father, and she's devoted to flowers; she'd never have run over them wittingly. Therefore they were run over in the dark. She couldn't have done it herself, as the battery had run out. Therefore somebody must have borrowed the carriage and pushed the body up to the quarry in it; which suggests that Blick was attacked by the murderer somewhere near the Little Manor."

"How do you explain the sleeping draught, then?"

"Blick must have taken it at the Little Manor. Either he felt the need of a sedative, toward the end of his interview with Miss Chantmerle, and slipped it into his whisky without her noticing; or it was put into his drink by someone else."

"By one of the sisters?"

"Yes."

"Implying that one of them is the murderer, or at least an accomplice of the murderer?"

"That doesn't absolutely follow. Celandine might have felt she'd had just about enough of argy-bargy with her unwelcome visitor. The only way she could get rid of him was to make him feel so sleepy that he had to go. Or Rosebay—she's madly protective with her sister. It'd be quite natural for her to think, 'Sir A. is still badgering poor Celandine. Will he never go?'—and drop a powder into a glass for him; she admits she poured out their drinks."

"So what happened next?"

"Blick leaves the house. He's disgruntled and getting very sleepy. The murderer meets him, knocks him lightly on the head, or very hard; wonders how to dispose of the body, or has already planned it; borrows the invalid carriage."

"He might even have found Blick asleep on the ground somewhere, I dare say. Well, who is he, then?"

"Someone who could have impersonated Blick. Not Rosebay, I imagine."

"Why not? She could have left the body lying for a wee while, put on its hat and coat, made her appearance at the Hall, then returned. A woman would need the invalid carriage to transport the body; a man might just as well have carried it, if the distance was as short as your theory implies."

"What's Rosebay's statement about that period?"

Blount flicked through Randall's report. "Says she went to bed immediately after bringing the drinks, went to sleep as soon as Blick had left. No proof. No alibi."

Nigel looked worried. "There's a little discrepancy here. Celandine told me that Blick left about eleven-twenty. 'He was not absolutely sober,' she said; 'he drank rather a lot of whisky here.' Rosebay said she brought in the drinks 'not long before' Blick left the house—about eleven-ten, she thought. That gives him only ten minutes to drink a lot of whisky."

"I can drink a lot in five," commented Blount.

"Blick was normally an abstemious man, though."

"I'll find out if their maid heard the bell when Miss Chantmerle rang it, and if she noticed what time it was. Randall doesn't seem to have taken that up. Pass on now. I know what motive Rosebay had. And the others?"

"The vicar and Daniel Durdle were wandering about that night. Durdle was drunk, the vicar has a gammy leg; either might have given the impression of the unsteady walk which the Hall cook noticed. Both wear dark clothes. At least the vicar does; and Durdle—"

Blount referred to Randall's report again. "Aye, it

seems Durdle had on his Sabbath garments when he visited the New Inn."

"Both had strongish motives." Nigel enlarged upon these for a few minutes.

"But would they commit murder, under the circumstances? You know them both."

"Mark Raynham might, in hot blood. And of course a man with a gammy leg would be more likely to use the invalid carriage. I've seen him lifting Miss Chantmerle a short distance; but to carry a drugged Blick up to the quarry from a spot somewhere between the Little Manor and the Hall—that'd be pretty hard work for him. Durdle—well, I'd put nothing past him. He's a fanatic, all right; and a fanatic with a keen eye for the main chance. But it seems pretty certain that he gave Blick his nasty information about Raynham's wife, which means that he exposed himself to Blick as the writer of the anonymous letters. Now Durdle wouldn't have given Blick this information gratis. And I fancy the *quid* for his *quo* would be Blick's assurance not to go on with his intention to turn Durdle and his mother out of the village. So Durdle's obvious motive for doing in Sir A. is gone."

Superintendent Blount gazed quizzically at his companion. "I've never known anyone build so many bricks with so little straw as you do, Strangeways."

"I draw the outlines. Your job is to fill them in. You can have a jolly time tomorrow collecting facts and knocking holes in my arguments with them."

"And have you any more of these—e-eh—skeleton theories for me?"

"Oh yes indeed. There's Stanford and Charles."

"Guid presairrve us! Not again?"

Nigel pointed a dogmatic finger at him. "What evidence have you that they both went to bed early and didn't get up again till next morning? Only their own word. The man the cook saw might have been Charles Blick returning, after killing his father. He's the one of our suspects who most resembles the dead man physically. What he'd done would tend to make him walk unsteadily. He's the obvious accomplice, supposing it was Rosebay who doped the drink."

"I doubt you're talking sense at last."

"Unfortunately, there's an outsize snag in this theory. Just now, I overheard Charles say to the girl, 'What happened to you last night, Bay? Why didn't you come?' Take it how you like, that's a damned odd thing for a murderer to say to his accomplice, even when he didn't know—or was past caring—that someone else was listening."

Blount's face was transformed by a look of excitement and intelligence, which he seldom allowed to be seen upon it.

"I'll ask ye two things, Strangeways. First, if there'd been no murder, what would ye have said this Charles laddie was refairring to?"

"A lover's assignation," replied Nigel at once.

"And now"—Blount's Scots accent grew more marked, as it always did when he was most serious—"and now, forget everything else, ignorr the mateerial fa-acts, juist consider motive—pure motive. Which of all these people wud ye say had the strongest motive, by and large, for wishing Sir Errchibald Blick dead?"

Nigel's answer came less readily this time. Finally, his pale-blue eyes absently regarding the tankard of beer before him, he said: "Celandine Chantmerle, I suppose."

The next morning, while Blount and Detective Sergeant Reid were about their business, Nigel was meditating upon two anonymous letters which Randall had shown him the previous evening. They had been delivered by the same post as the letter Sir Archibald had received, and their envelopes too bore the Moreford postmark. It was reasonable to suppose that all three had been posted together, in the box opposite the New Inn. And, if this was so, to be delivered by the afternoon post, they must have been put in the box some time between 3:15 the previous day and 8:15 the next morning. Daniel Durdle had been under observation during this period. It was established that neither he nor his mother had gone near the New Inn post box. Yet the letter Blick had received, both in its style and in its malignant exposure of Rosebay's secret, was very much after the manner of Daniel Durdle.

But did Daniel know that Blick was coming down to Prior's Umborne next day? The visit had been decided upon very suddenly. A telephone call to Stanford now produced the information that he had, in fact, mentioned to Durdle on the previous day that they were expecting his father. So the only problem which remained was the actual posting of the letters.

Suddenly Nigel saw how it might have been done. Durdle could have put them, unstamped, among the outgoing mail which the van collected in the morning. They would be sorted at the G.P.O. in Moreford, stamped there, and sent back to Prior's Umborne for the afternoon delivery. But they should have been stamped at the Prior's Umborne post office. Surely the sorters at Moreford would notice three letters which failed to bear the official stamp. Nigel rang up Inspector Randall, to be categorically informed, after a pause for investigation, that no such letters had been received at the G.P.O.

It was extremely aggravating. And the other two

anonymous letters offered no sort of clue. They had been sent to Rosie, the village tart, and a smallholder named Biddle, accusing the latter of too great familiarity with his sister, the former of familiarity with every male in Prior's Umborne. Routine stuff, thought Nigel. The voice was the voice of Daniel; but it seemed the hand could not have been his. Some talented pasticheur had been at work. But who? and why? There seemed three possible explanations. Either Daniel Durdle had contrived to post the letters in some way yet to be discovered, or they had been written by some other crackpot, touched off by the earlier poison-pen campaign, who knew of Sir Archibald's visit; or—and Nigel thought this the most likely—they were part of a calculated plan, the letters to Biddle and Rosie being a blind to conceal the real purpose of the letter which Blick had received. But what was this purpose? On the face of it, Charles and Rosebay seemed to be the targets. Was it possible, however, that this letter might have been part of the plan for murdering Blick? Whatever its purpose, its effect had been to send Blick raging up to have it out with Celandine. She had refused to see him, yet he had forced his way into her presence—that much was established.

Nigel directed the searchlight of his mind upon Celandine Chantmerle. It was perfectly true, if one considered motive alone, she stood out from the rest. She held Blick responsible for her father's death, and Blick had been made to meet his end in the same place. Blick had threatened to cut off her income, and had exposed her idolized father's lapse—perhaps taunted her with it. There was almost a superfluity of reasons why she should have killed him. But physically, it was impossible for her to have killed him in the way he was killed; while practically, all her possible motives but the first—

revenge for her father—failed to fit in with the idea of a *planned* murder, for it was only just before his death that Blick had threatened and insulted her.

Suppose, however, she had planned ahead to kill Sir Archibald. She would still need an accomplice to manage the physical part of it. Charles? the vicar? Stanford? Rosebay herself? Nigel's theory about the field glasses eliminated Stanford and Rosebay. The vicar loved Celandine; but was he so besotted about her that he would commit murder under her influence? Nigel could not see him as another Macbeth. In hot blood, he might have struck; but throw a sleeping man over a cliff—surely not?

So there remained Charles Blick, that elusive, unsatisfactory creature whose ordinariness cloaked him like a hurriedly-assumed disguise. Nigel could imagine him playing Macbeth to Celandine's Lady Macbeth. Indeed, it was far easier to imagine him committing murder for her sake than for Rosebay's. What if Charles had fallen in love with Celandine again, or never fallen out of it? No doubt his father would put the same veto on his marrying her as Rosebay; they were both tainted stock. The "understanding" with Rosebay might have been a blind, to conceal the murderous intention he shared with Celandine. Anyway, even before the crime Charles had given the appearance of anguish, uneasiness, guilt; and to look guilty is not inevitably a sign of innocence. His words to Rosebay, "What happened to you last night? Why didn't you come?"—they took a different color now. Perhaps he had arranged a meeting with the girl, to establish an alibi, and she had failed to turn up. The words had seemed to make nonsense of the theory that Charles and Rosebay were accomplices; but they rang very differently tested against the idea of Charles and Celandine.

As Nigel explored this new idea, he saw Rosebay Chantmerle walk rapidly past the window. Then she came into his room, very pale and breathing hard.

"I must talk to you. No, not here. Can you come out?"

Her eyes avoided his, but he felt her will tugging at him like a child's hand.

They went over to the crossroads; past the post office, where Mrs. Durdle regarded them bleakly through her window; and turned off the village street to the left. Not till the cottages were behind them did Rosebay speak again. Then she said abruptly: "Let's stop here. I can't go back. There are policemen everywhere up there. I'm frightened."

"Have they interviewed you yet?"

"No. Not till eleven o'clock. Superintendent Blount wants to see Dinny and me then."

She spoke fast, jerkily, her hands clenched on the bar of the stile where she was sitting, her eyes darting at him timidly.

"Blount won't bully you. He's not the strong-arm type," said Nigel.

The girl looked at him and down again, with a pathetic gratefulness. "I wish you'd be there, though. . . . Oh, damn and blast! It's my last decent pair." She must have laddered her stocking as she climbed onto the stile. "I'm always hitting things, knocking things over—" Her voice quavered away, and she began to sob desperately.

Nigel took her thin wrist and held it, feeling the pulse beat like a frightened animal's and thinking—not for the first time—that Charles Blick ought to be in his place, supplying the consolation.

There were ragged, rainy clouds in the low sky. Rosebay's hair flamed sullenly, flickered by the gusty wind.

She is passionate, Celandine is sensual, said Nigel to himself, then wondered why so naïve and irrelevant a thought should come into his head. Rosebay's manner, by turns direct and evasive, seemed to be infectious.

Her tears had stopped suddenly, like an April shower, but leaving no freshness and fragrance behind. From her body, as he stood close beside the stile, came an animal smell of fear, stuffy, almost rank. Or was he imagining this too? He felt an overmastering desire to clear the air. Holding her wrist firmly still, and stroking it a little, he said: "Look, we simply must get this field-glasses business out into the open. How can you expect me to help you, if—?"

The girl moved sharply, trying to jerk away from his hand. "There've been a lot of policemen, walking up and down in the little wood. In lines. Like hunting for a golf ball. I watched them for a bit on my way down here. They found a handkerchief. A man's handkerchief, it looked like. Do you think it was a clue?"

"Never mind about the handkerchief. I want to talk about you and Stanford. . . . No, don't try to get away from me. You've got to listen. Better have it out with me than Blount."

Rosebay's free hand suddenly lashed out, the fingernails scoring down his cheek. It was like a terrified, treed cat attacking its would-be rescuer.

"Oh, I'm *sorry*," she was saying the next moment, in an absurdly inadequate tone, as if apologizing for spilling a teacup over him. "I *am* sorry. I didn't mean—"

Nigel couldn't help laughing; and after a few seconds' pause, in which she seemed to be warily testing the quality of his laughter, she smiled at him.

"I've never hit a man—anyone before. I've left an awful mark, you know."

"About time you did, then." Nigel was about to add that Charles might have been the better for a clump over the ear, but he refrained.

Rosebay dabbed fussily at his cheek with her handkerchief. "Well, what about me and Stanford, then?" she said.

13. All This Dead Body of Hate

"Stanford gave away the truth about the binoculars quite early on, though I didn't grasp it at the time," said Nigel. "He used the same words as were in the message that came with them—'bright eyes.' But this might have been a coincidence. The real give-away was when Randall said to him that your sister was none the worse for her experience, and Stanford said, 'But none the better, either?' This fitted in perfectly with what you were overheard saying to Stanford on the telephone—'It hasn't worked.' You and he put up an excellent smoke screen over this. But I saw through it before long."

Nigel gazed ruminatively at the girl sitting beside him. She was staring across the fields which separated them from the village, her shoulders hunched in that familiar posture, her whole body tensed for the blow.

"You wouldn't care to go on with it yourself?"

Rosebay shook her head, looking like a recalcitrant child.

"Well then. The field glasses, which seemed the work of some fiendish maniac, were in fact meant to do good—to be a piece of shock therapy. Weren't they now?"

The girl remained obstinately silent. Nigel sighed, then went on: "You wanted to marry Charles. You felt you couldn't leave your sister as long as she was a cripple. Perhaps you thought she would oppose the marriage, too, for reasons of her own. You opened your heart to Stanford. You had consulted Celandine's new doctor, some years before, when first he took over the practice. He told you then the nature of her illness. It occurred to you and Stanford that a violent shock, such as had originally caused her hysterical paralysis, might cure it. Stanford's father had told him about the baited binoculars in Scotland Yard's Black Museum. Stanford's unconventional mind seized upon this as a method; he had the skill to rig up the glasses, and the temperament—a mixture of good-heartedness and childish audacity—to put the thing into practice. For *your* sake, Rosebay, not for your sister's. He loves you, I fancy, in his peculiar way."

Rosebay flashed her green eyes at him. "Oh, that's absolute nonsense!"

"Well, let's call it pure quixotism, if you like," he said patiently. "Stanford fixed it so that the screw was very stiff to turn. That fact alone convinced me from the start it was not a murderous attempt. You were standing close to Celandine, in an obvious state of extreme anxiety, ready to snatch them from her if she persisted in trying to turn the screw with the glasses up to her eyes. Presently you did take them. And then you gave yourself away. When the needles shot out of the eyepieces, and the binoculars fell to the ground, you staged a terrific horror act—picked them up, held them in front of Celandine's face, did everything you could to *increase* the shock for her. It wasn't at all what one would expect from the devoted sister who'd always been so thoughtful and protective."

Nigel paused for a little, but the girl still made no comment. Her face was strained white with some apprehension or anxiety.

"But the well-meant trick didn't work. You waited a day. Celandine was still a cripple. Then you rang up Stanford. You'd had a bad dream that night. You dreamed you heard your father walking in the room above. That was a symbol, wasn't it? You so desperately wanted Celandine to walk that you dreamed footsteps. But you felt guilty about the method you'd used: so your sister had to be kept out of the dream, and your father substituted for her."

"I don't understand that," said Rosebay in a dazed voice.

"What *I* don't understand is why you shouldn't have owned up about it. To me, not the police. You knew I knew, didn't you?"

"I know you're a very clever man." Rosebay was making a great effort to get a grip on herself. "And it's a wonderful theory. But you are rather wonderful. And very frightening. Those hypnotic blue eyes of yours—I believe you'd make me confess anything, do anything for you."

The unpredictable creature was gazing dreamily down at him; and Nigel had hardly time to register the fact that she was making an all-out attempt, in her gauche, unpracticed way, to seduce him, when she murmured, her voice suddenly low, dark and vibrant, "Don't look at me like that," and pulled his head into her breast, as if to hide his eyes away from her.

They stayed so for a few moments.

"What are you thinking?" she whispered.

Nigel was thinking, as it so happened, that the vagaries of the human mind are really intolerable.

She said, "You won't tell the police, will you? Not yet."

Nigel, with the slight, enormous effort of one pulling himself out of a dream, drew away from her.

"About the field glasses? I have told them, my dear."

Her mouth, bending above him, seemed swollen. The stubborn look came back into her eyes.

"I thought you—you were on my side," she said drearily.

"It's not a game, this."

"Oh yes it is," she exclaimed, with astonishing bitterness. "One of the manly games. Like hunting down some wretched animal. All conventions and codes of honor. It makes me sick. Justice!—you'll tell me that's all you care about next. Well, go up and get your prize, like a good little boy!" She broke off, flushed, looking rather ashamed of her outburst, and very beautiful.

"You do talk wonderful rot sometimes," said Nigel.

She gave a half smile, timorous again; then, looking at her wrist watch, cried: "Oh God! It's just on eleven. I must go back."

She set off rapidly up the field path, Nigel at her side.

"What was rather naughty," said Nigel, "was for you and Stanford to incriminate Daniel Durdle over the binoculars. That bloodcurdling message in the style of the anonymous letters: Stanford's idea, no doubt. And then young Rosebay luring the unfortunate Durdle up here that night, so it could look as if he'd delivered the parcel."

"I'm not *young* Rosebay. I'm nearly thirty, and I feel fifty. And I don't want to hear any more of your theorizing."

Rosebay hurried on, her lips compressed. She has darted from mood to mood, and presented several personalities, thought Nigel, in the last fifteen minutes. She is really a much more interesting woman, possibly a subtler too, than her sister. She tells lies, of course; but women have such a temperamental attitude toward truth. Opportunist, rather. The truth is made for woman, not woman for the truth. One wouldn't mind that, if only they didn't make it so infernally difficult for men to be truthful with *them*; one's always being tempted to soften or sweeten or pare down or exaggerate the facts for them, so as to satisfy their vanity or avoid wounding their quivering sensibilities or bolster up their perpetually crumbling egos. Yet they're hard as nails too. Wretched Charles, having to steer an anfractuous course between Rosebay and Celandine.

"Are you really in love with Charles?" he asked.

She gave him a surprised look, which turned into a strangely sly, secretive one.

"I've not had much opportunity of knowing what it's like to be in love. I suppose I am. Of course, I can't respect him very much, since—Oh!"

It was almost a scream. They had come out onto the road which led up past the New Inn to the Little Manor. Opposite them stood the gate of the Chantmerles' drive. Beside it, immobile and wooden as a gate post, stood Daniel Durdle.

"He's always hanging about nowadays," Rosebay muttered. "I can't stand it. He frightens me."

Nigel took her arm, to lead her past that motionless, bizarre and somehow menacing figure. Durdle took off his hat as they approached. Along the broad top bar of the gate, something had been written in chalk. Nigel bent down to read it. *Whoso sheddeth man's blood, by man shall his blood be shed.*

"So you've been scribbling again," said Nigel sternly.

"I have testified unto the truth. 'And I saw the Woman drunken with the blood of the saints.' "

Nigel felt a violent tremor pass through Rosebay's body. It was as though Durdle cast an aura of chill about him. They went up the drive, and saw a uniformed policeman at the door.

"Superintendent Blount is expecting you, miss. If you'll come this way."

Blount was sitting at one end of the mahogany table in the dining room, wearing his semi-official look—serious, confidential, bland, like a bank manager about to interview an old client on the subject of a well-established and not excessive overdraft. He appeared, as always, to have all the time in the world at his disposal. At the side table sat Detective Sergeant Reid, sharpening a pencil carefully into the wastepaper basket.

"Now you'll be Miss—e-eh—Rosebay Chantmerle?" Blount rose, shook her hand and solicitously drew out a chair for her, near his own. A cozy little chat, thought Nigel; he'll ask her next if she minds sitting opposite the window.

"And you're the young lady who—e-eh—found the body? A fearfu' shock it must have been." Blount clucked sympathetically. Bloody old serpent in hen's clothing, said Nigel to himself. Aloud, he said: "D'you mind if I stay, Superintendent?"

"By all means. Come and sit ye down. Just a few questions to ask this young lady."

Blount's few questions multiplied like protozoa. He took Rosebay backward step by step from the moment when she had seen the body of Sir Archibald Blick in the quarry. The girl seemed outwardly composed enough, but Nigel sensed an apprehension and wariness which Blount's reassuring manner failed to dispel. The

Detective Sergeant bent studiously over his shorthand. Nigel, gazing at the portrait of Edric Chantmerle, fell into a brown study from which he was presently aroused by a subtle change of tone in Blount's voice.

"Now, Miss Chantmerle, those drinks you brought in. About ten past eleven, you told Inspector Randall?"

"Yes."

"You're sure of that? You looked at your watch, or saw a clock?"

After the briefest hesitation, Rosebay said, "No. But it must have been roughly then. I heard Sir Archibald leave about ten minutes later, and Dinny—my sister told me next morning he'd left at eleven-twenty."

"Oh well now, so it was a bit of deduction on your part?" said Blount, beaming at her like a favorite uncle. "But something's gone wrong. Your maid—e-eh—Charity Cooper tells me she heard the bell ring just on ten-thirty. She'd just gone to bed, and she noted the time on her alarm clock. She'd have got up to answer it, but that she heard you go downstairs first. You must have mistaken the time, don't you think?"

"You're trying to catch me out," she said, with a petulant thrust of her underlip.

Blount's expression was genuinely scandalized. "My dear young lady! Come, this won't do. I'm trying to establish the facts."

"Well, I still think Charity must be making a mistake."

"Mightn't you have snoozed off a wee while after you'd brought in the drinks, and been woken up by Sir Archibald's leaving? So you'd think it was only ten minutes later, when in fact it was about fifty?"

"No, I was keeping myself awake because I wanted to ask Dinny what he'd said. A lot depended on it for me."

"Just so. According to your first statement, to Inspector Randall, you undressed and went to bed after fetching the drinks. You heard Sir Archibald leave. By the bye, how did you know it was he? Hear him bidding your sister good-by?"

Rosebay's green eyes opened wide. "But who else could it have been? I didn't actually hear him say good-by. Probably he didn't. He was in a foul temper. He just stamped through the hall and then the front door closed."

"I see. You'd been staying awake to hear the result of the interview. So, when Sir Archibald left, you'd go downstairs at once to see your sister?"

Rosebay twisted the handkerchief she held on her lap. "No, I didn't. It sounds awfully strange, but I must have gone to sleep the next minute. Relief that he was out of the house, perhaps."

The Superintendent, gazing at her benevolently, allowed himself just enough silence to suggest polite incredulity. Then he asked her to describe exactly what had happened when she brought in the drinks. By her account, Rosebay had gone to the drawing room; said good evening to Sir Archibald, who gave her a stony look; fetched a tray of drinks, at her sister's request, from the dining room; put it down on the table beside Celandine. Blount examined her minutely over all these movements, but she did not hesitate or contradict herself. She had poured out a strong whisky for Sir Archibald, a weaker one for her sister. She was only a minute or two in the room, during which Sir Archibald had maintained an adamant silence.

"Did you not take a drink yourself?" asked Blount.

Rosebay knitted her brow, as if in an effort to remember. "I—no, I don't think so."

Nigel wondered just what Blount was driving at. Inspector Randall, questioning Charity Cooper the day after the murder, had learned that she had washed up two dirty glasses from the drawing room immediately after breakfast. The contents of the decanter had been analyzed later, and no drug found. Clearly, if Sir Archibald had taken the sleeping draught at the Little Manor, it must have been put straight into his glass.

"But can't you definitely remember?" Blount was saying.

"No. I mean I didn't take a drink."

"Can you remember another thing? Why you didn't keep your appointment with Charles Blick that night?"

Blount's tone was still smooth, but Nigel felt the sudden constriction of the iron hand beneath it. Rosebay seemed thoroughly flustered by the sudden change of direction.

"My appointment? Whatever—?"

"Mr. Strangeways heard Mr. Blick ask you what had happened to you last night—the night of the murder, that was," Blount heavily underlined. " 'Why didn't you come?' he said. Come where, Miss Chantmerle?"

"Oh, I see. There's nothing guilty about it." Rosebay spoke rather resentfully. "I'd wanted to have a private talk with him. We fixed it up the day before, as soon as he heard his father was coming down."

"Fixed it up how?"

"How? Oh, I see. By telephone. I rang him up from here, at the works. He told me of his father's visit. I said he must be firm and tell his father that we intended to get married. He was going to talk to him after dinner the next night; but Sir Archibald came up here instead, so Charles didn't get the chance."

"The idea was that, after he'd talked to his father, he should meet you and tell you the result?"

"Yes. That's right."

"Where and when?"

"Well, of course we had to leave the time rather vague. It was to be as soon after eleven as possible—he knew he'd have to have a long session with his father. We were to meet on the path between here and the Hall, in the field, just the other side of the road."

"Why not here? or at the Hall?"

"Because I wanted it to be private," replied Rosebay impatiently. "I didn't want to risk meeting his father."

"But you failed to keep this appointment?"

"Yes." She looked down into her lap.

"Come now, Miss Chantmerle," said Blount after a pause. "You must tell me why."

"Well, I kept on expecting Sir Archibald would go soon. I thought I'd wait till he went, and ask Dinny what he'd said, and then go out to Charles. But instead I fell asleep immediately he left."

For the first time, Blount gave her his hardest look: "Yet, after bringing in the drinks, you got undressed and went to bed. That's what you told Inspector Randall. Why did you undress if you meant to go out of doors any minute?"

Rosebay's slight body writhed. She looked for a moment almost distraught. Finally she said, in a low voice: "Oh, all right, I was ashamed to tell you. You wouldn't understand. I was furious with Charles, and I'm ashamed of myself now. You see, when Dinny rang and I came downstairs, I listened at the door for a few seconds before I went in. I heard Sir Archibald say—I can't remember the exact words—that Charles had had plenty of opportunity to talk to him. He said it so contemptuously, as if Charles was too cowardly or just didn't care enough about me to face him, I decided to let Charles stew in his own juice—couldn't bear the idea of meeting him that evening. It was humiliating."

Yes, thought Nigel, a woman so identifies herself with her man that she feels personally insulted by him, outraged, when he shows himself up in a bad light before anyone else. But she'll even lie, as Rosebay had just lied, to cover up his weakness from others.

"Thank you, Miss Chantmerle. That will be all for the present. I'll ask you to sign your statement later."

She got up, looking bewildered at this abrupt termination of the interview, yet relieved as well.

"An unsatisfactory witness," remarked Blount austerely. "I'm seeing Miss Celandine in the drawing room. You'd better come along."

They went straight away. Celandine was sitting in a high-backed chair, a rug over her knees, looking out into the garden. She received the two Scotland Yard men graciously, and gave Nigel a special smile.

"I'm all ready, you see, Superintendent. Even facing the light for you."

"Oh well now, oh well now!" Blount briskly patted his bald head. "Then I'll take the window seat, eh? Must do these things properly, ma'am, as you say. And if Sergeant Reid may have that wee table over there? Splendid! Now I'm afraid I'm going to ask you a lot of questions you've been asked before. Policeman's lot, ma'am, asking questions."

"I'm sure you love it really." Celandine's mouth curved humorously: her eyes danced at him. The Superintendent rubbed his hands in glee. Blount being gallant is like an elephant dancing a polka, thought Nigel sourly. Old Twinkletoes. Blount's opening surprised Nigel considerably, however.

"Would this be yours, ma'am?" he asked, drawing a fine linen handkerchief from his pocket.

Celandine leaned forward. "A clue, is it? How exciting. But what made you think it's mine? It's a man's, surely?"

"It has a monogram on it. C."

"But that must be Ch—"

"Charles Blick's?"

"Hadn't you better ask *him*?" There was a touch of frost in her voice, but Blount entirely disregarded it.

"Of course. I will, soon. We've only just found it, you see."

There was quite a long pause. Celandine looked mystified.

"It must have been lying on the ground a night or two. Damp, you see, and a bit greenish," the Superintendent pursued, shaking out the handkerchief for her to look at. With equal deliberation, he put it back in his pocket.

What's all this? thought Nigel. Has he tumbled to the possibility of Charles as Celandine's accomplice? Was he trying to fray her nerve by dangling this evidence in front of her nose? If so, he's having singularly little success. She looks merely interested and baffled.

"Can't think how Randall's men missed it. T'ck, t'ck, t'ck."

"You're being very mysterious," she said. "I suppose you found it when you were searching the wood just now."

"Yes. Just so." Blount seemed oddly *piano*, as if he had been somehow outmaneuvered. Well, it was disconcerting that, if Charles had been her accomplice, she should take so calmly the finding of his handkerchief near the scene of the crime.

The Superintendent took her painstakingly through the preliminaries to her interview with Archibald Blick. He had rung up that afternoon, demanding to see her, but she had refused. Why? Because she disliked him personally, and had no desire to fight his battle against Charles and Rosebay. Did she suspect he might come to see her, in spite of this refusal? Yes: he was *capable de tout*. Had she discussed the situation with Charles Blick? No: he seemed to have been avoiding her since her birthday party. With her sister? A little, but Rosebay was very secretive. So Sir Archibald arrived just before ten o'clock: who let him in? He just walked in; the front door is only locked last thing at night. Was he in the habit of just walking in like that? Oh no; indeed, she had not seen him for at least a year, and had never exchanged more than the barest civilities with him since her father's death; but no doubt he considered he owned the house, since—as he was shortly to divulge—the Chantmerles were supported by his money.

Blount read through the statement she had made to Randall about her conversation with Sir Archibald.

"Have you anything to add to this, ma'am? Can you remember anything more that was said, which might help us? He was here for an hour and twenty minutes. A long time."

Celandine's eyes were closed: there was an expression of distaste on her lovely face.

"I simply couldn't get rid of him. He went on and on. Raving about Rosebay, threatening what he'd do if I didn't help him prevent the marriage. He was quite bloody-minded. But you know all this. I thought if I gave him a drink he might take the hint and go, or at least become a little more civilized. But he just went on helping himself and battering away at me."

"That was about half an hour after he came, you rang the bell?"

"Was it? I thought it was later than that. But I'd lost all sense of time."

"How soon after you rang did your sister come in?"

"I really don't know. A minute? Two?"

"Think hard. This may be important."

Celandine opened her eyes wide at him, a puzzled frown on her brow. "I'm sorry. I can't be more precise."

"Where do you keep your sleeping powder?"

"In my bedroom. I sleep in what used to be the morning room. On this floor."

"You keep it locked up?"

"Oh no, we never lock anything up."

"Did you notice if any was missing that night? I dare say you'd feel the need of a sedative after your ordeal?"

"My ordeal? Oh yes, Sir Archibald had been rather overstimulating. I did take some. But I didn't notice if any was missing."

"Your sister's fingerprints were found on the bottle, as well as yours."

"Naturally. She often mixes it for me."

"Did you actually watch your sister pour out the drinks?"

"Yes, I think I did," said Celandine slowly. She smiled, and turned her wrist in an exquisite gesture which made one think of fans and lace ruffles. "But this is absurd, you know. The glasses are amber-colored. If Bay wanted to administer a drug, she could have slipped it in outside the room. One wouldn't have noticed the powder in the glass. But she'd never do such a silly thing."

"One thing you didn't mention in your first statement, Miss Chantmerle. From evidence received, I understand that Sir Archibald, soon after his arrival, made a reference to the anonymous letters. Something about his son marrying into a family of poison-pen writers. Can you tell me any more about that?"

Celandine's blue eyes went dark. "Goodness gracious, was Bay listening at the keyhole after all?"

"You're not answering my question, ma'am."

She smiled sadly. "No more I am. I didn't mention it to Inspector Randall because it's a very sore spot with me. Yes, Sir Archibald did say that. I couldn't make out what he was talking about. Then he told me that Daniel Durdle was my—is my brother. It was a terrible shock." Celandine's face looked for a moment like a death mask—rigid, withdrawn, empty. "Apparently Durdle wrote the letters. Is that true? Sir Archibald said so."

Blount looked at her gravely, making no comment. "After Sir Archibald left, you went straight to bed?"

"No. I stayed up a little. Quarter of an hour or so. Trying to pull myself together. It had been a most disagreeable experience."

"You have—e-eh—assistance in getting to bed?"

"Yes, of course I do. I'm a cripple. There's no need to be tactful about it. I called up to Bay: she usually helps me. But she didn't answer. Fast asleep. So I rang for Charity and she came down instead. I told all this to Inspector Randall."

"Just so. You use the wee wheeled chair indoors, and your electric carriage when you go out. The shed where you keep the carriage was not locked that night. The battery was down at the garage, being recharged. You'd done a lot of traveling in it that afternoon." Blount seemed to be talking to himself. "The mileage needed to use up a battery is thirty-five. Ye-es. Or it can be discharged in—e-eh—forty-five hours by leaving the lights turned on, or else by screwing a resistance across the terminals."

"I see you've studied the subject, Mr. Blount," said Celandine gaily.

"Och, we policemen collect a deal of useless information in the course of our misspent lives. Do you never recharge the battery at home here? You could do it overnight by plugging it to the A.C. mains through a rectifier, you know."

Celandine, glancing at Nigel, gave a delicious giggle which resurrected the schoolgirl of thirty years ago.

"I'm sure I could. But Herbert—our gardener—he's terrified of what he calls 'the electric,' in any shape or form. It appears that a distant relative of his was once stricken down by it in London. Old Arthur, he goes to turn on his wireless—at Christmas it was, his missus and the nippers around him: there's a blinding flash, old Arthur drops down dead, and every single light goes out in the Commercial Road."

The Superintendent chuckled genially, massaging his scalp. It had all turned into a jolly party, with Celandine as ever the centerpiece. Blount seemed quite captivated by her charm and intelligence. But Nigel, knowing his Superintendent of old, suspected this relaxation of the atmosphere had been contrived by Blount for his own purposes.

"By the bye, ma'am, you know of course that your sister had arranged to meet Mr. Charles Blick after eleven o'clock on the night his father was murdered?"

"I—meet Charles?—no, indeed I did not. *Where?*" Celandine's voice was faint, except upon the last word, which came out with involuntary violence. Nigel had never seen her look so discomposed since the episode of the field glasses. The pure, vivacious face suddenly turned haggard, as if a mask had been torn from it.

"In the upper meadow between here and the Hall," replied Blount, studying her intently.

"But—but she couldn't have—she was asleep when Sir Archibald left. I don't understand—"

"You mean, you called up to her and got no reply."

"You're not suggesting—?"

"I'm only saying, Miss Chantmerle, that your sister had made an appointment which she says she didn't keep, and that there's a strong reason for believing Mr. Charles Blick did keep it—on the path which Sir Archibald would take when he left you. If—here! hold up, ma'am!"

Celandine had drooped forward in her chair, like a daffodil with a broken stem, fainting.

14. A Wounded Thing with a Rancorous Cry

Rosebay had been sent for, to attend to Celandine. Nigel, pacing the garden, was consumed by curiosity. What were the two sisters saying to each other now in that delightful, dated, shabby drawing room, with its Shannon-and-Ricketts aura eloquent of Edric Chantmerle's prosperous days? No doubt Detective Sergeant Reid was straining his ears outside the door: and no doubt, if Rosebay or Celandine had anything to conceal, she would not be blurting it out now. Nigel saw the two heads through the window, golden and dark, as Rosebay knelt beside her sister, who was still in the high-backed chair. It was like a tableau designed by some Edwardian painter. The two were talking, but Nigel could not see their expressions. It would be strange if Celandine were not asking Rosebay about the assignation with Charles; for, if anything stood out clear in this murky case, it was that Celandine had been ignorant of the assignation and woefully shocked to hear of it. But why?

There seemed two possible explanations. Either Charles had been Celandine's accomplice, and she was startled out of her senses to learn that, at the very time he should be carrying out his part of the plan, he'd arranged also to meet Rosebay; if Rosebay did keep the appointment, she might well have seen everything. Or else Celandine had fainted because she realized what grave suspicion the episode threw upon Rosebay herself.

No, there was a third possibility. Suppose Celandine had had some accomplice—Mark Raynham, Stanford even. The knowledge that Charles and perhaps Rosebay had been so near the scene of action would be enough to turn her faint. But one came back always to the two crucial questions: who was the figure the Hall cook had seen? how was the sleeping powder administered? And the latter, Nigel now realized, raised a still more important question—*when* was it administered?

If the figure the cook had seen was Sir Archibald himself, then he had probably been drugged after his return to the Hall. But the time factor alone, apart from other considerations, made this highly unlikely. Well then, it must have been either Celandine or Rosebay who doped his whisky. And here there was the curious discrepancy of evidence. Rosebay said she took in the drinks at about 11:10: Charity Cooper said the bell rang at 10:30: Celandine said she thought it was later than 10:30, but wasn't sure. Charity had actually looked at her clock, and the police had presumably made sure it was in order. Could it have been tampered with that night? Surely, if the murderer wanted to confuse the time issue the clock would have been put on by forty minutes, not back? For, whether it was Celandine or Rosebay, she would want to give the impression that Blick had left the Little Manor in possession of his faculties, and walked home.

Nigel, aware that he was becoming snarled up in suppositions and complexities, took another line. The analyst's report of the amount of drug found in the stomach showed that, depending upon his resistance, it would take effect in ten to fifteen minutes. Rosebay had had only one chance to dope the drink. If it was 10:30 when she brought in the tray, Blick should have been asleep by 10:45; if it was 11:10, he might just have been able to get home. Celandine could have doped any of the numerous glasses of whisky he'd had, from 10:30 onward: she would presumably have timed it so that her accomplice would be in position when Blick left the house. In her first statement, to Randall, she'd said that Blick got up to go, "looking tired and rather sleepy" soon after 11:15, talked for a few more minutes, then left. The "sleepy" touch was bold, but not out of character.

The position, then, seemed to be this. If Charity Cooper was right about the time, it could not have been Rosebay who drugged the whisky: which made it all the odder that Rosebay should have persisted in contradicting Charity's evidence. But there was a still odder contradiction, Nigel perceived, in the idea of Celandine's having administered the drug. She must have realized that the autopsy would bring it to light, and that the police would find out it could only have been administered at the Hall or the Little Manor, thus directing suspicion against herself and/or Charles Blick. Therefore, thought Nigel, Charles cannot have been her accomplice. The only pattern the facts would fall into, then, was this: Celandine had drugged the whisky; her accomplice had carried out the murder, then gone to the Hall impersonating the murdered man, so that suspicion would be thrown upon Charles and Stanford. But who was this accomplice?

Nigel walked round the house, up toward the quarry. Somewhere, in this little wood, Blount's men had found the monogrammed handkerchief. Celandine had said, quite calmly, "I suppose you found it when you were searching the wood." Had she expected it to be found then? a bogus clue laid by her accomplice to incriminate Charles?

Nigel made his way along the narrow ride, toward the quarry. Blount had drawn off the main body of his searchers to go over the ground between the Little Manor and the Hall, particularly the spot where Charles Blick had arranged to meet Rosebay. But there was one uniformed man left, assiduously poking through the undergrowth with a stick. He recognized Nigel, and straightened up, groaning. It was Police Constable Clotworthy.

"Any luck?" asked Nigel.

"We found a handkerchief yurrabouts, earlier on, sir."

Nigel got him to demonstrate the exact spot. It had been discovered, just inside the wood, some thirty paces from the quarry and a couple of feet to the left of the ride, rolled up in a ball, at the roots of a clump of bracken. Nigel suspected that, in the first, rather hurried search, it had been trodden underfoot by the large boot of one of Randall's men. Looking up from the spot, he could see the ride ascending through a tangle of trees to the little ridge which hid the Chantmerles' house from sight.

As he looked, he became aware that one of the trees in the coppice was not a tree, but the tall, motionless figure of Daniel Durdle.

"Got some amateur searchers out too, I see," said Nigel, indicating the man.

Clotworthy executed what is known in theatrical

circles as a slow burn. "Amateur searchers? Oh no, sir. What? Hey you! Oh, it's Mr. Durdle! You're not allowed here. Don't you know you're trespassing?"

A sleek, resonant voice came through the shades of the tousled branches. "It's mine as much as theirs. I have a right to be here. 'Lo, we heard of it at Ephratah, and found it in the wood.' "

"What's that, Mr. Durdle? You found something?"

Clotworthy's question elicited no answer. Durdle picked his way through the undergrowth toward them.

"Now you've no business here rightly, Mr. Durdle, look so," Clotworthy began. Nigel had time to notice a deprecating tone, almost a deference, in Clotworthy's voice; he realized that Durdle had not spoken wildly when he said he was a man not without authority in the village. Ignoring the Constable, Daniel addressed Nigel.

"I wish to speak to you."

"What about? If it's anything to do with the murder, you must speak to Superintendent Blount."

"Then I will go unto him."

"I've no doubt he's extremely busy just now."

"Then I will await him in my habitation."

Daniel Durdle departed toward the quarry track, his long stride and weird figure reminding Nigel disagreeably of the Scissors Man.

Nigel went to look for Blount. The Superintendent was still directing the search around the spot where Charles Blick had awaited Rosebay. Nothing had been found so far except a couple of cigarette stubs under the hedge on the far side of the road. No sign of a struggle. As Blount said, "They're proof he came here, if they're his, but no proof he stayed here all the time. He could drop two old butts, just to give the impression he'd never shifted from this spot."

Nigel told him of Durdle's request, and presently they set off for the village, with Reid, leaving one of Randall's men to superintend the search; every foot of ground was to be examined along the route which Sir Archibald could be presumed to have taken on leaving the Little Manor.

"What did you make of the Chantmerles?" said Nigel.

"Vairry interesting. Would you say they were on good terms? Confide in each other, normally?"

"About average, I think. Rosebay's always been rather overshadowed, of course; but she doesn't seem to resent it unduly. I just don't know whether they confide. Why do you ask?"

"Because Reid tells me that, after we left, they hardly said a word about—well, what you'd expect. From what he could hear, the elder one began to rate her sister for making assignations with men late at night, and the younger said she'd only done it because she couldn't wait to hear whether Charles Blick had won his father over or stood up to him. Miss Celandine then said something about how peculiar it was her sister should have gone to sleep when she'd been so anxious to see Charles. And Miss Rosebay replied, it *was* peculiar, but she supposed she'd been exhausted by everything that had happened. Then her sister said, 'Obviously the police think one of us must have doped his whisky.' 'Oh, but that's absurd, Dinny,' Miss Rosebay said. And that was all. Just a lot of small talk and uneasy silences after. It's no' natural. It's as if they suspected each other."

"They probably suspected there was a flatfoot with his ear gummed to the keyhole. Has either of them tried to get in touch with Charles?"

"Not yet. And that's another curious thing—if they're both innocent."

"Oh, I don't know. Innocent people are apt to take fright and behave guiltily when they feel they're under suspicion."

Blount pounded along with his rolling gait for twenty yards or so in silence. Then he said: "You go in for too much of the mental fancy-work, Strangeways. What's the point this case turns on?"

"The sleeping draught."

"Quite so. Now answer me this: why would you give a man a strong, *but not a lethal*, dose of sleeping draught?"

"To send him to sleep, ducky."

Blount ignored this. His face was grim. "I'll tell you what's in my mind. If either of the Chantmerle sisters had a male accomplice, why should she drug Archibald Blick? He was an old, wee fellow. Any man could kill him easily. And the drug in the stomach could only throw suspicion on the Chantmerles. But suppose a woman was to put him in the quarry. She'd want to have him groggy or asleep first."

"What are you driving at?"

"The sleeping draught doesn't make sense unless this was a woman's crime. In all your fancy permutations and combinations, Strangeways, you've never included this—*the two sisters having done the murder together*. Celandine dopes the whisky; Rosebay drags the sleeping man out of doors, puts him in the electric carriage, dumps him in the quarry, leaves Charles Blick's handkerchief to incriminate him, and—"

"But why make an assignation with Charles? And who was it the Hall cook saw?"

"It was Charles Blick she saw, returning from the appointment Rosebay had failed to keep. He's the one who could most easily be mistaken for his father. And the assignation was made—just on the path Sir Archibald would return by, mark you now, but well away from the wood and the quarry—so that we'd think Sir Archibald ran into Charles there, as he was going home, made him go back to the Hall with him, started blowing off about Rosebay, quarreled, took a sleeping draught, was killed by Charles. The sisters couldn't take into account that the Hall cook would wake up, look out of the window *and see only one Blick returning*. What about that?"

"If that's what we were meant to think," Nigel replied, "I can only say we've been singularly slow in the uptake. It's a wonderful theory, Blount, wonderful. And it collapses into thin air on one point—Celandine was obviously knocked all of a heap to hear about Rosebay's assignation with Charles."

"You're green yet, I doubt. You tell me Rosebay's a natural actress. Hasn't it occurred to you her sister is a better one still?"

Mrs. Durdle led them into the cheerless, poky parlor, saying that her son would be down in a minute. She was painfully ill at ease with them, twining and untwining her fingers in front of her bosom as she sat stiffly on the edge of a chair. Blount's affabilities were received with little, harassed dippings of the head; the craggy face, the scraped-back hair, the angular figure—all was graceless and unyielding. And, even as Nigel was about to turn his eyes away from the unlovely spectacle, her face flushed red and she was leaning toward Blount, saying:

"You won't do anything to my boy, will you, sir? He's different from other boys, I know. But he's always been real good to me. He wouldn't harm anyone—not meaning to."

For a moment Nigel could hardly believe his eyes or his ears. The intensity of her voice almost scorched him. In her tone and expression he suddenly felt the embers of a passionate young girl—the girl who had loved Edric Chantmerle thirty years ago. Yes, only a creature of strong will and passion could have tempted the refined, subtle, romantic, aging Edric. Her simplicity would intrigue him, her fire consume him. And then, in a moment, it was over: the flame went out, leaving behind a coarse, violent village girl, and a man appalled by what he had done, ready to twist and turn any way to avoid its consequences: a bit of a worm, in fact.

"I guessed about those letters, and spoke to him," she was saying. "Oh, it was downright wicked, and I told him so. But it's my fault, sir. He was all I had, and I spoiled him. Can't you lock me up, instead? He'd never do it again, I swear to you. He's brooded so long over what he thinks his rights—you understand me, sir?—he gets mazed at times. He wrote them to rebuke sin, so he told me. I'm a religious woman myself, but I don't hold with making trouble like that. He'd never do anything real bad, though. Not—not what was done to Sir Archibald."

Glancing at Blount, Nigel saw that he was genuinely moved. It was tragic, the woman's love for that unlovable creature upstairs.

"I must do my duty, ma'am," said Blount. "But if there are—e-eh—extenuating circumstances, you can be sure they'll be taken into account. Hrr'm. Medical opinion. Testimonials to character. Unfortunate history. Hrr'm. Must remember, though, damage done by letters. Suicide. Attempted suicide. Feeling in village. Full severity of law."

As always on the rare occasions he was moved, Blount had fallen into the idiom of Mr. Jingle.

"Fully sympathetic with your position, ma'am. Do all we can to make things easy for you."

"It's not for myself I'm asking, sir. I've had trouble before and lived it down. My age, you don't worry so about what people say." Her plain, harsh face lifted proudly. There was a kind of beauty in it now. They heard footsteps on the stairs.

"My mother has been entertaining you, gentlemen?"

"You have a better mother than you deserve," said Blount, not unimpressively.

"We all have, praise the Lord. A little refreshment for you?"

"Thank you, no."

Mrs. Durdle, with a backward glance at her son, slipped out of the room.

"And what can I do for you?"

"I was told you wished to see me."

Durdle's head wriggled on the long neck. He gave a sickly ingratiating smile, and began to speak. The enormity of what he proposed soon began to show through his veiled language; he was offering to trade some vital information about the murder in return for immunity over the anonymous letters. Not that he ever admitted in so many words that he had been responsible for them: he had the sea lawyer's tongue and the peasant's slyness, overlaid with an oleaginous religiosity which made Nigel feel nauseated. Blount soon cut short these overtures.

"If you know anything relevant to the murder of Sir Archibald Blick, it is your duty to inform me of it, and failure to do so will get you into serious trouble. Worse trouble than you're in already. I'm not bargaining with you, my lad. And I'm a busy man. So get on with it, if you've anything to say."

Durdle's thick spectacles flashed malevolently at them. For a moment, Nigel thought Blount's treatment had been too drastic; but Durdle was the kind of man whose rancor increased in proportion to the size of the audience before whom he was humiliated. And now, as soon became apparent, vindictiveness was stronger in him than wounded vanity.

His previous story—that, after leaving the New Inn on the night of the crime, he had fallen asleep in a ditch—was amended. He had fallen into a ditch, the worse for drink, but not gone to sleep. He was brooding over his recent interview with Sir Archibald. In spite of his having been useful to that gentleman—

"You told him a piece of scandalous filth about the late Mrs. Raynham, eh?" Blount interjected. "What else?"

Durdle's mouth hardened, while his head swiveled as if he were turning the other cheek.

"I told him who my father was."

So Durdle had given Sir Archibald this powerful weapon against Celandine, Nigel ruminated. He could imagine the eminent financier stressing his objections to his son marrying into a family which had produced, not only the erratic Rosebay, but this ill-favored, schizophrenic creature.

In spite of that, Durdle was saying, he had distrusted Sir Archibald's promise to reconsider his intention of expelling him and his mother from the village. So he decided to go up to the Little Manor and confront Miss Chantmerle herself with the truth. It was the sort of resolution a cowardly man, unaccustomedly flown with liquor, might well take, Nigel reflected. Daniel's intention, wrapped up now in somewhat evasive terms, had clearly been to blackmail his elder sister: if she did not intercede for him with Sir Archibald, or consent to give him "his portion," he would "publish her father's iniquity abroad, yea, that I am the seed of his chambering and wantonness," as Daniel, with a brief return to his Chapel manner, expressed it.

He had walked up to the Little Manor, found the front in darkness, gone round to the garden at the back. There, to his surprise, he saw Celandine talking to Sir Archibald. He decided to wait for a little, in case her visitor left.

"What time was this?"

"I heard the church clock strike half past ten soon after I arrived."

"I see. So you stood there a while, in the dark, spying upon them."

" 'But Joshua had said unto the two men that had spied out the country, Go into the Harlot's house.' "

"None of that now," said Blount, looking extremely shocked. "Get on with it."

Durdle testified that Blick had been "exceeding wroth against the woman Celandine," though he could not hear what was being said. Shortly after the half hour had struck, Blount's questions elicited, Rosebay came in, went out again, and returned with a tray.

"And they filled themselves with strong drink," Durdle sanctimoniously added.

"Who filled themselves?"

According to Durdle, Sir Archibald had drunk one glass poured out by Rosebay, and almost immediately poured himself another. Celandine had taken a few sips from hers, also mixed by Rosebay, then given it to her sister, who drank it off before retiring.

"Did you then, or any time later, observe any tampering with the drinks?"

Daniel looked surprised. But it was still not generally known, since the inquest had not yet been held and Blount had succeeded in keeping it from the press so far, that the dead man had had a sleeping draught: Blount's most pertinacious questioning, however, gained nothing here. From the position where Durdle had been standing, he could not see the drink tray. All he could say was that Sir Archibald had been pacing about the room a good deal, and it would have been quite possible for Rosebay, or later Celandine, to have doped his drink without his noticing it. Daniel gave this evidence with an ill-concealed, mounting relish; its implications were not lost on him.

After twenty minutes or so, he had lost interest in the scene. Sir Archibald showed no signs of going, and Celandine would probably be off to bed as soon as he did leave. So Durdle had wandered away, with an idea in his fuddled mind of intercepting Sir Archibald on his return home and having it out with him again. He went out through the garden gate, toward the upper meadow across which Sir Archibald would walk home by the short cut to the Hall. But, before he had crossed the road into the meadow, he became aware that "one was lying in wait there."

"Lying in wait? Why did you think that? It might have been a couple spooning, mightn't it?"

Durdle shuddered, almost imperceptibly. His lank, red hair showed a line of sweat beads where it met his forehead.

"I heard no sounds of lewdness. There was a smell of tobacco smoke. It was the woman Rosebay's paramour, concealing himself privily to—"

"How do you know that? It was quite dark."

"He lit a cigarette. By the light of the match, I recognized the face of Charles Blick."

Durdle had at once moved away. He wandered aimlessly round to the west of the Little Manor, toward the wood. He'd been feeling sick, he said, and it was better if he kept moving.

"What time was this?"

"The clock struck eleven a few minutes after I turned back."

According to Daniel Durdle's account of his movements, which Blount was marking on a large-scale ordinance map, he had stood for some time in a field to the west of the Little Manor and the wood, at a point equidistant about a hundred yards from them both, waiting.

"Waiting for what?"

The man's head went up; the nostrils of the long thin nose distended. "I smelled evil in the air," he said.

"You thought Miss Rosebay might be coming out, and you wanted to play Peeping Tom, eh? Wasn't that it?"

"She, or her sister," Durdle snarled viciously. "They are both rotten with the appetites of the flesh, corrupted by the pride of the eye, going to and fro in fine raiment—"

"Shut up!" roared Blount. "Answer my questions, and spare us this canting talk! How long did you wait there?"

Durdle thought it might have been ten minutes. Then he had heard faint sounds from the direction of the house—he could not describe them; they were not voices, more like footsteps, but very slow and irregular. He hung about for another ten minutes or so, then decided to go home across the upper meadow. He was just in time to hear the footsteps of someone crossing the road into the meadow; it was too dark, apart from his bad eyesight, for him to see who it was. It could not have been Rosebay, he thought at first, for no voices came from the place of assignation; and when Durdle presently went into the field, there was no trace of Charles Blick either. Durdle had next walked cautiously round the edges of the field, ending up at a haystack near which he listened a while in case Charles and Rosebay might be disporting themselves there. But again he drew a blank. As he stood there, he heard somebody coming up along the field path from the direction of the Hall. He reckoned this was some ten or twelve minutes from the time he had heard footsteps cross the road. It was a sort of quick, shuffling, dragging sound; and one moment, when the person paused, he heard hard breathing, in the stillness of the night.

"Had you heard the dogs barking at the Hall?"

"Yes, a few minutes before."

"And this next sound you heard. What did you think it was, at the time?"

Durdle's spectacles glinted. "Might have been someone carrying or dragging a heavy sack. But not at that time of night. I couldn't make it out."

The man was silent for a minute, his thin white fingers twisting like worms on the sofa where he sat. Then he burst out uncontrollably, shockingly, almost incoherent with the hatred that had fermented in him all these years. Sin had stalked abroad that night like the Adversary. . . . The woman Rosebay, slinking up from the Hall covert, panting and exhausted after . . . Filth, adulteresses, murderesses . . . Flaunting their fornications; running about the city like dogs, and grinning . . . The woman Celandine—she had flouted the Elect, clothed herself in gold and fine raiment, left the hungry to beg their bread. . . . Vengeance is mine, saith the Lord. . . . Her iniquities would find her out, though she fled even unto the ends of the earth.

Blount let him rave for a while. Then, signing to Nigel and Reid, he got up and walked out.

15. A Shuffled Step . . . a Dead Weight Trail'd

Daniel Durdle's evidence had at once thrown light and confusion upon the whole case. Although Durdle had been fuddled with drink on the night in question, and although his mind was warped with hatred and religious mania, Nigel was inclined to consider seriously the facts which emerged from his statement. In making it, Durdle had revealed his presence near the scene of the crime at the relevant hour. He was so evilly disposed toward the Chantmerles that he had been willing to take this risk of putting himself under suspicion; yet, if he had been merely telling lies to incriminate them, it was surprising he had not gone much further.

Sitting alone in The Sweet Drop after lunch, Nigel worked out a timetable:

Times (approx.)	*Movements*	*Witnesses*
10 P.M.	Sir A. arrives at Little Manor.	Celandine Charity
	Durdle leaves New Inn.	Landlord
10:10	Vicar, in Little Manor garden, overhears conversation, then "walks about for an hour or more."	Raynham

Times (approx.)	*Movements*	*Witnesses*
10:28	Durdle arrives at Little Manor.	Durdle
10:30	Celandine's bell rings.	Charity
10:31 10:32	Rosebay enters drawing room, goes out again, and returns with drinks.	Durdle
10:33–35	Rosebay leaves room.	Durdle
10:55	Durdle goes out of garden.	Durdle
10:57	Durdle sees Charles at rendezvous.	Durdle
11:00	Rosebay has arranged to meet Charles.	Rosebay
	Durdle in field to W. of house.	Durdle
11:10	Rosebay *says* she brought in drinks.	Rosebay
11:10	Durdle hears sounds from house.	Durdle
11:20	Sir A. leaves Little Manor.	Celandine Rosebay
	Rosebay falls asleep.	Rosebay
11:25	Durdle returns to road; hears someone crossing it. Charles no longer at rendezvous.	Durdle
11:30	Sir A., or impersonator, back at Hall.	Hall cook
11:35	Durdle hears someone coming up from Hall.	Durdle
11:40	Durdle seen on road from Hall to village.	Village chap
	Celandine calls up to Rosebay, who is "asleep," then rings for Charity, who helps her to bed.	Celandine Celandine Charity

Several points emerged from this tabulation. First, Rosebay must have either lied or been mistaken about the time when she brought in the drinks. Both Charity's evidence and Durdle's put it shortly after 10:30: Celandine's was vague—"thought it had been later." Second, Charles had lied; said he and his brother went to bed soon after 10:30: but Rosebay had made an assignation to meet him some time after 11:00, and Durdle had found him at the rendezvous a little before the appointed time. Third, the person Durdle heard crossing the road was presumably the person whom the Hall cook saw five minutes later; therefore it was either Sir Archibald or an impersonator. The times Durdle had given, after his hearing the clock strike 11:00, could not be very accurate, but they fitted well enough. It seemed probable, but was by no means certain, that the person he had heard coming up the field path from the Hall was the same one as he had heard going down toward the Hall ten minutes earlier; and if so, it must have been an impersonator—why should Sir Archibald have walked home, and then straight back to the Little Manor again?

If Durdle was telling the truth, and his times were reasonably accurate, Sir Archibald could hardly have been attacked at the Hall. Even if he had been knocked on the head immediately after his return, how could the attacker have done this and got the insensible body as far as halfway across the upper meadow in five minutes? Yet there was Durdle's curious remark that "it might have been someone carrying or dragging a heavy sack." It was possible, of course, that Sir Archibald had started back for the Hall earlier than 11:20; but only if Celandine and Rosebay were lying or mistaken about the time he left: and besides, if this had happened, what sense could be made of the Hall cook's evidence, and who was it Durdle had heard crossing the road at 11:25?

Nigel pushed aside the timetable impatiently. One could get no farther with it till Charles Blick's story had been told. If he was at the rendezvous just before eleven, and smoked two cigarettes there, he must have moved off not long before Durdle returned to the spot at 11:25. The simplest explanation was that, hearing Durdle's footsteps and somebody else's converging upon him just then, he'd decided the place was too public for meeting Rosebay, and had gone quietly off home again. Then it might have been he, after all, whom the Hall cook had seen.

Nigel could not imagine any other explanation of Charles's movements which was both natural and innocent. But suppose he were not innocent. Suppose he agreed to the rendezvous with Rosebay as the ideal device for getting her away from the house and grounds while he was disposing of his father's body, drugged by Celandine. Nigel sat up in some excitement, and studied his timetable again. Charles could have smoked one cigarette on the way up—the one Durdle smelled—and dropped its butt together with an old one beside the hedge. He would arrive several minutes too early at the "rendezvous," *so as not to meet Rosebay.* He would hear Durdle move off, lie low for a minute, then go on toward the Little Manor, making a detour to avoid Rosebay, and be ready on the scene of action at 11 o'clock. This would give him twenty minutes to do what had to be done. The "slow, irregular steps" Durdle heard at 11:10 could be Charles dragging his insensible father to the electric carriage. He would push the body in it silently up to the quarry, unaware of having dropped his handkerchief on the way, return to the house, replace the carriage in the shed, and go straight home, being heard by Durdle crossing the road at 11:25. It could all be done comfortably in the time.

But what about the person Durdle had heard

returning ten minutes later? Nigel struck his fist on the table in excitement. He'd got it! Charles, arrived at the Hall, finds his handkerchief is lost and goes stumbling back in panic to look for it, knowing he has left a damning clue behind somewhere.

At this point, Nigel's thought processes were interrupted by the arrival of Blount, who invited him to walk up to the Hall, where he was going to take a statement from Stanford Blick. Nigel beguiled the way by expounding his latest theory. After hearing him out in somewhat discouraging silence, the Superintendent remarked: "The trouble with you, Strangeways, is that you think too much and don't use your imagination enough."

"Well, I *must* say!"

"I'll not deny," Blount remorselessly continued, "that your theory has points of interest—e-eh—academically speaking. Aye, it's a beautiful frame. It only lacks the picture inside it. Isn't that so, Reid?"

"I dare say you're right, sir," said the Detective Sergeant diplomatically.

"The picture now," Blount expatiated with mounting enthusiasm. "There's Charles Blick outside the house, Miss Chantmerle and Sir Archibald in the drawing room. Charles is waiting for a signal from his accomplice to tell him the old man's asleep and he can enter."

"Surely he'd just look in through the drawing-room windows? Why a signal?"

Blount beamed at him in a pitying manner. "D'you suppose Celandine would leave the curtains undrawn when Rosebay was outside the house and might look in and see the dirty work going on?"

"But—"

"No, wait a minute. At some point Celandine asks Sir Archibald to close the curtains; or maybe she does it herself in that wheel chair. Maybe that's the signal Charles was awaiting. Charles enters. He has to convey the sleeping man outside to the electric carriage. Picture it. Use your imagination. Now then, Reid, what would you do first?"

"Make sure the other sister was really out of the house."

Blount smacked his large hands together. "Exactly! There'd be no danger from Charity Cooper. She's deafish. Her room is at the other end of the house, and faces away from the drive and the shed where the carriage is kept. But how could they be certain Rosebay wouldn't come back from the upper meadow and surprise them? or that she'd kept the assignation at all?"

"That's surely a risk they'd have to take?"

Blount's eyes twinkled at Nigel from behind his old-fashioned pince-nez. "Why take the risk when it could be avoided?"

"I don't get you."

"Think back to what that loon, Durdle, told us. Something that contradicted a bit of Miss Rosebay's evidence."

Nigel thought hard for a minute. "Oh lord, yes! You're perfectly right. The drink she took."

"Precisely. Durdle said she knocked back a dram of whisky her sister had sipped from. Now, here's *my* picture of it. The assignation in the upper meadow was the original plan. But Celandine's an intelligent woman. She sees how risky it is. And, when she finds there's an opportunity to dope a glass of whisky, she seizes it; takes a sip or two herself, hands the glass to her sister. Rosebay is neutralized for the rest of the night—the stuff has half an hour to work before Charles is due. And it's later Celandine drops a powder into Sir Archibald's glass."

"Yes, I admit that's much more plausible. But how do you account for Rosebay's telling all those fibs, then?"

"She's a vairy loyal, protective kind of lassie. I agree with you there. She'd wake up the next morning with a bit of a head. And when she hears about the dead man having had a sleeping draught, she'll put two and two together. She thinks to herself, if I say I heard Sir Archibald leave at 11:20, and brought the drinks only ten minutes earlier, it'll help to clear Celandine, for it'll strongly suggest that the drug could not have been administered to him here, before he left."

They were now turning in at the Hall gate. Emerging from the avenue, they saw Stanford Blick reclining in a hammock under the cedar tree which overspread the lawn. They also caught a glimpse of a woman's figure and red hair just disappearing round the side of the house. The dogs broke into their demented barking.

Stanford, looking bizarre as ever in his muffler and stained cloth cap, rose to greet them.

"Have I the honor of addressing Superintendent Blount? Your fame is known even in these remote parts, dear sir. There are deck chairs behind the cedar. Pray draw them up, and let's have a jolly confab."

Blount wore an expression, familiar to Nigel, which being interpreted meant, "All right, laddie, I'll sort you presently." For the moment, he was content to offer formal condolences, which Stanford received with a kind of inattentive dignity.

"I'm hoping, sir, you may be able to amplify the statement you made to Inspector Randall."

Stanford nodded absently. Then he raised a vivacious finger: "Ah, I thought so. The willow warbler. Hear it?

A very sporting little songster, don't you think?" He peered up into the branches of the cedar. " 'Birds in the high Hall-garden,' " he remarked. "A much underrated poet, Tennyson, you agree? 'What matter if I go mad? I shall have had my day.' "

"Just so, sir. You inherit all this property?"

"The estate? Yes, I believe so."

"And your father's money? How does that go?"

"There are a number of bequests, to dotty things like his eugenics society. My brother and I are the residuary legatees. I get two-thirds and he gets a third."

"A very large sum it will be, I dare say."

"Oh yes, a tidy whack. Unless of course he altered his will recently."

"Had he threatened to do so, sir?"

"My dear old Super, Pop was always threatening to cut us off with a shilling. But he'd never have done it, really; he believed in The Family, you see." Stanford's voice had its rueful, husky tone which might break out any moment, one felt, into a chuckle.

"Did he make any such threats on the afternoon of his death? I understand you had a quarrel with him."

"Oh, I must explain. That was about Susie. He thought I was spending too much money on her. The fact is, of course, he was quite interested in her himself. But I'd been having a lot of trouble with her—her bearings would keep overheating, poor girl. Pop had rather lost his nerve, and said he couldn't go on financing her."

Detective Sergeant Reid's pencil appeared to have frozen to the page of his notebook during this explanation.

"But that would have blown over anyway," Stanford went on. "And I was able to persuade him Susie was ready now for any bench tests he cared to have made."

Comprehension dawned on Sergeant Reid's fresh young face.

"No, the big bang came when I tried to put in a word for Chas and Rosebay. Couldn't shake the old boy on that."

Blount questioned him at some length over this point, then moved on to dinner that night. It had been rather a grim affair, Stanford conceded. They had started late, which upset the cook, which upset his father's temper and digestion; conversation had not flowed. They did not rise from table till nine o'clock, and Sir Archibald had gone straight to the room he used as a study, to deal with some urgent work which his interviews that afternoon had compelled him to postpone.

"It was damned awkward for old Chas. He'd been screwing himself up to have a *démarche* with Pop after dinner. But it's always been a tradition in our family, when Pop retires to work, he's left undisturbed. Chas thought he'd beard him when he'd finished. But then Pop put his head in at the door and told us he was going up to the Little Manor, so poor old Chas was balked again."

"This was a bit before ten?"

"Yes."

"What state of mind would you say your brother was in? Did he—e-eh—express indignation at your father's attitude toward his engagement?"

Stanford's brown, shining eyes regarded Blount steadfastly.

"He didn't threaten to bump him off, if that's what you mean."

"Really, sir, you mustn't twist my words."

"I wasn't twisting—only interpreting them."

The air between them seemed to quiver, as if after an inaudible clash of steel on steel.

"Chas was nervy, down in the mouth, rather perplexed. My impression was that he didn't quite know where he stood, about young Rosebay—stood with himself, I mean."

"So, shortly after ten-thirty, you both went to bed?"

"That's correct."

"And you didn't hear your brother going out, a quarter of an hour later, to meet his fiancée?"

If Blount intended this as a bombshell, it quite failed to detonate. Stanford, in his chattiest manner, replied, "No. Chas is a secretive chap, rather. Young Rosebay's just been telling me about it. Puts Chas on the spot a bit, I suppose?"

"It puts him on the scene of the crime at the relevant period," Blount formidably replied.

"Yes, so it does." Stanford didn't seem at all perturbed. "Rosebay also told me you suspect her of doping Pop's drink. Or her sister."

"They both had access to sleeping powder."

"So have Chas and I. Kept in the bathroom cupboard. Same prescription as Celandine's. So did Pop."

"I don't quite follow you."

"Pop often carried it about with him. Not in powder form. Pills. Same ingredients, though, I believe. Or rather, *a* pill."

There could be no doubt of the effect of Stanford's countermine, if such it was designed to be. Sergeant Reid's pencil was paralyzed; even Blount blinked hard, as if he had cracked his shin in the dark.

"Why haven't I been told of this?" he demanded.

"Well, the point hadn't arisen when Randall came to see me."

Stanford, his blackened teeth showing in an amiable grin, enlarged on it.

"I expect Strangeways noticed that little silver matchcase Pop used to fiddle with. He generally had a sleeping pill in it. His valet was supposed to replenish it. He'd never carry more than one at a time, because he was afraid of contracting the drug habit—he'd a number of rather quaint phobias like that, poor old boy. Did you find the matchcase on his body?"

It had been found near Sir Archibald's body, Blount told them, having apparently fallen out of his waistcoat pocket. It was lying, open, in a pool of water. At Blount's request, Stanford now summoned Sir Archibald's valet—by ringing a large, brass hand bell which stood on the grass near the hammock. The valet testified that he had put a pill in the silver box when laying out his employer's clothes for dinner that night.

This information, Nigel reflected, altered the whole aspect of the case. Two possibilities arose from it. The box having been found empty proved nothing, since it had also been found open; the pill might have fallen out of it; and if so, it would have been dissolved in the water where the body was lying. But suppose Sir Archibald had swallowed the pill—just before or after leaving the Little Manor? It was not unthinkable. The fact that he was in the habit of carrying one about with him suggested that he was prepared to take a strong sedative when and where he needed it, not necessarily in his own home before going to bed. Suspicion was, at any rate, no longer concentrated upon the Chantmerles. Daniel Durdle, Mark Raynham and Charles Blick had all been near the scene of the crime that night; any one of them might have met Sir Archibald on his way back to the Hall, stunned him and hurled his still living body into the quarry—granted always that the composition of his sleeping pills corresponded with the analysis of the sedative found in his organs.

Nigel gazed round him, at the cedar, the lawn, the elaborate facade of the Hall. They had become strangely unreal in this dull, lowering day, as if a gauze had been interposed, making the scene behind it ghostly. It *was* unreal, of course. The theories spun by his active brain, even this group of solid men conversing beneath the cedar tree, seemed insubstantial compared with the activity which had been going on all over Prior's Umborne: the policemen quartering the upper meadow; Blount's assistants, at the Hall, the Little Manor, the post office, the vicarage, minutely examining clothes and shoes for telltale traces, interviewing servants, searching, making inquiries from house to house in case any suspicious movements had been noticed on the night of the crime; all this background activity, patient, deliberate, relentless, was the real thing.

With an effort, Nigel dragged his attention back to the scene upon the lawn. Superintendent Blount had returned to the night when Sir Archibald was killed. Stanford went to sleep, he repeated, soon after getting to bed. The dogs awoke him. Then he went off to sleep again. He did not know when his brother returned; Charles had breakfasted before him next morning.

"So you can tell us nothing more about that night? Your brother has never discussed it with you?"

"He has not discussed his own movements, no." Stanford hesitated. An enigmatic look, half calculating, half teasing, came over his face. The rich, husky voice took on a deeper resonance as he said: "I remember the time, for the roots of my hair were stirred by a shuffled step, by a dead weight trailed, by a whispered fright."

Nigel felt a queer chill between his shoulder blades. Sergeant Reid glanced covertly at Blount, as if inquiring whether this should be taken down in evidence.

"Meaning precisely what, sir?" asked Blount. "You've remembered something, you say?"

Stanford gave his wild, leprechaun smile. "That depends. I don't suppose you consider dreams as evidence?"

"I think we might as well hear it," Nigel put in quickly. "You had a dream that night—a nightmare? which has something to do with Tennyson?"

"Good old Strangebugs. Knew I could rely on you. Not about the eminent poet, but—"

"Look here, sir, I'm a busy man," Blount began.

"I'll not detain you long. And you really should keep an open mind about these things. Extrasensory perception—for example—what you call telepathy—there's been a great deal of experimental work on it, and positive results obtained. Prophetic dreams are a branch of the subject. I don't mean the real prophetic dream, which has to be explained by a theory of time slipping out of gear into neutral, so to speak. I'm talking of the apparent hallucination behind a lot of ghost stories—chap's wife, mother or what not appears in his room at what turns out to be the very moment she died fifty miles away. Old wives' tales can teach the scientists plenty, believe me."

Stanford's eyes were glancing brilliantly, almost feverishly, between Blount and Nigel.

"You're telling us you had a dream about your father's death?" Blount's manner was curt and restive; but, like the Ancient Mariner, Stanford gripped his unwilling audience.

"Yes. A very queer dream indeed." The man's voice took on the muted, thrilling tone of one who tells a ghost story. "The extraordinary thing about it was that I saw two Pops."

"*Saw two pops?*" muttered Detective Sergeant Reid involuntarily, his pencil jerking suddenly as if a planchette board, not a notebook, lay beneath it.

"I seemed to be looking down from above. It was night, but I could see Dinny's electric carriage standing on a lawn. For some reason, it was absolutely horrifying—just the sight of it standing there, empty, and unattended. I'd no sense of place. Or rather, it hadn't any significance at first. It must have been the strip of lawn outside their front door, bordering the drive. I suppose the sensation of something horribly wrong came from, or was symbolized by, the carriage being on the grass, not on the drive itself. There it was, anyway, waiting. I knew it was waiting for something. So was I. Then two figures emerged right below me. One was holding the other under the armpits and sort of shuffling backward with it, dragging it toward the carriage. I wanted to scream out—to stop the whole thing; but I couldn't. I knew that, if the two figures reached the electric carriage, it would be the end. But they did. And it wasn't. I remember there was a sort of break in the film, so the next thing I saw was one of the figures in the carriage and the other starting to turn it and push it away. Like a kid pushing a Guy Fawkes dummy in a hand cart. The peak of the nightmare came then. You see, the figures were the same figure."

"The same figure?" muttered Blount, and audibly swallowed; he made an irritable movement, as if brushing a cobweb from his face. "What the devil do you mean?"

"Just that. The figure in the carriage was my father, and the figure pushing it was my father. It was a dream. I couldn't see their faces; but I didn't have to. I knew.

The figures were identical. Both wore dark overcoats and those curly-brimmed Homburg hats—the Edwardian fashion that has come in again. Pop was quite a dandy. Well, Father started pushing Father away, and I woke up."

There was an uneasy silence. Nigel felt Stanford's eyes upon him, a cryptic urgency in them.

"You're suggesting—e-eh—you saw the crime in your dream?" said Blount at last. "Pity you didn't see the criminal's face."

Something impelled Nigel to ask, "What time was it you woke up from this nightmare?"

"I looked at my watch—you know, sort of to shake myself free of the dream, get a grip on normality again. It was nine minutes past eleven. The next minute, I went to sleep again."

16. O Father! O God! Was It Well?

"Well, what did you make of that?" asked Blount, as they drove, a quarter of an hour later, toward Moreford.

"Rather instructive, the dream, I thought. And disagreeable. Made my flesh creep."

"Och, the dream! No, what interests me is the time he told us he awoke. Nine minutes past eleven. Just about the very time yon Durdle said he heard sounds from the Little Manor—slow footsteps, you remember?"

"Do I not! Stanford seems to have dreamed the murder at exactly the time it was taking place. Supports his theory of telepathy."

"Telepathy my foot! I'll ask you two questions, Strangeways. How did he come to fix on that precise time? And why did he tell us the creepy tale at all?"

"I see you're bursting to answer your questions. Well, why?"

"I've had tabs on Stanford Blick, and you can take it from me Durdle's not been in communication with him. So how could Stanford know that eleven-nine was a crucial moment in the night's doings, unless he was there, on the spot, himself? And why should he come out with that rigmarole about a dream except to give himself an alibi, for that very time?"

"A dream is not such stuff as alibis are made of."

"I disagree. It'd be of no earthly value in a court of law. But it could be a devilish subtle way of suggesting to an average clever policeman that one was at home and in bed when really one was somewhere else. He's got the 'fluence, yon laddie. I'll confess he almost had me crossing him off the list—it was all so weird, and so natural forbye, you couldna begin to suspect he was making it up."

"But, because it was so natural, your nasty, perverse mind goes assuming it must have been faked."

Arrived at Moreford, they went first to the police station, where Blount was closeted awhile with Inspector Randall. In the meantime, Nigel perused a carbon copy of Randall's report on the investigations into the new batch of anonymous letters. A good deal of work had been done upon this. There seemed to be no possible doubt now that they had not been posted by Daniel Durdle or his mother. Moreover, the field was narrowed to those who could have known, on the previous day, that Sir Archibald Blick was coming down from London. This eliminated the possibility of the letters having been written by some other Prior's Umborne free-lance inspired to emulate the original poison pen. Apart from the servants at the Hall, who had been too busy making preparations for Sir Archibald's arrival to go down to the village and gossip, the only people cognizant of it were Stanford and Charles Blick, the Chantmerles and the vicar.

Randall's inquiries disclosed that any of these could have posted letters in the New Inn box during the relevant period. Stanford and Charles denied having done so; Mark Raynham said he had posted several in the main box, but none in the other one; Rosebay had posted in the New Inn box three of her sister's letters and one of her own. These letters had been traced to their recipients, and all was in order. Finally, a Scotland Yard handwriting expert, after comparing the three latest letters with specimens of Daniel Durdle's efforts, had given the opinion that they were by a different hand. The pertinacious Randall had collected specimens of the handwriting of all six suspects and these were now under examination at Scotland Yard.

Twenty minutes after their arrival at the police station, Blount collected Nigel and they set off, with Detective Sergeant Reid, for the factory. Blount was uncommunicative on the way and at his grimmest when they got there. Charles Blick's office, a smallish, functional room on the upper floor, had a pleasant view over the railway sidings to the green and brown patchwork of country beyond. Charles himself, neat, watchful and worried-looking, seemed more of a personality here on his own ground. He gave a number of instructions to his secretary before he dismissed her and indicated that he was now at Blount's disposal for a quarter of an hour.

"I hope we shall not need to take up any more of your time," the Superintendent replied smoothly. "And I must warn you, Mr. Blick, that anything you say will be taken down and may be used in evidence. You are, of course, under no compulsion to make a statement. You understand that?"

As always, when the official warning was uttered, Nigel felt a constriction of the heart, a mingled apprehension and excitement such as one feels when the bell rings for the first round of the major contest.

Charles had bowed his head affirmatively, saying nothing.

"In view of evidence that has recently come to light, sir, I think you may wish to alter your original statement, made to Inspector Randall."

"What evidence is this?" asked Charles.

"You told Inspector Randall you went to bed on the night of the twentieth, shortly after ten-thirty, and were at home all that night. We now learn you had made an appointment to meet Miss Rosebay in the upper meadow, at some time after eleven P.M., and were in fact seen there a few minutes before the hour."

Charles Blick sighed, and drew down the corners of his mouth ruefully. "Yes, I suppose it was bound to come out. Who saw me? Rosebay never turned up, you know."

"You admit your first statement was false then?" Blount's voice and face were bleak as his native hills.

"Oh yes. I—well, I didn't want her to be mixed up in—"

"Mixed up in what, sir? When you made that statement, the cause of your father's death had not been established."

"I never supposed he walked over the edge of the quarry on purpose, or accidentally." Charles gave a wry little smile, which reminded one of his brother. "It was stupid of me to lie about it. The fact is I was fagged out, overwrought. And of course a bit windy too—I knew I'd be under suspicion if it came out I'd been up there that night."

"Just so." Charles's boyish, charming candor had broken as ineffectually as a wavelet upon Blount's granite front. "I understand you quarreled with your father about Miss Rosebay?"

"Well, no. There would have been a quarrel, no doubt, but it never came to that. He went out before I could have a talk with him."

"You'd arranged to meet Miss Rosebay later so as to tell her the results of that talk. You never had it. But you still went up to the rendezvous?"

"Naturally. I wouldn't want her to be waiting about there—"

"Wouldn't it have been simpler to put off the appointment by telephone?"

"I dare say," Charles replied dryly. "If it had been a business appointment. But it was a meeting with my fiancée. I'd want to see her anyway. Nothing unnatural or criminal in that, is there?"

"But you gave your brother to understand you were going up to bed. You wished to keep the—e-eh—rendezvous a secret from him?"

"If you like to put it that way, yes."

Charles is a more orthodox duelist than his brother, thought Nigel, but not ineffective. Odd there should be no photograph of Rosebay on his desk. Or is it odd? Perhaps he put it away for Sir Archibald's visit, and just hasn't put it back.

"So you went out, sir, to keep this appointment. At—?"

"About ten to eleven."

"Hat and overcoat, I suppose?"

"Overcoat. No hat."

"You're sure of that?"

"Quite sure. I usually wear a hat. But Rosebay's trying to get me out of the habit. Says it looks starchy in the country."

"You'd go out by the back door and across the court—the quickest way?"

"No. By the front. Then through the kitchen garden. Didn't want Stanford's hounds to wake everyone up. He's trained them to bark only if people go near his workshop. I came back the same way, for the same reason. O.K.?"

By luck, skill or pure innocence, Charles seemed to be neatly sidestepping Blount's minor pitfalls. But the region he now approached was a thickly-sown minefield. Led on into it by the Superintendent's questions, he described how he had walked across the upper meadow, smoking a cigarette. At the rendezvous, he threw it away and lit another. He heard someone moving on the far side of the road, but did not call out, in case it was not Rosebay. It evidently had not been, for the person went away at once. Shortly after this, it struck eleven. According to his statement, Charles waited for about ten minutes—time to finish his second cigarette. He then moved off.

"You didn't wait for—e-eh—your fiancée very long?"

"No. You see, our arrangement was that she should be there at eleven, and wait for me; I didn't know how long my talk with father would go on, and I'd said I might be a bit late. As you know, things turned out differently. Father went up to the Little Manor before I could have my talk with him. Rosebay is usually very punctual, so I assumed she was being detained by him at the house and wouldn't be able to get out."

"I see. Did you hear any sounds from the Little Manor while you were waiting? Or anyone else on the road?"

"No."

"And about eleven-ten you moved off?"

"Probably a bit earlier. Time always seems so much longer when one's hanging about."

"Where did you go?"

"Through the gate into the road. Turned left. Walked to the crossroads—Fenny Cross, it's called—then turned left again onto the road which takes you down past the Hall. I got home about a quarter to twelve."

"A long walk, Mr. Blick."

Charles glanced sharply at the Superintendent. "What do you mean by that?"

"You couldn't wait more than ten minutes for your fiancée. But you could spare half an hour for walking the night. Why didn't you go straight home?"

"If I'd known I was going to be mixed up in a criminal investigation, no doubt I would have."

"You've not answered my question, sir. Are you unwilling to do so? I have no powers to compel you to answer."

Charles Blick, looking at Nigel markedly, as if normal human understanding could not be expected from any other quarter, said, "I was in rather a state. I felt I'd failed Rosebay by not having it out with my father. I wanted to get it all straight in my mind."

"Get it straight whether you really loved her enough to go through with the consequences of your father's opposition?" asked Nigel.

"No, of course not . . . Well, not exactly." Charles was ill at ease and confused. "It'd have meant poverty for us, if . . . Damn it, one must have some prospects to offer one's wife."

"Did you meet anyone in the course of your—e-eh—ramble?" inquired Blount.

"No. Those roads are deserted at that time of night."

"And you didn't go through the wood above the Little Manor, or anywhere near the quarry?"

"*No.* I've just told you I—"

"Have you been there, in the wood, any time during the last week?"

"No. Why?" Charles sounded genuinely mystified by this last question.

"Do you recognize this handkerchief?" Blount spread it out on the desk at which Charles was sitting.

"Yes, indeed," said Charles slowly. "It's my monogram. However did it get so dirty? Where did you find it?"

"In the wood. Near the scene of the crime. Have you any explanation how it came to be there?"

Nigel could almost pity Charles Blick at that moment. His face was blank, all emotion sponged off it by the shock; only his eyes were desperately alive, with the look of one who has to do a complex, lightning calculation in his head, against time.

"I simply can't understand it," he said at last.

Blount pointed to the handkerchief. "There seems to be a bloodstain just there. It's very faint; and frankly, our analyst may not be able to get anything from it. It looks as if the handkerchief had been rubbed very hard on the ground—on a patch of grass or moss—to hide the stain. Have you any comments to make?"

"Comments? Good God, man!" There was dawning horror on Charles Blick's face; and as if to conceal it, he buried his head in his hands, bowed over the desk. At last, in a muffled voice, he said, "Am I supposed to be defending myself? Are you charging me?"

"Not at present, Mr. Blick. I am only asking for an explanation."

"Now look. If I—if I'd killed my father, and got his blood on my handkerchief, do you really suppose I'd leave it lying about, for you to find?"

Nigel could almost hear counsel for the defense hammering home the argument. It would sound singularly convincing to the less imaginative jurymen. But was it not just what a murderer might well have done?

Particularly a murderer with his father's blood on his hands? Out, damned spot! Rub the blood off your hands. But there it is on the handkerchief. Rub it off the handkerchief. But it's dark. You can't see. You only felt it on your hands. You know you can't rub it off, ever; and physically, you can't even rub it off the handkerchief—only rub it in, hide it with moss stain, earth stain. The bloodstain is still there: you know you ought to take the handkerchief away and burn it; but you simply cannot bear to put it in your pocket, with your father's blood upon it. A terrible revulsion makes you thrust it away—out of sight, if not out of mind, into the bracken roots.

Blount had held a long silence. The old trick: the best way to break down defenses was to let silence undermine them. Finally he said: "It wasn't exactly left 'lying about,' you know. It was hidden among the stems of a clump of bracken."

Charles was staring at the handkerchief. "How do you know it's blood? I can't see anything. It just looks dirty to me."

Nigel wondered too. Was it a bluff on Blount's part? Surely not? Blount didn't go in for dubious maneuvers like that.

"We've done a preliminary test here. Microscopic examination seems to show something besides the obvious green staining. The handkerchief will be sent to Scotland Yard this evening for the analysts to work on. I don't say it is necessarily blood. I'm not specially interested in that. What I'm interested in is how your handkerchief came to be there at all."

"Yes. Of course."

"Have you missed a handkerchief lately? Lost one anywhere?"

Charles Blick's head came up. Again there was that look of feverish calculation in his eyes.

"No," he said. "No, I haven't. Not as far as I know. I'm sure I haven't."

"You leave me no alternative, sir," said Blount, after a pause. "You say you have not been near the wood lately, and have not missed one of your handkerchiefs. Do you suggest somebody stole one from you?"

"I don't suggest anything." Charles's voice had the rough edge of exhaustion on it. "I simply don't understand."

"Could anyone have access to the drawer where you keep them?" Blount was leaning over backward to be fair.

"Not a drawer. A big inlaid-wood box. My mother gave it to me when I was a boy. It's not kept locked."

"What is it, Strangeways?" asked Blount sharply. "Have you a question you—"

"No. Not just now. I can wait." Nigel was staring at the handkerchief. But what gave him that mesmerized look was the point of light he had just seen at the end of a dark passage. Carefully, in his mind, he began to walk toward it. Yes, he believed he was on the right track now. The pinpoint grew larger, was opening out into an incredible yet inevitable solution. He hardly heard the rest of Blount's inquiry, or his warning that Charles Blick must notify the police should business require him to travel out of the district.

Absentmindedly he rose to follow the Superintendent and Reid out of the room. At the door, he turned. Charles Blick, standing by his desk, was gazing at the spot where the handkerchief had been spread out; his lips were firm, his shoulders squared; he looked a picture of stubbornness—the weak man who, having made a decision, clings to it as a drowning man to his proverbial straw.

Nigel closed the door quietly. Charles looked up, a wincing expression on his face.

"Tell me," said Nigel, "you must have talked it all over with your brother—about your father's death. What did you make of his dream?"

"Dream?"

"The nightmare he had the night your father was killed?"

"I—nightmare? He never mentioned it," Charles replied in a dazed way.

"Stanford is the only person who seems to have been really hard hit by your father's death," said Nigel musingly. "That struck me from the start."

"He got on with him. Better than I did. Yes, he's genuinely cut up. But I can't make out what you're driving at."

"What's his relationship with Miss Chantmerle like?"

"Relationship? Well, he's very fond of her. Sort of favorite uncle. She always goes to him when—"

"No, I meant Celandine Chantmerle."

"Oh, Dinny? I don't think he likes her very much. Why?" Charles looked more puzzled than ever.

"Was it he who persuaded you to break off your engagement with Celandine, when her father died?"

"Certainly not. Look here, I consider it's damned impertinence on your part to—"

"I quite agree. And now I'm going to be still more impertinent. Has it ever occurred to you that Stanford's feelings for Rosebay might be more than a favorite uncle's? He even got a poison-pen letter, accusing him of 'goings-on' with Rosebay."

"That's utter nonsense. Put it right out of your head."

"You know that he and Rosebay were behind the business of the field glasses?"

"Bay told me that was your theory."

"But didn't admit it was true? Why not? It may have been ill-advised, but there was nothing discreditable about it, surely—an unorthodox attempt at a cure by shock treatment?"

"I'm really not in a position to judge the ethics of it," replied Charles stiffly.

"But, if it had been successful," Nigel persisted, "anyone would have agreed the end had justified the means, wouldn't they?"

Charles Blick had begun to tremble uncontrollably. "God damn it! Will you leave me alone! What the hell's it got to do with me?"

"All right, we'll talk about something else," said Nigel, his pale eyes regarding Charles expressionlessly. "Your hand, for instance. Healed up O.K., has it?"

For a couple of seconds Blick stared at him uncomprehendingly. Then, putting his hand in his pocket, he nodded. He was making a tremendous effort to get himself under control. Walking over to the window, he gazed out. Nigel addressed his back.

"Who do *you* think murdered your father?"

"I've no ideas about it."

"Not interested?"

A vein in the back of Charles's neck was violently throbbing. He made no reply.

"Not even when someone has tried to incriminate you? Unless of course you did it yourself. You had motive and opportunity, and you've no alibi."

Silence.

"You're in a jam. Fighting a lost battle. Don't you

think you've done enough? Why not confess? You're only postponing the—"

"Confess?" Charles had turned round at last. There was the old anxiety on his face, the haunted look in those dark eyes; but, welling up as it were from beneath, a sort of calm despair. "What should I confess?" he asked, quite quietly.

"That you lied to Blount just now."

"And why should I confess it, supposing I did?"

"For your own—no, I think chiefly for Miss Chantmerle's peace of mind. She can't stand this strain indefinitely. You're putting too much of a load upon her, and you've no right to."

"Oh, Bay'll come through. Don't you see?—the one thing she'd never forgive me would be if I—"

Charles broke off as the telephone started ringing.

"Damn it all, do you love her or don't you?" asked Nigel urgently. "Surely you've paid off the mortgage, *now?*"

Looking harassed beyond endurance, Charles took up the receiver. "Hallo, Charles Blick here . . . Bay? What is it, darling? . . . God! Yes, of course, I'll come at once."

He turned to Nigel. "There's been an accident. I must go straight away." He sent for his works manager and rapped out some orders, then ran downstairs. At the door, a policeman moved forward, his hand raised; but, when he saw Nigel at Blick's heels, he stepped back, and let them go out. They jumped into Charles's car and set off at top speed for Prior's Umborne.

17. The Fault Was Mine, The Fault Was Mine

Had Superintendent Blount been present at the Little Manor during the next few hours, he would undoubtedly have been shocked by Nigel Strangeways' activities; indeed, being both in his public and his private affairs a stickler for decorum, he would soon have put a stop to them—and as a result the case might have dragged on for days or weeks, or never been broken open at all.

But Nigel was not bound by official rules. Etiquette and convention meant nothing to him, when a problem had arisen which could only be solved by unorthodox methods. And this problem was much more than a criminological one; there were people involved whose sanity, whose lives perhaps would be endangered if the situation dragged on much longer. Besides, Nigel was angry. His eyes burned with a cold flame, as he listened now to Charles. Rosebay had rung up to say that her sister's wheeled chair had somehow caught fire while she was sitting in it; fortunately Mark Raynham had been on the spot and managed to put it out before Celandine was badly hurt, burning his own hands in the process. That was all they knew at present. But it was enough for Nigel. The time had come to put a stop to all this; he was going to set the cat in among the pigeons, stir up trouble with an apparently irresponsible hand, and see what happened. The criminal was sitting pretty, behind impregnable defenses, and must be somehow bluffed or tempted or forced out into the open.

They were waiting in the drawing room when Nigel and Charles hurried in—the vicar, his hands roughly bandaged, his mouth firmly set against the pain; Celandine Chantmerle, propped up on the sofa, hectic spots of color glowing through the delicate make-up on her cheekbones; Rosebay, pale with exhaustion, bright hair disordered, nervously chewing the red lacquer off her fingernails. Charles Blick strode over to her at once. His voice was shaky:

"Are you all right, darling? Are you sure you're all right? How did it happen?"

Something dawned, flickered and went out in her eyes as she looked up at him. Then she gave a sort of childish whimper and turned her face away from him.

"It's I who had the accident, Charles," said Celandine coolly. "But I'm getting quite used to being in the wars. Do please persuade Bay not to fuss about me any more—she takes everything so tragically. Bay, darling, I swear to you I'm *really not hurt*. Just lightly toasted on one side. Honestly. It's poor Mark ought to get the sympathy, *and* a medal. When *will* that wretched doctor come?"

"Don't worry about me, Dinny. Bit of luck I happened to be here," said the vicar, a gruff, embarrassed note in his voice. He held up his bandaged hands. "Everything I have is yours, if you want it. You know that."

Celandine gave him a dancing, glancing look. "You're very sweet, Mark. But I don't want you charred."

"Well, now we've all taken our hair down," said Charles, gazing at Rosebay's averted face, "what did happen?"

"Oh, thank goodness, here he is at last," said Celandine as the doorbell rang. "You must let him see you first, Mark. . . . No, please do what I say," she added imperiously, as the vicar began to demur.

While the doctor was examining him in another room, she told the story. Early in the afternoon, two of Blount's assistants had unexpectedly come to search the house. She had made no objection to this. But when, after a couple of hours, they asked to see the locked room on the top floor—her father's room—she was at first unwilling. "I couldn't bear the idea of them tramping about there, sticking their noses into everything. It's absurd of me, I dare say, but—well, that room is a sort of shrine to me. I keep my memories there. Or do you think piety is very sentimental and old-fashioned?" she said, with a serious, proud look at Nigel.

"No, I've nothing against piety."

"Of course, I knew they could get a search warrant. I didn't want to be obstructive. Whatever could they find there, anyway? It was just routine, they said. Wonderful formula! So I asked if they'd mind my being there when they made the search. It evidently didn't quite suit their notions of official propriety; but they agreed after a bit."

One policeman had carried Celandine upstairs, the other brought her wheel chair. She unlocked the door, but then remembered that the keys to her father's desk, wardrobe and chest of drawers were in her bureau downstairs.

"I sent one of the policemen to fetch them; and then I had to send the other after him with the key of the bureau, which was in my bag. I suppose they must have thought it rather sinister, my getting them both out of the room, but they were very gentlemanly about it. Not that I could have done much destroying of evidence during the minute they were away."

They had asked her to unlock the wardrobe for them first. This she did; and then the other articles of furniture in turn, wheeling herself from one to another. It must have been a bizarre scene, reflected Nigel, this painstaking examination of the effects of a man dead twenty years ago; he could imagine the stolid, impersonal faces of the plain-clothes men, and Celandine's beauty shining in the dusty room; being Celandine, she would not try very hard to conceal her sense of outrage at this desecration of the shrine.

"They took away one of my father's overcoats. It was horrible. Especially when they gave me a receipt for it. I wish I knew what it was all about."

"But the accident," Charles blurted out impatiently. "Did they set fire to you before leaving?"

"Oh, *don't*, Charles," Rosebay exclaimed. "It's not funny."

"I thought it might have been another practical joke. Like the binoculars," said Charles.

There was a hush of shock, as if a ghost, as if Edric Chantmerle himself had suddenly materialized in the pretty, faded drawing room. Charles seems to be doing my work for me, thought Nigel. Celandine slowly turned her cornflower eyes to him, with a deep look of complicity.

"I'm afraid it was no more successful than the binoculars, Nigel," she said. Her significant tone told him that she had guessed the truth of the baited field glasses. Or perhaps Rosebay had confessed to her? No, a glance at the girl's agonized expression told him she could not have done so.

"I bear no malice, as they say, about that," Celandine remarked. Her exquisite face gleamed with humor as she added, "It was neither kill nor cure, was it?"

Rosebay flushed painfully, unable to answer or to meet her sister's eyes.

"But this time it was a pure accident. Really." Celandine gave her delicious giggle. "Spontaneous combustion."

When the policemen left, she had stayed up in her father's room. She wanted to "disinfect it" from their activities, though they had meticulously replaced everything which they had disturbed during their search. She had heard Mark Raynham arriving just before, and knew he could carry her downstairs presently. So she locked the door behind the policemen, to ensure solitude for a while, lit a cigarette, and began to think about her father, the old happy days with him. She had some relics of him, unwrapped from their tissue paper, on her lap.

"I don't know if I dozed off. I don't think so. But there was a sudden fuff—the box of matches had exploded."

"Good God! Yes, it does happen," said Charles. "I had a box went off in my pocket one day, at a cricket match."

The blazing matchbox on her lap set fire instantly to the tissue paper. She made a convulsive movement to brush it off, but only succeeded in pushing down the burning paper between herself and the side of the chair, where it set fire to the Paisley shawl over her knees.

"I yelled out like fury—afraid my dress was beginning

to catch; and I couldn't get out of the chair. It all happened so quickly, I lost my head altogether. I heard Mark tearing up the stairs. But of course the damned door was locked, and I couldn't wheel myself toward it because the left side of the chair was on fire and I couldn't get my hand onto that wheel. I was just going round in circles."

"We heard her screaming the door was locked," said Rosebay, "so Mark hurled himself at it and broke it in. There was Dinny, helpless in the chair, with smoke and flame going up. Mark dragged her out of it, and put out the fire with his hands."

"Good for old Mark," said Charles. "But you must have got burnt a bit, Dinny—aren't you in pain?"

"It's nice of you to be so solicitous, Charles. I won't pretend the patient is altogether comfortable. But one advantage of my unfortunate limbs is that I don't have much sensation in them. No doubt God was taking a long-term view when He afflicted me with them." She glanced round at the others, with that look of excitement bubbling up irrepressibly into her eyes. "I really do seem to bear a charmed life, don't I?" she said.

"I wouldn't bank too much on that," remarked Charles, and at the same moment Rosebay was agitatedly saying, "Don't, Dinny! Don't say that! It's tempting providence."

"Bay darling, when *will* you get over your extraordinary suspicions—superstitions, I mean. Oh lord! That was a prime old Freudian error, wasn't it? One has suspicion so very much on one's mind just now."

"You've no need to worry about that anyway," said Charles harshly. "It's me the police are after. They found a handkerchief of mine, bloodstained into the bargain, near what they call the scene of the crime."

"Oh, Charles!" Rosebay, her own handkerchief pressed to her mouth, stared at him with affrighted eyes. "It *was* yours they found?"

"*Pas possible*," breathed Celandine. "There must be some explanation. I mean—"

"You're damned right there must be. Someone put it there to get me into trouble."

"Charles told the police he had no idea who could have got hold of a handkerchief of his," said Nigel levelly.

At that moment the door opened to admit Mark Raynham and the doctor. Nigel became aware of Rosebay's eyes fastened upon Charles in a brooding look, both anxious and puzzled. The doctor said he would examine Celandine where she was, upon the sofa. The others started to go out.

"Will you stay and help me, Rosebay?" said the doctor.

"No," she muttered. "I'm no good at—I'll send Charity."

The young doctor raised his eyebrows disapprovingly, but said no more. Whether it was that Rosebay wanted to be alone with Charles, or not to be alone with her sister, Nigel was determined not to let her out of his sight. The pot must be kept boiling. He drew Mark Raynham aside, and whispered to him for a few moments, while Rosebay was telling Charity that she was needed in the drawing room. Then she found Nigel firmly walking her toward the garden, Charles and Mark Raynham following.

"I saw you leaving the Hall this afternoon, just as we arrived. Did Stanford tell you about his dream?" asked Nigel.

"What *is* this about a dream?" said Charles irritably.

"Dream? Yes, he did. It frightened me."

"When you got back here, you told your sister about it?"

"Yes," the girl muttered. "Was there anything wrong about that?"

"Did she have any comments?"

"Oh well, how extraordinary it was. You know. That sort of thing."

"Did Stanford tell you *when* he had it? What time he woke up from it?"

"Yes. About ten past eleven, he said. It was an extraordinary coincidence, wasn't it?"

"What was?"

"His dreaming it just—" Rosebay's eyes suddenly flinched, and her hand flew to her mouth—"I mean, his having had the dream that night."

"You were going to say 'his dreaming it *just then*.' I call that the very opposite of a coincidence. You told the police Sir Archibald was alive at eleven-twenty; you heard him leave the house."

"You're twisting my words."

"You know very well I'm not. I suggest you never heard him leave. You were in your room, fast asleep. Or were you by any chance waiting for him outside?"

"Charles!" the girl cried faintly. "Stop him! He's accusing me of—"

"Look here, Strangeways!" Charles Blick thrust himself between them. "If you say a word more to Rosebay, I'll hit you for six. Who the hell d'you think—?"

"That's better. At last we have a human reaction. Now let's see if someone can't tell the truth for a change. Come on, let's sit down." Nigel set out the deck chairs. There was a purposefulness about him now which the others found they could not resist.

"Within the last hour," he outrageously continued, "I've heard stunning lies from you two. Let's see what the vicar can do in that line."

Mark Raynham made an embarrassed sound, between a laugh and a throat-clearing.

"Do you still say, Vicar, you remember nothing about that long walk you took, the night Sir Archibald was murdered?"

Nigel was facing the open French windows of the drawing room. Ever since they had come out in the garden, his voice had been loud and aggressive, and unconsciously the others were raising their voices too.

"I don't remember anything to the point," replied Mark Raynham, the eyes watchful now in his haggard face.

"Surely you have some idea where you went?"

"Oh well, I do remember vaguely finding myself at Fenny Cross. I sat on a stile there for a bit."

"And then?"

"Then I started for home. It was after eleven—later than I'd thought."

"By which road?"

"The one that goes past the end of this garden."

"So you'd pass here about eleven-forty?"

"About that."

"And you met no one on the way?"

"I told you that, when all this first arose. If you're looking for an alibi, I haven't got one. You don't meet people on these country roads late at night."

"Apparently not. But you ought to have. You see, Blick here told the police he set off on that road, *toward* Fenny Cross, at eleven-ten or a little before. You should have met. So which of you is lying?"

Mark and Charles, looking sheepish, avoided each other's eyes.

"Well—hah—I suppose we just missed each other somehow," said the vicar, with his nervous, hearty laugh.

Upon the distant hills, the mist hung low. Uneasy puffs of wind from the southwest stirred the daffodils into macabre little dances. The fruit blossoms, thick and oppressive, were losing their color as the daylight drained away, pink and white changing alike into a dingy gray. Presently the doctor came out. Miss Chantmerle, he said, must have had a remarkable escape; there were inflamed patches on her left side and flank, but no serious burns; he had dressed them and given her a penicillin injection. He would call again early tomorrow, to make sure no infection had set in, but there was very little danger of that. She refused to go to bed yet, so her sister must see that she at least stayed on the sofa and avoided excitement.

Excitement, however, was just what Celandine seemed unable to avoid. As they returned to the drawing room, Nigel saw in her eyes that strange exhilaration which he had been noticing, off and on, since her birthday party.

"I couldn't help hearing some of what you were saying out there. I can't wait to hear the sequel. Charles and Mark passing each other on a narrow country road, both so deep in thought that they didn't notice each other. So then—?"

"Celandine, don't you think you ought to go to bed?" said Mark Raynham. "You know what the doctor—"

"And miss the denouement? Not for anything, my dear. Now stop fussing about me. Let's go on with the truth game."

"I don't like it. It's a game apt to end in tears," said the vicar, his rough voice softened and sad now.

"Nobody's even started playing the truth game yet," said Nigel. "You don't seem to realize you're all involved in a murder investigation. And lies, whatever motive you tell them from, won't in the end save the guilty. The innocent don't need them. Charles now—"

"Well, what about me?" Charles Blick was sitting on the arm of Rosebay's chair. He had kept close to her ever since their arrival at the house.

Nigel pointed a dogmatic finger at him: "You and your handkerchief. You know perfectly well when and where you lost it. You tied it loosely round your hand when a needle of those binoculars drew blood from you. You ran out of this house soon after, and in your agitation you didn't notice the handkerchief had dropped off. It was *your* blood on it. Why didn't you tell the police that? Because you suspected Rosebay had picked it up, somewhere in the hall or the front garden where you dropped it. Rosebay had picked it up, and planted it in the wood; and therefore Rosebay was a murderess."

Charles had been on his feet, vainly trying to speak. Now he exclaimed, "You're utterly wrong! I never thought it was *Bay* who—"

"Then who did you think had found it? Who did you think you were protecting?" asked Nigel sharply.

"You've got it all wrong, damn you," Charles replied with a sort of obstinate energy. "I wasn't protecting anyone. I didn't lose the handkerchief here at all. It was on my hand when I got home."

"So you naturally put it in the dirty-clothes basket?"

"I—no, I didn't. I just stuffed it in a drawer, I expect."

"Or into your pocket, perhaps? So, a night or two later, when you thought you'd got your father's blood on your hands, out it came again and—"

"Nigel!" Celandine's cool voice, with a touch of

rebuke in it, made them all look at her. "Nigel, please! I'm sure you have some reason for talking like this, but it's terribly melodramatic—and these are my friends, you know."

"I'm sorry, but you asked for the truth game. It's not a game one can play in kid gloves. Shall we stop it? Are you all too afraid of the truth to go on?"

There was a stir and then a silence in the drawing room.

"If Charles did not do it, he is lying to protect either Rosebay or Stanford; they're the most likely ones to have found the handkerchief, and committed the crime. The police will very likely arrest Charles if further evidence doesn't turn up."

Rosebay gave a sobbing gasp, and reached for Charles's hand.

"He had a strong motive. He was on the spot. His handkerchief was found there. And now—the police don't know this yet—he has been caught out in a flagrant lie. Why should he say he walked home by Fenny Cross, when he didn't? Because he had to be somewhere away from here when the crime was committed. It sounds like the lie of a guilty man."

"But look here," said Mark, "I thought it depended upon some sleeping draught Sir Archibald took. How could Charles have given it to him?"

Nigel told them about the sleeping pill which Sir Archibald carried in his silver matchbox. "He may have taken it before leaving here."

"Oh, thank heavens for that," exclaimed Celandine. "I knew the police suspected Rosebay or me of giving it to him."

"I'm afraid that doesn't clear things up at all," Nigel said. "The murderer might have removed the pill while

Sir Archibald was asleep from a drug administered to him in his drinks here—it was not a secret that he often carried a sleeping pill with him. Or it may just have fallen out of the box and been absorbed in the water where his body lay. But, if he did take it here, then the field of suspects is widened to include Charles, and the vicar, and Daniel Durdle. Are you quite sure you didn't see him taking it, Celandine?"

"No. I didn't *see* him. But that means nothing."

"Very well then. It's possible—I'm giving you the Superintendent's view—that Mark or Durdle is lying about his movements that night. But there's no material evidence against them whatsoever. Nothing but a possible motive—not even a strong one in Durdle's case. So we come back to Charles."

"Stop it! I can't stand this any more! It wasn't Charles!" Rosebay had dragged her hand away from his, and was on her feet in front of him.

"How do you know?" asked Nigel.

"*Because I did it.*"

"Bay! What are you saying? Do pull yourself together!"

"Don't listen to her! It's crazy. She—"

"No, Charles, I've had enough. You must listen." Rosebay's voice was steady now, and deep. She looked a different woman; standing there with her head thrown back, upright and tense, her hands clasped in front of her, she reminded Nigel of a student facing the ordeal of her first public performance. The green eyes, the pallor, the glorious bay-red hair—it was as if one saw them for the first time, heightened and composed into breathtaking beauty by the exaltation that seemed to possess her. She had found herself at last; awkwardness, self-distrust, immaturity all dropped off like ill-fitting clothes. And she held her audience, for the first and perhaps the last time.

"I was listening at the door nearly all the time that night. Of course I was, Dinny. I heard everything he said. I knew he would stop our money, and stop my marrying Charles. I've always been a coward. You know why I'm so frightened of Daniel Durdle?—because he's not right in the head, and he made me think I might have inherited madness too. I think I did go mad that night for a while, but I stopped being a coward. Something sort of snapped in my head as I listened, and I felt different—quite calm and cool. I determined to catch Sir Archibald when he left the house, and if he didn't listen to my pleadings, I'd kill him. I knew I'd be suspected if his body was found near here, but I wouldn't be able to take it far away. My brain was working beautifully. I saw at once how to do it. I went up and fetched a dark coat of father's, and a hat of his like Sir Archibald was wearing, and took them outside, to the place where I was going to meet him. The only thing I was afraid of was Charles's turning up. But I heard footsteps going away along the road at the end of the garden, and I knew that must be Charles. Soon afterward, Sir Archibald came out. I intercepted him on the path, well away from the house, so nobody should hear us. He wouldn't listen to me. He said an awful thing, and I saw red. I just hit out at him wildly—hit him on the temple with my fist—and he fell down. His eyes seemed to go white in the darkness. I thought he was dead, and I suddenly realized I hadn't really meant to kill him—it had been sort of a phantasy—you know?—which had come true in spite of me. Oh, I can't explain that. Well, I thought he was dead, and I didn't want him dead any more; but I had to get rid of him. I couldn't stand his white eyeballs staring up at me. I wheeled out Dinny's carriage and dragged him into it. It was then I heard him breathing. A beastly snoring noise. I might have spared him if he hadn't made it. But it disgusted me—like the noise something makes that hasn't been killed properly, and you just want to finish it off. So I wheeled him up to the quarry and pushed him over and put the carriage back in the shed. It didn't seem like me doing all this, but somebody else inside me. Perhaps I really was mad. Anyway, I put on father's long coat and hat, and hurried down to the Hall. I knew the dogs would bark if I went through the back courtyard, and they'd think it was him returning home. And if anyone happened to see me, they'd only see a figure in a hat and coat like him. Then I came back here. But there was still a light on downstairs, so I had to wait till Dinny went to bed before I could creep in. It wasn't till nearly midnight that her bedroom light went out. I was terrified that she might have wanted me to put her to bed, and somehow found out I wasn't in my room. But she got Charity instead. . . . I'm sorry about your handkerchief, Charles. I'd been keeping it here"—she touched her breast—"because it was yours. I wanted something to wipe my hands on, after I'd—after I put him in the quarry. Then I crumpled it up and threw it away. I didn't really think whether anyone would find it. But next morning I went in the wood to look for it, and I couldn't find it myself; it was dark when I threw it away, and I couldn't remember just where. I never meant it to incrim—incriminate you."

Rosebay Chantmerle paused. Whatever emotions she had aroused in her audience—and goodness knows, thought Nigel, they must be a remarkable assortment of emotions—none of them in the room was able to say a word. Rosebay looked round at them, the light visibly dying from her eyes. Then, in a quiet tone: "I don't think there's anything more for me to say now."

"Well, actually there is one thing. What did you do with the hat?" asked Nigel.

"The hat?"

"Yes, your father's hat. I imagine you replaced the coat in his wardrobe: that would be the one the police took away this afternoon. But the hat—you might have left hairs in it, or—"

"I burnt the hat that night in the incinerator. I would have burnt the coat too, but I was afraid the buttons mightn't be destroyed. So I just brushed it very carefully and put it back." She gazed sadly for a moment at Nigel, as if he had somehow betrayed her. Then she said, "Is that all? I'd like to go now, please."

Nigel nodded to her. The moment the door was shut, he said urgently to Charles, "Go along. Don't leave her alone. Don't let her out of your sight. Please do what I tell you."

When the three were alone, Nigel turned to Celandine. "Have you missed one of your father's hats?"

"No. They were there when the police opened the wardrobe. A tophat, a boater, a light gray Homburg, and a few caps."

"I simply can't understand it," said the vicar. "Rosebay? No, I don't believe it. Do you, Strangeways?"

"Her account of her movements fitted the timetable. And there was a lot of convincing psychological detail."

"Bay is a very imaginative girl," said Celandine. "I didn't know she was all that much in love with Charles, though—enough to try and put her head in a noose for him. Of course she didn't do it."

Something in Celandine's voice made the two men

look at her sharply. She was reclining gracefully upon the sofa, her profile clear-cut against the flowered wall-paper. And she resembled Primavera no longer, but an avenging Artemis. Her words came cold and hard, as if chipped out of marble. "I know she did not do it. And I won't allow her to take the blame for a—for a coward and weakling like Charles. Not for him, of all people."

"You *know*?"

"Yes, Nigel. I know because—well, I have been protecting him too. A woman never forgets her first lover. He's like her firstborn: whatever he may do to her, she keeps a soft spot for him in her heart—a special niche."

"*You've* been protecting him?"

"That night, when Sir Archibald left, I wheeled my chair down the hall after him. I felt as if he contaminated my house. I opened the front door, to air it. He'd only gone twenty or thirty yards, I suppose. I heard him say, 'Charles? What on earth are you doing up here?' That's all I heard. I closed the door and went back to the drawing room."

"You'll swear to that in court?" asked Nigel.

"Certainly." Her beautiful lips were set firm as a statue's. "I'd have kept it a secret forever. But not now, not after he's let Bay crucify herself to save his skin. Oh no."

Ten minutes later, Nigel and the vicar were walking down the track from the quarry, up which they had come on Nigel's first afternoon at Prior's Umborne. Mark Raynham looked grim and deeply disturbed. "I never ought to have done it," he said, slashing with his stick at a wayside weed. "I don't know what your game was, but I don't like the taste of it."

"Nor do I. But we're dealing with someone who is

clever and wicked. Really wicked. You played up very well."

"Charles wicked? Oh no, you're wrong there."

"I don't mean Charles Blick."

Mark limped on a few strides, then stopped dead. "But in that case—"

Nigel returned his gaze, somberly and in silence. The countryside about them, under the darkening sky, had the isolated look of a deaf mute. Mark's face flooded with an apprehension such as Nigel had rarely seen.

"No. It's not possible." He repeated it, louder, desperately—"I tell you, it's not possible. . . . Are you trying to tell me they were both in it together? That doesn't make sense."

"No," said Nigel gently, "it doesn't."

"But then—" Mark's voice thickened and choked, as if the word which lay on his tongue were a hideously rapid cancer. He moved on again, stumbling fast down the rough track: he might have been trying to shake Nigel off, or to escape some invisible Fury.

"You can never prove it," he said at last, breathing hard.

"Possibly not."

"Why in God's name did you have to pick on me as—?"

"I'm sorry. But you couldn't want the innocent to go on suffering. It was the only way."

They were approaching the village now. Mark Raynham's face, taut with anguish, turned to Nigel: "You said, 'the only way.' Very well. I'm going home now to write out a confession. Good-by."

18. I Hate the Dreadful Hollow

"This is a case," said Nigel, "which has been fogged from the start because the innocent—three of our suspects—insisted on behaving as if they were guilty. And they did this because they were in fact laboring under heavy loads of guilt, but not about Sir Archibald's death."

It was nearly 11:30 on the same night. Nigel and Superintendent Blount were sitting in their room at The Sweet Drop. Nigel had given Blount an account of what had happened since they parted at the Moreford works; it was a somewhat censored version, but the Superintendent's outraged sense of decorum could not be restrained throughout. He puffed, clucked, gave scandalized ejaculations; and when Nigel came to the trap he had laid, which involved Mark Raynham, Blount exclaimed, "Och no! That's beyond everything! I'd lose my pension if I did that. See here, Strangeways—"

"I've no pension to lose. I had to smoke the criminal out. And that did it. The bait was snapped up very nicely."

"M'phm, I dare say. But—"

"Are you absolutely certain that chap's reliable you sent to the vicarage?"

"Don't fash yourself about that. He'll not let the vicar out of his sight. Were you afraid he'd try to make a run for it?"

"No. I'm afraid he might cut his throat after writing this confession."

Mark Raynham sealed up the envelope and sat back with a glance at the plain-clothes man stolidly entrenched in his armchair. They never took drinks when on duty. Nor did he have any sleeping drugs. Mark shivered at the image that came into his mind. He had loved, not wisely but too well. Not once, but twice. He had been exalted, then cast down; transfigured, and fooled—utterly fooled. Yet his love, against all reason, against disillusionment even, survived.

"Charles Blick, for instance," Nigel was saying. "He's been hamstrung throughout by a sense of guilt at having let Celandine down twenty years ago. All his evasions, his lies, his quixotic behavior, and his ambivalent treatment of Rosebay, can be traced back to that. Rosebay's is more complex—genuine love for her sister, some disgruntlement at always being overshadowed by her, mixed up with the guilt a healthy person feels who is in an intimate relationship with a cripple—*and* the guilt she feels about her own resentment at being tied to a cripple."

Rosebay Chantmerle had gone to sleep. There was a smile on her face. She was dreaming, but not the bad dreams she had feared would come. Her last thought had been, "Charles does love me. I know that at last. I can't understand anything else, but I don't need to, now."

The church clock struck half past eleven. At the Hall, Charles was saying good night to his brother. "It's all clear between me and Bay," he told him.

"I'm glad. Of course she's too good for you. But—"

"If they arrest me tomorrow, you'll look after her, won't you?"

"They'll not arrest you. I've seen it in the crystal. I'm psychic, old scout."

"Look here, what is all this about a dream you had? Everyone keeps yammering about it."

Blount gave Nigel a skeptical look. "And who's your third guilty innocent?"

"Mark Raynham. His first wife came to a bad end. But, being the man he is—a bit of a saint, you know—he took her guilt upon himself; if he'd been different, a better husband, she'd never have gone bad—that sort of thing. He's a born self-torturer. One look at his face tells you that. So he fell in love again. With a beautiful and intelligent and difficult woman who is a cripple. Asking for more torture, wasn't it? He's the sacrificial type, like Rosebay. So now—well, he failed to save the first woman he loved; and when her successor looks to be in need of salvation, he goes and does a Sydney Carton. It's not rational, it's not sensible, it's not very moral. But love and guilt have sparked together and blown all those considerations to Jericho. He's beyond even realizing that a false confession won't stand up to a moment's expert scrutiny—is much more likely to expose the person it's meant to shield."

*　　*　　*

Celandine Chantmerle lay awake at the Little Manor, listening. Her burns itched badly, and the penicillin had sent wave after wave of icy depression through her. Fire and ice. There was something she must do before she slept, though. Charity had told her that the plain-clothes policeman had settled down in the kitchen for the night, and the village constable was patrolling somewhere outside. They were taking good care of her, Charity said. Yet there was a feeling of deadly apprehension in her heart. Were these men really guarding her, or—? The police surely could not be so bone-stupid, after what she'd told them.

The wind, which had been rising for several hours, danced and dandled the new moon in the boughs of the trees outside Celandine's window.

"The one figure in this case who most certainly labors under no sense of guilt whatsoever for anything," said Nigel, "is Daniel Durdle. He is convinced of his own salvation. He's self-righteous, and sees himself as an instrument of the wrath of God. He's cunning enough, but not so clever as he thinks. The ruling passion of his life is envy—acrid envy of the power and position he feels he ought to have as Edric Chantmerle's son. The Chantmerle sisters are his supplanters. He gratified some of his lust for power by writing the anonymous letters. But Celandine, who had mocked him in public, remained untouched. If it was she, not Blick, who had been murdered, I know who the murderer would have been. Daniel's vindictiveness toward her would go to any lengths."

A tall question mark of a figure, blacker than the night around him, Daniel Durdle was standing on the far side of the hedge, facing Celandine Chantmerle's window.

The rising wind flicked the lank red hair straggling over his temples. His attitude was one of strained attentiveness; and had anyone been close enough to observe it, he would have seen a gloating expression on the man's face. Daniel was hugging a secret to himself. He could have told the police more, but they were fools and might have misinterpreted it. He was the Sanctified Vessel, the Sharp Sword in the hand of Jehovah, and to him would vengeance be given. He stood there, listening hard, awaiting he scarcely knew what. Presently the extra-keen hearing, which compensated for his shortness of sight, caught a faint sound from the house.

"Stanford Blick's share in the proceedings has, to all appearances, been that of the enthusiastic supporter on the touch-line, if one can imagine such a person bellowing advice in the cryptic words of a Delphic oracle. He's the only one who has kept his head throughout. He's given the impression that the whole thing was a game: and so far he's not had to pay any forfeits, even over the binoculars. He's a living example of the advantages of sitting tight and boxing clever. Of course the last dark hint he threw out was broad enough; but he must be wondering if we've taken it in the right way."

In his study at the Hall, lit by oil lamps, Stanford Blick pushed aside the blueprints on his desk. He could not concentrate. Surely something must happen soon. Strangeways was a cultivated sort of chap; he could take a hint, one imagined. Then he could get back, out of this morass of human emotions and moral maneuverings, onto the high dry ground of scientific abstraction—formulae and equations, stresses and resistances. The only question was, he thought, tapping his teeth with grubby fingernails, whether to let things ride or give them just one more gentle, oblique push.

"We've both been so warm," said Nigel. "Right up against the hidden truth. But we couldn't see it. When you asked me who had the strongest motives for the crime, what did I answer? And when you brought a hypothetical case against Celandine Chantmerle for having done it with an accomplice, you were absolutely boiling, as the children say. Durdle's evidence, that he'd seen Rosebay drink up her sister's glass of whisky, is crucial. I wonder did he see any more, though. I've a hunch he's been keeping something from us—playing his own game. And I don't like the thought of that. He's a dangerous man."

Daniel Durdle followed the figure he had heard emerging. It had moved too silently for Constable Clotworthy, patrolling the garden, to hear. But Durdle's keener ears were sharpened by his vindictive hatred. Pausing now and then as he followed in the figure's wake, listening to the stealthy, slurred footsteps which led him toward the little wood, he exulted.

"I'm not sure the murderer isn't in an impregnable position. Can you imagine bringing a case? It'll have to be one of those 'unsolved crimes' where the police know but cannot act. Or will you try to persuade the Public Prosecutor that there's some hope of convicting a helpless cripple for committing this murder single-handed?"

"Celandine Chantmerle? Aye, it should have been her all along," said Blount, eying Nigel watchfully. "But it's not possible—psychologically, I mean—that a woman whose powers had suddenly been restored should be able to conceal the fact, at that very moment. *Why* should she? You're not telling me she contemplated murder as early as that?"

"No. But the binoculars released more than a pair of needles. They released a spring of deadly hatred in her. I'll come to that presently. Let's take the hypothesis that the binoculars, Stanford's shock treatment, *did* work. It's the only one which fits together all the bits of evidence we've got into a coherent pattern. Rosebay's dream, for example, and the Hall cook's story. On the night of the binoculars episode, Rosebay dreamed she heard footsteps—'sort of slurring footsteps'—in her father's room above. She'd often had the dream before. But this time she dreamed his door was opening, and the footsteps were coming downstairs. She woke to hear Celandine calling out to her from the room below. Now this last stage may not have been part of the dream at all; she would assume it was, in her dazed condition; but in fact it was the real thing—Celandine practicing walking, at night, when everyone was asleep. She had to relearn it, you see, after twenty years. Like an infant. And what did the Hall cook say about the gait of the figure she glimpsed in the courtyard below? It was 'not exactly like a limp; *more like the way a toddler walks.*' Yes, the cook handed it to us on a plate. But, as Daniel Durdle no doubt would say, we had ears and heard not."

The figure entered the ride through the dark wood, moving silently now on turf. Daniel crept up closer. Glints of moonlight revealed the figure's not quite normal gait: it walked like a clever machine, or like a person who must still exercise conscious control, pushing the feet alternately forward, working out a continuous problem of equilibrium, propping itself along with a walking stick. The branches overhead, tangled and unkempt, made snickering, whimpering noises as the gale rubbed them together. Needle points of moonlight stabbed through the shifting branches, darting here or there, then going out. One of these revealed to Daniel Durdle what looked like a large white envelope in the hand of the figure he was pursuing. A grin, like a rictus on the face of a corpse, came involuntarily upon his blanched face. He stopped dead for a moment, as if in thought, then turned back, skirted the wood's edge, and was running at full speed, with his Scissors-Man stride, down to the village.

"What made Celandine conceal her regained power from the very start, before she could have contemplated any murder? Ah, but she had a murderous feeling in her heart, even then. I was there. She saw Charles—the man who had once loved her, and who now, so she believed, was under her spell again—saw him turn to Rosebay, heard him say to Rosebay, 'Are you all right, love?' I noticed an extraordinary look of incredulity, horror, anger, on her face. Then she fainted. It wasn't chiefly because of the binoculars she looked like that. It was the revelation that she'd been tricked. All Charles's visits to the house, which she'd believed were signs of a reawakened passion for herself, had been for her sister's sake—her dim, unconsidered sister. Hell hath no fury . . . From that moment, she was out to get Charles. And his father's visit gave her the opportunity. She'd hated Sir Archibald from of old. But the real victim of his murder was to be Charles.

"Every time I saw her after that, I was struck by an

air of subdued excitement she had, a sort of exhilaration. It came from the secret knowledge that she could walk, and the power this gave her. You see, her power had been on the wane. As Joe Summers told me, she wasn't the queen of the village any more—not with the younger generation, anyway. She took this out a bit on her sister, whether consciously or not I don't know; but I noticed a sort of gentle bullying, undermining Rosebay's self-confidence. And later she threw out subtle hints about Rosebay's mental instability. I suspect this was partly to foul her relationship with Charles—which, of course, Celandine cleverly pretended to have guessed at for some time and to approve—and partly to counter any awkward revelations Rosebay might unwillingly make. Like all hysterical types, Celandine is exacting, imperious, obstructive and impulsive, with a craving both for sympathy and power. Under stress, that sort can easily split into a dual personality. With her, it was controlled and made infinitely more dangerous by her charm and a first-rate *feminine* intelligence; her instinct was sharpened to a razor edge. And of course she had a glorious, irresponsible feeling of being invulnerable—as long as no one knew she could now walk."

Celandine Chantmerle came out of the wood onto the sward which lay between it and the quarry. She frowned at a clump of daffodils jigging wildly in the wind; before the storm was over, many delicate stems would be broken. Her father's voice, reading aloud to her some lines of Virgil, sounded in her head:

> *purpureus veluti cum flos succisus aratro*
> *languescit moriens, lassove papavera collo*
> *demisere caput, pluvia cum forte gravantur.*

Those broken daffodils—she felt them as a comic injustice. But for them—Yet she was glad of the storm tonight; its sounds had covered her as she opened the window, stepped out, closed it behind her, choosing a moment when Clotworthy was at the other end of his patrol. In spite of her itching burns, her perplexity and tiredness, a kind of exhilaration flooded over her again. She had outwitted Clotworthy; and as for that other policeman, he could keep guard over the incinerator for the rest of his life, for all she cared.

"If Celandine hadn't accidentally run the wheel of her carriage over some daffodils that night, she'd be sitting pretty till Kingdom Come. We should never have suspected the carriage had been used, and Charles Blick would have been for the high jump. As it was, though, we knew it *had* been used, and that suggested it was a woman's crime—that and the sleeping draught."

"Not the only mistake she made, though."

"Not the only one," Nigel agreed. "As soon as she heard Archibald Blick was coming down, her mind started to work. She devised the plan for paying off two scores at once. First she wrote an anonymous letter which would be calculated to fetch him up to her house. She walked down to the New Inn that night and posted it, with two others as blinds. But she wanted us to think the original poison pen had written them; and she made the mistake of asking me more than once to be sure and let her know when the poison pen was going to be arrested—obviously so that she shouldn't post the letters *after* his arrest, and queer that part of her plan."

Daniel Durdle was halfway to the village, still running hard, streaming with sweat, the black coattails flying out behind him. He reckoned he'd have at least ten minutes, after he got there, to put his plan into operation. However it worked out, it could only work out ill for the woman Celandine: and it might do him a bit of good in quite another way. He ran on, his eyes hard as the pebbly glasses which covered them.

"She could be pretty sure, after that letter and what she said to him on the telephone, that Sir Archibald would come up to see her that night. During the day she had gone for an unusually long ride in her electric carriage, to exhaust the battery, so that it would be impossible for anyone to have transported Sir A.'s body under power to the quarry, and therefore impossible for her, a cripple, to have done the murder. That was rather too elaborate a safeguard, rather a fussy, feminine touch.

"Well, as she'd calculated, Sir A. turned up. Now I think it's quite possible that, till then, her plans and preparations may have been more than half phantasy; you know—I'll lay the fuse but, when the moment comes, there'll be no compulsion to light it. But the compulsion did come. Sir A. threatened to cut off her money. And worse. You remember the snatches of conversation the vicar heard? 'Charles marry into a family of poison-pen writers!' . . . 'Are you daring to suggest that Bay—' And then Sir A. said something like 'Your brother has *two* sisters.' What does that sound like, Blount?"

"By jiminy, as if he'd somehow got suspicious that Durdle hadn't written all the letters, and that it was not Rosebay but Celandine herself who had written the others."

"Exactly. She may have given herself away to him on the telephone. It may have been a shrewd guess on his part; or merely part of his general offensiveness. That doesn't matter. What matters is that Celandine now saw yet another reason why she must get rid of the old man. And here she made another mistake, though it was an unavoidable one. She gave him drinks, and she apparently talked with him for a whole hour and more—a man she admitted to hating for having caused her father's death, a man she had refused to have in her house—she actually gave him drinks and allowed him to stay all that time. It wasn't in character. But of course she had to. Had first to drug the glass she handed Rosebay, give time for it to take effect, drug Sir Archibald, and wait till he was asleep."

The old track was rough, and in the dark Celandine floundered as she walked down it, in spite of the help her father's walking stick gave. But there was no hurry, she reminded herself—not like that other night when she had to push the electric carriage, walking beside the sleeping man's shoulder to hold the steering wheel, up the slight slope into the wood until it reached the summit and rolled easily down toward the quarry. She shivered a little now, forcibly preventing herself from turning her head. It was ridiculous to imagine a man, a dead man, climbing out of the quarry behind her and following. She felt tired, queerly oppressed. Where had her strength come from that night? from fear? hatred? or simply from exasperation at the semi-animate object which lolled in the invalid carriage like a dummy? If only she'd had more time to find her feet. A practice the first night, when she'd nearly given everything away by waking Rosebay. Practice the next day, at times when she was alone in the house; and the walk down to the village that night. And the next day the twelve-mile drive to a lonely wood where she could practice again, undisturbed. But for that long drive, there'd have been enough power left in the battery to get him to the quarry without having to push the damned thing. Perhaps it was just as well, though, since her bad luck over the daffodils had made the police suspect the carriage had been used.

Celandine gave a sharp, frightened sob, as a claw of bramble lashed out at her ankle. Everything was turning against her. She stopped to disentangle it, and it lacerated her hand. She whimpered a little, almost decided to turn back; but the envelope she carried must be posted. Once that was done, she would be really safe.

"So Celandine somehow gets her sleeping victim into the electric carriage, pushes him to the quarry, drags him out and tips him over the edge. Rubbish to be shot her. Her arms must be pretty strong, trundling herself about for years in that wheel chair. She'd found Charles's handkerchief on the day of the binoculars episode—the doctor said she refused to stay in her bedroom, and no doubt she spotted it as she wheeled herself back to the drawing room; he must have dropped it in the hall. It was to turn out useful, though she didn't know that at the time. She rubbed it hard on the turf now, to cover up the bloodstain Charles had left on it."

"I suppose that was to prevent anyone identifying the handkerchief, when it was found, with the one Charles had wrapped round his hand that day," Blount suggested.

"Possibly; though we'd only have Charles's word for it that he'd lost the handkerchief at the Little Manor. And in fact he refused to say even that much. I think he'd already got vague suspicions about Celandine before you interrogated him. And when you produced the handkerchief, they were confirmed. But he wouldn't say anything to betray her. That silence of his paid the last installment of his debt to Celandine, for what had happened in the past. I admire him for it, damn silly though it was. He gave himself away to me soon afterward, incidentally. I threw out the idea that he had refused to come clean because he suspected Rosebay of having found the handkerchief and put it in the wood. And he said, 'You're utterly wrong! I never thought it was *Bay* who—' Then he stopped in confusion. The inference was obvious. No, I fancy Celandine may have had some notion about blood groups in her head when she tried to cover up the stain. To be thoroughly incriminating, it ought to have Sir Archibald's blood on it; but, for all she knew, he was a different blood group from Charles. Anyway, she left it there. And then she made another bad mistake. When you showed her the handkerchief and said it had only just been found, she failed to ask the natural, immediate question."

"*Where* had we found it?"

"Exactly. Any innocent person would have asked that automatically. But she was being a bit too cautious. She didn't want to give the impression of being greatly interested in the handkerchief, and she overdid the incuriosity. Of course, she knew damn well where you'd found it. A less subtle criminal would at once have asked. Later, perhaps realizing her lack of curiosity might have seemed a bit odd, she said, 'I suppose you found it when you were searching the wood just now.' But she couldn't see men searching the wood, not from the ground-floor windows of the Little Manor. If the handkerchief had been *accidentally* dropped there by an accomplice, she ought to have shown some trace of alarm. Therefore the handkerchief must have been *deliberately* planted. Whom would it incriminate? Charles, and only Charles. Who had reason to hate Charles? Celandine, and only Celandine.

"But, being a fundamentally decent chap, and having a load of conscience on top of that, Charles refused to hit back at her. Rosebay had begun to suspect her sister, too; but she tied herself into knots to protect Celandine. She was jumpy at the very start, when Randall began questioning Celandine about the electric carriage. She wouldn't admit the purpose of the binoculars, because that might put into my head the possibility that Celandine's powers *had* been restored. She tried to vamp me. She told various stories, all more or less false, about what happened on the night of the murder, in the attempt to deflect suspicion from Celandine. And she was terribly disturbed when she saw what Durdle had chalked on the front gate—'Whoso sheddeth man's blood, by man shall his blood be shed.' It seemed to her a direct accusation against her sister. And I wonder, by the bye, was it. I've a feeling Durdle may have seen more, or know more, than he told us—something he's keeping in reserve for purposes of blackmail, or for his vendetta."

Daniel Durdle had reached the outskirts of the village. As he approached, he saw a curtain drawn across the lighted bedroom window of a solitary house: someone was still up in the sleeping village. Smiling to himself, Daniel recalled the thing he had not told the police—how, just before he had crept out of the Little Manor garden that night, a figure had walked to the drawing-room windows and pulled the curtains across them: the figure of Celandine Chantmerle; walking. It had scared him out of his wits at the moment, made him retreat as before an apparition. But presently fear gave way to curiosity, so he'd hung around in the vicinity. And the next day, when the news came that Sir Archibald was dead, his heart leaped exultantly. Now he had her in his grip at last—that fine, contemptuous sister of his, that whore of Babylon. He had bided his time, gloating like a miser over the hoarded secret. Now she would have to yield up to him his rights, the money, everything. At any moment he could make her go down on her knees to him. But tonight, up there on the wood's edge, he'd seen a richer revenge.

Daniel Durdle ran to the cottage of Greta Smart, and began furiously knocking upon her door.

"When she'd put back the invalid carriage, Celandine put on her father's coat and hat, which she had ready, and went down to the Hall, impersonating Sir Archibald. This was to be another strand in the rope to hang Charles.

" 'I seem to have a charmed life,' she said to me this afternoon. By God, she did too, that night. Charles Blick had only left the place of assignation ten minutes before. No wonder she fainted when she heard Rosebay had made that rendezvous with him. And both the vicar and Durdle were about the place as well. However, she got away with it. Perhaps that made her overconfident. Anyway, she did nothing about destroying the clothes she had worn."

"Are you just guessing now? That hat wasn't there, you know."

"It's a theory based on the way she behaved when your men came to search the house. First, she insisted on being present when they searched her father's room. Then, once they were in the room, she sent them down to fetch the keys of his furniture. That would give her time to take the hat out of the wardrobe and conceal it beneath the rug which covered her knees in the wheel chair. The wardrobe was presumably not, in fact, locked; but, when your men returned with the keys, she pretended to unlock it for them. I must say, the whole transaction showed great nerve and presence of mind on her part."

"But why should she be so frightened of their finding the hat, and not bother about the overcoat?"

"Ah, that's where Stanford Blick comes in."

"Wait a minute, Strangeways. Would she have set fire to herself trying to burn the hat after my men had left?"

"Just possible. But I don't think so. I believe she was getting a bit rattled. The police were apparently still interested in her. Charles Blick had not yet been arrested. And Celandine suspected that Rosebay had suspicions about her—that came out later in an interesting little slip of the tongue. I think she wanted to give one final, conclusive demonstration that she could not have murdered Blick."

Celandine was nearing the village now. The burns were itching worse than ever, and the dressings seemed to impede movement. She asked herself irritably if she hadn't wasted her time as well as her skin. It was easy enough to set fire to her chair and coverings, having first got out of it and locked the door; then to scream; then to get back into the chair just as Mark started to break down the door. It gave Mark an opportunity of playing the little hero, and herself only a few seconds of pain. But, she now thought with mounting vexation, it hadn't really proved anything. Anyone convinced she could not walk would need no proof of it: the police, with their filthy suspicious natures, and Nigel Strangeways who had turned out so heartless and disloyal—if they suspected she could walk, no doubt they were capable of suspecting that she had only got back into the burning chair at the last moment. Surely they must have arrested Charles, though, by now, after what she'd told them. It was intelligent of her to have waited till then before making the statement. Thinking of Charles Blick, she frowned. The moonlight showed her lips set in a cruel line, her face abstract and merciless as that of a carved idol demanding blood sacrifice. Damn them all—the horrible old man, and Charles, and Stanford. She might have known Stanford would be against her too, would betray her as Charles had betrayed her and as his father had betrayed hers. The Blicks—what an accursed race! A muttering of violent, childishly filthy abuse began to seep through her lovely lips. Then she whimpered a little in self-pity. But for Stanford, she'd never have had to come out tonight, walking this hard track in pain and misery.

"But Celandine finally gave herself away through sheer, calculated rancor," Nigel was saying. "This evening, after the 'accident' to Celandine, I arranged a little trap with the vicar's aid, as I told you. I'd previously stepped up the atmosphere by talking loudly and indiscreetly out in the garden, so that Celandine could hear from indoors. I mentioned Stanford's dream, for example, and discovered that Rosebay had told her sister about it. I was playing upon Celandine's nerves. Then, by arrangement, I made the vicar 'remember' that he'd walked back from Fenny Cross, past the Little Manor at the very same time when Charles had told us he was walking toward Fenny Cross. But he'd not met

Charles on the road. Therefore either he or Charles had lied. Of course, it was Mark who really lied; and he'll never forgive me for persuading him to do so. It wasn't a nice trick; but Celandine isn't a nice murderer. Anyway, she overheard this. For her, it was a godsend. It destroyed Charles's alibi—convicted him of lying (for it would never occur to her that Mark wouldn't tell the truth). It was pretty safe now for her to say she'd heard Sir Archibald accosting his son shortly after leaving the house, for if Charles could have *proved* he was nowhere near the house then, he'd have done so by now.

"Celandine probably thought she chose her moment very cleverly. After Rosebay's 'confession,' she could no longer bear to withhold her knowledge about Charles, dear old friend though he was. But this is the point—a woman as intelligent as Celandine, though she was innocent of the crime herself, would have seen through that confession of Rosebay's at once. Indeed, she admitted she did. 'Bay's a very imaginative girl,' she said. 'I didn't know she was so much in love with Charles as to try and put her head in a noose for him.' So why should Rosebay's bogus confession, which wouldn't bear a moment's expert examination, wouldn't put the girl in any real danger from the police, compel Celandine to come out with a damning piece of information about Charles which far more pressing circumstances had failed to force from her?"

Nigel fell silent. In a lull between the gusts, he heard feet running and a knock on a door. Somebody knocking up the village midwife, he supposed.

In the darkness, close to the post box in the wall opposite the New Inn, Daniel Durdle was waiting. It occurred to him that, if he had miscalculated, he would be the laughingstock of the village. Had she heard him, and turned back? The little group around him was already restive, beginning to eye him covertly, with doubt and somber suspicion. Greta Smart was there: and the young laborer who had attempted suicide: and Rosie, from whom, even at this unconventional moment, Greta kept herself noticeably apart.

"You're not having us on, I hope, Mr. Durdle?" she said.

"It won't be long now. Just you wait. The evildoer approaches."

Two more figures, coats thrown on over their night clothes, joined the group. There was a minute's silence, uneasy and embarrassed. Then Durdle held up his finger. His keen ear had caught the sound of footsteps. Then they all heard them—slurring, stealthy footsteps approaching from the direction where the quarry track met the main road.

"Are we all here?" asked Daniel. "You know what to do. The Lord has delivered the sinner into our hands."

His voice, low but resonant, had them under a spell. The group dispersed, flitting one way and another into the deeper shadows.

"I'm still not sure I understand how Stanford Blick comes into this," said Blount.

"Stanford has a first-rate mind. From what Rosebay and others told him, he'd worked out how his father was killed and by whom. But he's a whimsical character too, and he prefers not to get deeply involved in things. It suited his humor to make oblique hints, never come out direct with his suspicions. He quoted *Maud* to us on the lawn, three times. And the narrator of

Maud, you remember, is a broody young man whose father committed suicide after being ruined by a rich company promoter living at the Hall. Substitute Celandine for that young man. Then there was Stanford's alleged dream."

"Yes, I was waiting for that."

"He said he'd awakened from it at eleven-nine. At first it sounded too pat to be mere coincidence—that he should have dreamed it within a minute of the time when Durdle heard those dragging sounds from the Little Manor. But it was neither coincidence, nor guilty knowledge on Stanford's part. It was pure deduction. He knew that the murderer, impersonating his father, had come to the back door of the Hall at eleven-thirty. He could reckon it would take Celandine the best part of ten minutes to walk down there, and that it would previously have taken her another ten to wheel the body up to the quarry and return and put the invalid carriage away. Ten and ten from eleven-thirty gives you eleven-ten. Stanford's 'eleven-nine' was just an artistic touch to make it sound more lifelike. He calculated the removal of his father couldn't have taken place any earlier, since Charles had only walked away from the rendezvous between eleven-five and eleven-ten, and he'd have heard suspicious sounds if Celandine had been doing her work before eleven-ten.

"Stanford's 'dream' gave us a sort of eerie, symbolic version of the murder. The reason he made it up was to point out—remember what he said?—'Both wore dark overcoats and those curly-brimmed Homburg hats—*the Edwardian fashion* that has come in again. Pop was quite a dandy.' Stanford banked on Celandine's having worn her father's hat to impersonate his. He used the word 'Edwardian' so as to inject that idea into our minds, without committing himself any further.

"We know he told Rosebay his dream, too, and she told her sister. That must have scared Celandine considerably. 'A dark Homburg hat' might mean anything: but the Hall cook could probably recognize a dark, curly-brimmed, Edwardian one, if she was shown it—the very double of the one which the dandified old Sir Archibald had worn that night. Which is why I asked you to have a man guarding the incinerator at the Little Manor. Celandine has got to get rid of that hat somehow, and she knows it."

A figure approached cautiously out of the darkness, the faint moonlight picking out the silver band on the walking stick and the bulky white envelope it carried. The watchers could hear its breathing, rasping and uneven. It moved, like a not quite perfected automaton, toward the post box. Daniel Durdle slid between the figure and the wall, his thick glasses dully gleaming.

"So we've got you at last," he said, and at the same instant Rosie exclaimed: "Oh dear lordy, it's Miss Chantmerle!"

Celandine whipped round, to see a semicircle of villagers hemming her in to the wall. She neither screamed nor sobbed. A hideous spasm went over her face, contorting its beauty as a flaw of wind twists an image in a clear pool: then it passed, leaving a cold, angry expression.

"Let me pass, please," she said to Daniel.

"Not so fast. We have caught you red-handed in your iniquities and—"

"Get out of my way, you greasy, canting clown! Are you going to listen to this figure of fun? a sickening hypocrite like—"

"Just let us see that envelope, Miss Chantmerle," said Greta Smart, thrusting forward, her arms akimbo.

"Certainly not. This is outrageous. Go home, all of you."

"Ah, I thought so," said Greta bitterly. "Pretenden you was a cripple, and all the time creepen down here to post your filthy dirty letters. You'm no better than a murderer. You killed my brother."

The group closed in on Celandine, like a ring of dangerous animals.

"You're making a terrible mistake," she said, a slight quaver in her voice. "I—I only found out I could walk a few—it must have been the shock of my accident. I got burnt quite badly this afternoon. I—"

"To hell with that!" growled the young laborer. "Let's take her off to the police."

"No, let the poor soul speak," said Rosie, the village tart. "Maybe she can explain. 'Tes only fair."

"The police will tell you it's this holy horror, Durdle, who wrote the letters; they've known it for days."

"Whyn't they arrest'n, then?" said a gaunt woman with her hair in curling papers.

"Won't you let us see that envelope, Miss Chantmerle?" said Rosie. "We'm glad you can walk again, aren't we, folks? A proper miracle, enn't?"

Celandine held out the envelope for her to see. The others crowded round. The young laborer flashed a torch on it and read out the address slowly.

"Why, that's in Scotland, right up north, see?" said Rosie. "She'm not written to any of we. Now let her go, do."

Durdle's sleek voice came, insinuating. "Don't you be taken in. Suppose there's a number of envelopes inside that big one, envelopes full of nastiness, to be posted back here from Scotland. She's clever. Shall we ask her just to open that envelope and let us see what's inside it?"

"Yes, that's right. Come on, Miss Chantmerle," said Greta Smart. "If you're innocent—"

"No, damn you—I'm sorry, Greta, I'm not very well. But really I can't let you—"

"She's afraid, the witch, the daughter of Satan!" Daniel Durdle made a grab for the envelope. Celandine stepped back. There was a rasping swish, and she had drawn the steel blade from her father's swordstick.

"Get back, all of you. Let me pass, or I'll use this. I mean it."

"So that proves it!" Durdle's voice had a demented ring. "Whore! Murderess!"

He lunged forward to seize Celandine, and his body was spitted on the blade.

"What the devil is going on?" said Blount. Between the gusts of the storm, they could hear more banging of doors and pounding footsteps. "Must be a fire. Let's go and see."

What they found was a group of people at the far end of the village, who had been aroused, some by Durdle's first knocking-up of victims of his own poison-pen letters, some by the following wind or rumor, bending over Durdle's body. Rosie was trying to staunch the blood which flowed from the left side of his stomach. Cries and shouts were borne on the wind from the direction of the hillside, and the dogs at Templeton's farm began to bark.

"She's got away. They're chasing her. Miss Chantmerle." It took Blount a minute to get the facts straight; then he ran over to the New Inn to telephone. By the time he came out again, Daniel was dead.

Nigel was running up the road to Templeton's farm. The gale rocked the elms behind it, and burred in the upland grasses. Everything was in movement, in flight. The new moon went tearing through the cloud rack overhead: by its light, as Nigel emerged from the clutter of farm buildings and ran diagonally right toward the quarry track, he beheld an extraordinary spectacle. Outlined against the sky, a woman's figure, moving with a queer, lolloping gait, appeared on the ridge of the hill. Other figures, four or five of them, were close behind her. There was a flicker of miniature lightning, as she turned to threaten them with the blade of her swordstick. They stopped, huddled together, then moved on again when Celandine moved, keeping their distance.

The progress of this spasmodic pursuit, taking its time from the fugitive no one dared to close with, was slow enough for Nigel, running hard on his right diagonal, to have some hope of intercepting it. Surmounting the incline, and coming out on the plateau, with the little wood ahead to his left, he had arrived level with the pursuers. They were toiling up the rough track, barely trotting now, behind them a straggle of other villagers who, awakened by Durdle's first alarm, had arrived at the New Inn in time to see Celandine break through the cordon and disappear into the darkness. A few minutes had been wasted in explanation, and attending to Daniel Durdle. Then most of them had followed the original five, the victims of Durdle's own letters who were casting about in the direction Celandine had taken. The dogs barking at Templeton's farm put them on the track. And here they were—women in curling pins, in hairnets, with wellingtons or bedroom slippers on their feet, nightdresses showing beneath the hems of their coats; men carrying pitchforks or shotguns, one wearing a nightcap. As they came up with Nigel, they all started babbling:

"It's Miss Chantmerle! . . . She's the poison pen! . . . Killed Mr. Durdle, she have! . . . She'm a witch!"

Nigel could not stop them. This was the witch-hunt, the lynching he had told Durdle would happen. They were going to lynch the right person, for the wrong reason.

"Stop!" he yelled. "She's not the poison pen! You—"

A cry came from the darkness, twenty yards ahead. Celandine had reached the sward where the daffodils tossed, only to see Constable Clotworthy, roused by Blount's telephone call, advancing upon her from the ride through the wood. The moon sailed out from behind a dark cloud. Everything else in the world seemed to stand stockstill for a moment. Then Celandine turned, ran a few yards with that terrible, pathetic gait of a child whose legs are in irons, and went over the quarry's edge. There was no scream, no faint cry from her, even: only, after the silence, a thudding splash. . . .

Presently Nigel became aware of the Constable at his side.

"She's dropped these, sir," said the man in a hushed voice, handing him a naked swordstick and a bulky envelope. It was addressed to some unknown in the far north of Scotland. Nigel opened it, and drew out strips of felt, a black ribbon, a leather sweatband—an Edwardian Homburg cut up into pieces: Edric Chantmerle's hat.